Mummy's the Word

OTHER BOOKS AND AUDIO BOOKS
BY KERRY BLAIR:

The Heart Has Forever

The Heart Has Its Reasons

The Heart Only Knows

Closing In

Digging Up the Past

This Just In

Mummy's the Word

a novel

Kerry Blair

Covenant Communications, Inc.

Cover illustration by Josh Yamamoto

Cover design copyrighted 2005 by Covenant Communications, Inc.

Published by Covenant Communications, Inc.
American Fork, Utah

Printed in Canada
First Printing:August 2005

11 10 09 08 07 06 05   10 9 8 7 6 5 4 3 2 1

ISBN 1-59156-907-9

ACKNOWLEDGMENTS

Gratitude and love to

Joan Sowards, Kristen Cannegieter, Jeri Gilchrist,
& the mysterious, anonymous Covenant readers
for their time, generosity, and honesty.

Angela Eschler, Shauna Humphreys, Melissa Stockdale,
& the miraculous, unheralded Covenant staff
for their talent, knowledge, and wisdom.

My family, my friends, & my flock
for their faith, hope, and endless charity.

DEDICATION

To Lance Corporal Matthew J. Blair, USMC:
*We're so very proud of your honor, courage, and commitment to
our country—but mummy movies and Twilight Zone
marathons here at home just aren't the same without you.*

And to the memory of John Wright Blair &
Daniel Christopher Wolfe:
*You taught our family of eternity and touched
countless lives—we miss you still.
(A portion of the author's royalties will be donated
in their names to Camp Sundown so that other extraordinary
children will always have a special place to run and play
and rejoice in childhood.)*

Chapter 1

For the second night in a row, I sat in my ancient, black VW on the seedy side of town doing what I do best—minding somebody else's business.

Beside me on the passenger's seat was a half-empty package of donuts—the itsy-bitsy white ones that contain more carbs than some people eat in a week. Carbohydrates and calories aside, they're a bad addiction for a girl whose wardrobe tends toward black-on-black. Those little donuts were designed to explode on impact with human lips, sending powdered-sugar particles careening into the atmosphere and, worse, down the front of one's shirt. Still, they're as necessary to me on a stakeout as a car radio, digital camera, and cross-word puzzle. Besides, I figure that the general idea of a stakeout is to be invisible. If I do my job right, nobody will know I eat donuts with the grace of a two-year-old.

If I do my job right. I might as well admit from the start it's the *if*s in situations that usually get me into trouble.

Wick Barlow had just signed off the airwaves with his trademark, "Stay tuned. Stay awake. Stay alert. Things are looking up!" so I knew it was 3:00 A.M. Barlow's three-hour talk show airs at midnight—prime time for UFOlogists, denizens of the street, and private detectives. Barlow is king of the first cult, the drug dealers and immodestly clad women milling across the street from my car were members of the second, and I, Samantha Shade, was trying my darndest to make a name for myself in the third. (Move over Sam Spade; there's a new gumshoe in town.)

I was sorry the radio show was over. Wick Barlow is offbeat to the point of being off his noodle, but he's always good for a laugh. With one hand I switched the dial to soft rock. With the other I reached for a two-liter bottle of Diet Coke on the floorboard. It was caffeine free, of course. I don't need loud music or artificial stimulants to keep me awake, even in the tiniest hours of the morning. Ever since my parents adopted Arjay nine years before, staying up all night has come naturally to all of us. Even our Weimaraner, Clueless, is nocturnal.

I'd just loosened the cap on the soda bottle when a car came slowly down the street. I screwed the top back on and dropped the bottle. It was the third time that car had circled the block, slower each time. It wasn't the car I was looking for. The man I was being paid to photograph drove a new BMW. This Chevy Cavalier was at least as old as the clunker I drive. The driver was wrong, too. He wasn't the middle-aged city councilman who'd lose his happy home and promising political future when I gave his wife the pictures I'd taken of him the night before. The guy in the Chevy was young, probably in his late twenties, and too good-looking to be picking up a date in this neighborhood.

I think it was because the guy seemed so out of place that I watched him so closely. Because of how slowly he drove, I knew he was looking for something in particular. *Someone* in particular. I frowned in disgust when it occurred to me that it might be the girl who'd just emerged from the shadows of a vacant museum. I'd spent the last two nights trying to talk to that teenager but had never been closer than fifteen feet before she ran away from me.

I raised the digital camera carefully. It was new, top of the line, and very expensive. I probably shouldn't have taken it from the office without Uncle Eddie's permission, but if you want to be the best, you have to have the right equipment. I want to be the best private investigator on the planet.

To be perfectly truthful, I want more.

Would you laugh if I confessed that I've always longed to be bitten by a radioactive spider, like Peter Parker, or to learn that I'd been adopted from another planet, like Clark Kent? (My parents adopted Arjay, after all, and he certainly seems alien to most people.) I'd settle for being transformed into Hulkette in a freak accident, but no matter how long I hang around my father's genetic research lab, there is never an accident, freaky or otherwise. At twenty-three I'm still mortal, petite, a little plump, almost pretty, and past the comic-book stage in every aspect of my life except in my heart of hearts.

But that night I stared across the street imagining how I'd use superpowers if I had them. I'd want the right kind of powers, of course. Forget sticky fingers or biceps of steel; I wanted the power to send druggies to rehab and misguided women to college or vocational school. Of course, that was just for starters. I wouldn't exactly turn down the ability to fly and/or leap tall buildings in a single bound.

I sighed, knowing my chances of saving the street (let alone the world) were pretty slim. Then I studied the guy in the Chevy again, thinking I could do some crusader-like moonlighting even without superpowers. After all, if a creep stalking a little girl didn't scream out for pro bono scum-busting, nothing did.

When his car rolled to a stop several yards ahead, I snapped a picture of its license plate, being sure to include the sign on the business behind it to pinpoint its location. (That's one of the first things my co-workers Knute and Delano taught me in Stakeout 101.) Then I focused on the driver's window as the car door opened. By adjusting the powerful lens, I not only had a perfect picture of the man's sandy brown hair, but I saw quite clearly that he had light gray eyes, a cleft in his chin, and a dimple in his right cheek.

Boyish, I thought. Then, *Too old to trail teenagers.*

I snapped off a shot of his long, jean-clad legs and well-fit leather jacket. Then I lowered the camera lens and watched with my own eyes as he approached exactly who I'd predicted he would.

The girl was huddled in the doorway of a long-abandoned planetarium. Despite her age, her image reminded me of myself as a little girl. I'd visited that museum on a class field trip accompanied by my mother. I wished this girl had a mother with her now. She looked like she needed one badly. But that was the end of our similarities. With her long, red hair and big eyes she resembled a My Scene Barbie doll. She seemed to have taken fashion tips straight from the pea-brained doll designers. Her tube top, low-slung jeans, and faux leopard-fur coat were what all the best-dressed fashion dolls—and worst-dressed teenagers—wore that year. I decided to call her "Bambi" because those doe eyes of hers made her look like a frightened fawn. A fawn who was being stalked by a hyena.

I turned my attention back to the scumbag as he approached the child. Bambi didn't run from him as she had from me. Instead she took a step closer. I shivered despite the fact that it wasn't cold in Phoenix, even in mid-October.

The man stood over Bambi, dwarfing her with his height and broad shoulders. Quickly raising the camera, I took a picture of him leaning down and speaking into the girl's ear. Bambi shook her head vigorously, but the scumbag kept talking. Minutes passed. Bambi's head stopped shaking, and her shoulders began to heave with sobs. The man put out a steadying hand to hold her in place. More minutes. More talk. More pictures. At last the girl wiped her eyes and nodded. The cretin led her toward his car.

I'd seen enough. Too much.

"Hold it right there!" I hollered. I bolted from my car, leaving the door open behind me in my hurry to right wrong and defend the innocent in my own little corner of Metropolis.

The other people on the street probably didn't mistake me for Supergirl as I charged across the street toward the abandoned museum, but they must have thought I was an undercover cop. They dissolved into the surroundings until only Bambi and the man remained. He turned toward me in surprise.

"Get away from her!" I ordered, extending my digital camera as if it were a ray gun. "I have a camera and I know how to use it!"

The man stepped between me and the girl. "I don't know who you are, lady," he said, "but—"

"I'm your worst nightmare," I retorted. (Sure, I'd probably copped the line from an action movie, but doesn't it seem worthy of a superhero?) I brandished my camera to strike fear into his heart. "I've got pictures of you and this . . . *child*. By tomorrow morning I'll have sent copies to the police, the newspapers, and everybody you've ever met." He looked more annoyed than alarmed, so I added, "I also got your license plate number, you pervert. And I have connections. Don't think I can't destroy you."

"Listen—" he said.

Before he could finish the sentence, Bambi darted out from behind him and ran. She was worthy of the nickname; deer in hunting season are slower to react than that girl.

For a split second I thought the guy would chase her, but he must have known it was futile. As she disappeared around a corner he let out a long breath. "Good job," he said. He actually had the nerve to sound sarcastic about it.

I smiled up at him, triumphant. "Thank you. All in a night's work." My shoulder-length bob of honey-colored hair swung over my shoulders as I turned back toward my car.

But before I could walk away, he gripped my arm. "I'll need to delete my pictures from your camera before you go."

My smile widened as I stuck the camera securely in the pocket of my jacket and deftly slipped my left leg into a defensive position. I'd just graduated from a course in tae kwon do, so I was confident that in the next minute this piece of crud would be lying on his back, looking up at me with a whole lot more respect.

But before I could remember the move, let alone complete it, he was standing in front of me with both my wrists locked in one of his hands. He used his free hand to reach into my jacket pocket for the camera. "Keep practicing," he said. "You're a little slow."

"You creep!" I screamed. "Let go of me! I'll—"

"You'll what?" The camera was in his hand, and his face was split by a grin that would have been incredibly attractive on anybody but a scumbag.

I looked down at my feet and smiled myself. *There's a reason I wear leather boots with reinforced metal toes,* I reminded myself. I wear them for just such occasions. I swung my foot toward the front of his leg. If he hadn't been quick I probably would have broken his kneecap. As it was, I delivered a glancing blow to his shin. Fortunately, it was enough to get the jerk to release me. Unfortunately, he didn't let go of my camera.

I was about to tear into him with all the wrath of a five-foot-three superhero wannabe when two things happened at once. A very tall, very large shadow separated itself from the blackness nearby, and a police car turned onto the street. The patrol car was still most of a block away when the shadow loomed over us.

I looked up—way up—into the dark face of the giant. He grinned down at me, revealing a row of straight, white teeth that were incongruous in the deeply lined, homely face.

"What are *you* doing here?" I demanded with my fists now on my hips.

"Eddie said to tell you it's called 'backup' if you caught me at it," the giant said.

I was appalled. "You didn't call Uncle Eddie, did you?"

"He called us," the man said. "Wanted us to know they got to Paris today. Delano filled him in. We thought—"

"I don't need a babysitter, Knute!"

The grin widened as he looked down at my sugar-coated black T-shirt. "Of course you don't, Sam. Did you save me any donuts?"

I brushed automatically at the white powder on my front, but I was more angry than embarrassed. I was mad at my associate, mad at my uncle, and mad at the lowlife who had taken the camera away from me. Mostly I was mad at the lowlife. After all, it was his sick proclivities that had started this. Whirling toward him I opened my mouth, then found I couldn't speak. The creep had drawn a gun. He raised it toward Knute's chest, lowered it, raised it again, and finally lowered it for good.

"Good choice, pervert," I said after I found my voice. "The cops are here. That stolen camera in your pocket guarantees you a free night in jail. Pulling a concealed weapon on us ought to cinch another week or more. And when I send them my pictures, I hope they'll lock you up forever!"

Once again, the expression on the guy's face didn't match what I thought he ought to feel. The scumbag *should* look scared—or at least sorry to have gotten caught—but he looked more annoyed than ever. As the patrol car rolled to a stop, he glanced inside it. At last his shoulders slumped as he said, "Oh, shoot."

I stared up at him, incredulous. I'd heard a whole lot of expletives since going to work on the streets as a PI, but *shoot* wasn't one of them. I figured I must have misunderstood. Regardless, the police were finally there, and they couldn't have come at a better time.

"Watch out!" I shouted at the officer who opened the door on the passenger side of the car. "He has a gun!"

In one fast, fluid movement the patrolman exited the vehicle, drew his service pistol, and used the door as a shield. The gun was aimed at Knute. "Drop it!"

"No!" I cried out in irritation. "Not him!" I swung an arm toward the cretin. "Him!"

When the officer ignored me, I stepped in front of Knute. *Isn't it always this way?* I thought. *Just because the creep is clean-cut and good-looking, and Knute is shaggy, dark-skinned, and unnaturally large, they suspect the wrong guy.*

The second officer, a tall, older man with a mustache, exited the car. He didn't draw a gun. "Drop the weapon," he told the cretin calmly.

Knute had raised his arms in the classic posture of surrender. The creep obediently dropped his gun, but he raised his hands only partway, and even then it seemed like an afterthought.

I glared at him and moved to retrieve the gun, but the older cop said, "Don't touch it." To his partner, he added, "Get their statements while I talk to . . ." He hesitated. "The suspect." He walked around the car, then picked up the gun himself and pocketed it.

Under the streetlight I could read the officer's nametag. *Dix. Captain* Dix. Good deal. What we needed right then was a guy with both experience and authority.

"Captain!" I said. "I'm so glad you're here. I—"

He waved me off as if I were a troublesome black beetle buzzing around his ear. "Take her statement, Monroe," he said again before motioning for the suspect to follow him down the sidewalk.

Although the young man was unarmed now and docile, the police were treating this thing way too casually. If ever a little police brutality was called for it was now. "He's a mugger!" I called after the captain. "He assaulted me!"

The creep turned. "Now wait just a minute. *I* assaulted *you?*"

"Yes!" I confirmed. "When I stopped him from propositioning a little girl, he attacked me and—"

"I never—"

"You did!" I insisted. To the officer I added, "And he stole my camera! You'd better—"

"Monroe will take your statement," the captain said tersely. But at least he gripped the creep's elbow and yanked him farther away.

Young Officer Monroe gazed down the street. I could have sworn I saw him stifle a grin. *At least there's one man on the force who wants to see justice done,* I thought. I rewarded him with a smile as he pulled a PDA from the front pocket of his shirt and turned to me with stylus in hand. "Your name, please."

"Samantha Shade," I replied. "And this is Knute Belanoff. We work together."

One eyebrow rose as he scribbled. "You're out here every night . . . working?"

I felt my cheeks burn with indignation. Although I've been told I dress like an undertaker—and/or a vampire—I've never been mistaken for a streetwalker. "I'll have you know—"

Knute dropped a restraining hand on my shoulder and extended the other to the cop. It held one of our white-on-black business cards that in the right light—or lack thereof—glow green. (I just love those glow-in-the-dark cards.) "We're private detectives," he said. "With Nightshade."

The officer took the card and then looked up at the giant. "Hey, I've heard of you. You're that weird outfit that's only open nights, right?"

Knute nodded as Monroe pocketed the card.

"Word is you're folding."

"Word is wrong," I said.

"Eddie Shade hasn't retired?"

Knute smiled. "He's trying to. Sam here has other ideas. She's Eddie's niece. She's kinda running things while the boss is in Europe."

In other words, I'd been given three weeks to prove myself.

Over the misgivings of his brother (my father), Uncle Eddie had taken me into his business and given me a chance to show all the Shades that I was better suited for a career at Nightshade than I was for one emptying bedpans and organizing bingo at our other family-owned-and-operated business, Shady Acres. Don't get me wrong. The Acres is a beautiful facility for the elderly, and my mother makes it a paradise on earth for her residents, but while it's *so* her, it *isn't* me. I'm all about mystery.

Mostly to please my parents, I earned a degree from ASU and completed an internship at the state mental hospital. But for the last six months I'd lived my childhood dream of working for Uncle Eddie. After all, being a detective is the next best thing to being a superhero, right? I love every minute of my job—even the long, sometimes tedious hours on stakeouts. (Being addicted to crossword puzzles helps with that.) By now I'd breezed through the training Uncle Eddie had provided and was weeks away from getting my private investigator's license. Then, if I made good on my own while he was in Europe, I'd have the chance to be his partner and maybe even take over the business when he actually retired. I wanted that more than anything, so I had to make good. I *had* to.

When Monroe turned to look at me I met his eyes and defied him to find me inadequate based solely on the fact that I look a whole lot more like *Bewitched's* Samantha Stevens than I do Sam Spade.

"So you're out here . . . ?"

"On a stakeout," I said, filling in the blank.

He looked surprised. "You mean you were watching for the guy over there?"

I shook my head impatiently. Busting a lowlife like him was frosting. I'd taken pictures of the cake the night before. Those pictures were still in my camera, thank goodness. I had a meeting with the councilman's wife the next night where I would bask in the glory of successfully completing one of Nightshade's more important cases. I mean, not even Knute has busted a dirty politician.

"No," I said to the cop. "I just happened to notice the creep. He showed up while I was waiting for . . . somebody else. I watched him proposition a girl who couldn't have been more than fourteen."

"Red hair?"

I frowned. "Yes. How did you know?"

"She's . . . uh . . . she's a regular."

"Him too?"

Monroe was too busy with his stylus to look up. "I, uh, haven't seen him before."

"But you'll arrest him, right?" I asked. "I want to press charges."

"I need the rest of the story."

I provided the details with alacrity—and maybe a little embellishment. While I talked I looked past Monroe toward the cretin down the street. He still wasn't in handcuffs. Even stranger, the police captain seemed to be doing most of the talking while the suspect stared down at the filthy sidewalk. "You'll arrest him, right?" I pressed when I'd finished giving my statement. "I want to charge him with assault."

"I've got that," Monroe said.

"You know," Knute interrupted, "I saw it go down. *Assault* might not be exactly what she means."

It's a good thing for Knute I don't have superpowers because the look I cast him would have stunned if not killed. "*Assault* is *exactly* what I mean," I insisted. To the officer I repeated, "He grabbed me. He stole my camera. I *want* to press charges."

"Right." Monroe pushed a button on the PDA. "I think I've got it, Miss Shade. Thank you. You'll have to come down to the station to file a formal complaint." I nodded, and he turned to Knute. "Now tell me what you saw."

"He didn't see any—" I began.

"If you can't be quiet," Monroe said, "I'll have to ask you to excuse us."

"She *can't* be quiet," Knute told him. "I'll guarantee that." He grinned at me before strolling a few feet down the sidewalk with the young officer on his heels.

I crossed my arms over my chest and glared after them. If Knute Belanoff hadn't been the best detective on earth—and the kindest man on the planet besides—I might have fired him on the spot.

Monroe and the captain finished their questioning at about the same time. I planted myself in front of the patrol car when they returned and smiled to see that the creep finally looked like I thought he should—crestfallen and very sorry he'd tangled with Samantha Shade.

"She wants to file a complaint," Monroe told his superior. "For assault."

The older man closed his eyes as if praying for patience, then opened them to glare at the cretin. "Cuff him," he said. When Monroe took half a second too long to comply, he barked, "Do it now. I've got better things to do tonight than hang around down here."

I smiled in satisfaction, then extended my hand. "My camera, please," I reminded the officer.

He patted his pocket. "It's evidence. You'll get it back. Eventually."

"But I need it now!" I protested. "It's my uncle's! Besides, I have other pictures on it. I need those pictures for a meeting with a client tomorrow night. A very important client. I *have* to have that camera, Captain! I—"

Unmoved, Officer Dix circled the car. "You can file a petition for its return when you come down to the station to file your complaint."

"But—"

Knute chuckled. "What do I keep telling you, Sam? Sometimes even when you win, you lose."

"But—"

As the creep was turned to be put into the back of the squad car, I got another look at his face. It was strong, finely chiseled, and ironically noble—the kind of face I saw more often in my dreams than in my line of work.

"Believe me, lady," the bad guy with the great face said. "You've got this all wrong."

I turned away as Officer Monroe closed the door. "Chalk one up for the good guys," I said, hoping the words were truer than they felt. Despite myself, I couldn't help thinking there *was* something disconcerting about the scumbag I'd busted—aside from his all-American good looks, I mean. I shook my head. Obviously I'd just saved the day like a true superhero. I should feel proud, not melancholy.

I looked up at Knute. As the big man watched the police car pull away, his brows knit together.

"He *did* proposition that girl," I said. "And he stole my camera."

"That's what it looked like, all right," Knute replied.

The patrol car turned the corner, and the denizens of the darkness began to reappear in ones and twos and dozens. I sighed. There is just so *much* wrong in the world that needs righting, you know? I sometimes doubt a bona fide superhero could handle it all.

"Your heart is in the right place, Sam," Knute told me as he walked me back across the street to my car.

"What's that supposed to mean?"

He looked down at me fondly. "You thought you knew what you were doing when you nailed that guy, and you thought you knew why you were doing it. What you don't know is what you did will do. We seldom know that."

I didn't have to understand Knute's homespun philosophy to know I didn't like the sound of it. The intuitive giant was seldom wrong, and he was hinting . . . what? I thought about the handsome perp and the scared runaway, and my heart turned over. Had I struck a blow for truth, justice, and decency, or had I made one of the biggest mistakes of my life?

I stared into my still-open car in dismay. Somebody had swiped the rest of my donuts, my Diet Coke, *and* my daily crossword puzzle. I had no goodies, no camera, no diversion—and no stakeout. I knew I might as well call it a night and swing by my parents' home to see if Arjay wanted to go to the Purple Cow with me. (My professional motto: *When the going gets tough, the tough get ice cream.*) Not that chocolate fudge could fill the pit that had formed in my stomach. The only way I thought I could fix that was if I could get back my pictures of the councilman, if I could find the runaway, and if I could see to it that I did learn what I'd just done would do.

Have I mentioned yet it's the *ifs* in situations that get me into trouble?

Note to the Reader Who Has Gotten This Far: *As much as I've always wanted to chronicle the many (mis)adventures of Nightshade Investigation, I've also long nurtured a desire to try my hand at putting together one of my favorite things on earth—a crossword puzzle. So, when this chance to tell my story came along, I thought, "Why not throw in a puzzle as well?" (One of my other favorite things is a hot-fudge sundae, but neither my editor nor I could think of a way to throw in one of those without making an awful, gooey mess of the pages.) Anyway, you can think of the story and the puzzle as two treats for the price of one. (Or you can ignore it altogether if you're one of THOSE people!) The puzzle and all the clues are in the back of the book, so don't think you have to solve it as you go along. (Unless you want to, of course.) I hope you like the idea, and I REALLY hope you'll find my crossword more puzzling than my writing! Have fun!*

—Sam

ACROSS

    58 *Above the horizon; Where things are always looking in Wick Barlow's line of work*

DOWN

    3 *Cretin; Creep; Miscreant*

    44 *Vital piece of "equipment" on stakeouts; Powdered sugar _____*

Chapter 2

Seventeen hours later, I began a new work night at Nightshade Investigation, Inc., a little worse for wear. Despite my sacrificing the hot-fudge sundae run to cruise the city streets looking for the runaway, I hadn't found Bambi. Despite three hours at the police station, I hadn't been able to get my camera back. Despite numerous inquiries, I still didn't know what had happened to the scumbag I'd busted.

I bet Wonder Woman never had days like this.

I leaned back in my uncle's chair and ran my hands over the soft, burgundy leather while I willed myself to relax. I love that chair, that desk, and that funky, impractical office. Although there are computers in the adjoining reception and workrooms, Uncle Eddie's inner sanctum contains only a few electric lamps and a telephone intercom system dating from the 1940s—the golden age of private detectives, according to Eddie. The glass-fronted bookcases are lined with manuals, law books, atlases, dictionaries, histories, and the complete works of Emerson, Ovid, Faulkner, and others—standing side by side with Uncle Eddie's vast collections of dime mysteries, science fiction, and a smattering of gothic horror.

The word *eclectic* was coined to define my uncle's workplace—and his life. His innumerable valuable, invaluable, and utterly worthless collectibles fill every available space between, in front of, and around his books. They had covered most of his desk as well, before I gathered them up and stowed them in a wooden crate in the corner of the room. I tried not to look at the box because it seemed to crouch there resentfully with its contents peering out at me between the slats, impatiently awaiting the return of the master of their domain.

And my uncle really is a master at what he does. Despite his unusual office, ridiculous business hours, and unbelievable staff, Edward Shade has found his niche. Or, more correctly, he's carved it out by the force of his considerable skill and intelligence. Although he isn't what the world considers rich, he spends every day doing what he loves— helping others. I believe that's the real reason Nightshade is not only economically successful, but also well regarded by everyone with whom we do business.

At least we *were* well regarded, right up until the time I became the temporary CEO.

As if to confirm my guilty suspicions, the intercom buzzed. It was my cousin Chaiya. (That's pronounced "ki-yuh." Her mother says it's Hebrew for "life force," but Delano thinks it means "fair game to tease unmercifully.") Chaiya is another niece who works for Eddie. As receptionist/secretary, she comes in from eight until midnight to enter reports into the computer and confirm clients' appointments. She isn't interested in detective work per se, but she needs the salary for tuition to cosmetology school. At least that's what she tells people. I think the real reason she "works" for Uncle Eddie is to meet the men who come and go from Nightshade's staff—particularly the attractive, unmarried ones. They are legion.

When Eddie hears of a young man in our stake who needs a job pre- or post-mission, he provides it. Ditto for older guys who are down on their luck or seemingly unemployable elsewhere. Most of these guys come and go before anybody but Chaiya and Uncle Eddie learn their names, but there have been two exceptions—Knute and Delano. Knute has worked with Eddie since before I was born; I think maybe they grew up together. Delano came along later. I don't know where Uncle Eddie found him, but I don't think it was the dog pound (like my father mutters under his breath). Delano pretty much defines "unconventional," but he's one of the savviest men I know.

"Sammy?"

Chaiya's disembodied voice coming over the intercom made me wince. It might not be as bad as the proverbial nails on a chalkboard, but it's pretty close.

"Sammy?" she repeated. "There's a mermaid here to see you."

I pressed a button on the antique intercom. "A what?"

"Oh, wait," Chaiya said. "*Mrs.* Mer*mann*. My mistake."

I caught my breath. Mrs. Mermann was the wife of the councilman—the low-down, cheating councilman who had no business on Van Buren Street in the middle of the night. (No legitimate, moral business, that is.) She was the client whose husband's pictures were still in the digital camera, which was still at the police station despite every threat, plea, and protestation I'd been able to muster.

"But I called her!" I said into the intercom. "I was up most of the day trying to get those pictures back for her. When I couldn't, I called and left a message on her answering machine telling her everything is fine, but I need a couple more days to—"

The heavy wooden door flew open and Mrs. Mermann appeared. She was dressed immaculately, but her makeup didn't match her ensemble. It was hastily applied with little attention to detail. The end result was that the red lipstick slashed across her face made her look comic and a little fierce.

"*Fine,* is it?" she said, crossing the room in a cloud of expensive perfume and righteous indignation. "*Fine,* you say?"

I gripped the desk. It felt solid and reassuring, like the right thing to hold onto when your career begins to slip out from under you.

As solid as it was, the desk shook when Mrs. Mermann slapped her Prada bag down on it. "Could you be so kind as to tell me just *what* about my situation is *fine?*"

"I—have the pictures!" I stammered. "I do! I just don't *have* them." I felt my eyes widen at the deepening color of Mrs. Mermann's face. Already it was darker than her rouge. "I mean, um, I don't have them *yet.*" In a few more moments Mrs. Mermann was either going to faint dead away or she was going to murder me.

She did neither. Instead, the middle-aged matron collapsed into Uncle Eddie's favorite chair, a thing of black lacquer and red Chinese brocade that everybody with taste and 20/40 vision or better finds atrocious. Then she dissolved into a torrent of tears.

I wish she'd have murdered me. It would have been less painful. I rounded the desk to her side. "It's all right—"

"Oh yes!" the poor woman wailed. "It's *fine!*" She blew her nose on a soggy square of Irish linen. "My husband left me today," she continued. "He said I was small-minded and suspicious and *delusional.* He said I'd hear from his lawyer." She looked up accusingly, the tears forming long rivulets of mascara down her plump cheeks. I looked away from the black puddles of the stuff that formed between her two chins. "*My* attorney said *I* should make the first move. He sent me to *you!*"

I knew at once the attorney she referred to was Uncle Eddie's longtime associate and good friend Mick Farrell. After struggling through law school together, Mick and Eddie had joined forces. Eddie left the bar and founded Nightshade, and Mick sent all his clients his friend's way. They'd worked successfully together now for what, thirty years? Forty? Longer? I closed my eyes but opened them again quickly lest I squeeze out tears that would ruin my own mascara.

"I saw him on Van Buren Street, Mrs. Mermann," I tried to reassure her. "I took pictures of your husband like you asked."

"Where *are* they?"

"They're . . . they were confiscated." I hesitated. "By the police."

The woman gasped. "Then you've lost them! Oh, why, why did I come *here?*" Her red-rimmed eyes took in the office with horror.

Suddenly, when I considered the room through my client's eyes, everything unique and appealing seemed suddenly anachronistic and tawdry—like a bad joke played by the set director on *The Maltese Falcon.* Then revelation struck. It wasn't the office that provoked the poor woman's disdain and dismay—it was the person behind the claw-footed mahogany desk. If there was a joke here, it was me trying to fit my tiny feet into my uncle's huge shoes.

I swallowed and squared my shoulders. Even if I *wasn't* capable of captaining Nightshade's ship of state on a permanent basis, I ought to at least be able to keep from running it into the ground on my third day at the helm. "I didn't lose them," I repeated. "I'll get that proof for you, Mrs. Mermann. I will." Unfortunately, I had no plan that would help me keep that promise. I'd already tried huffing and puffing, but the brick police station hadn't blown down.

The door opened again. Thank goodness. Reinforcements.

Chaiya stood, flanked by Knute in the doorway. In her hand she held a paper cup of water. It wasn't much as peace offerings go, but it was probably all she had in her office to offer besides metallic-hued nail polish, a curling iron, and six flavors of Altoids. I smiled at my cousin for all I was worth. She isn't particularly outstanding as receptionists or roommates go, but boy is she loyal!

"Would you like a drink?" Chaiya asked.

Under every other circumstance, Mrs. Mermann's eyes would have focused on Chaiya's outrageous outfit, cornrows, and Cleopatra-lined eyes, but Knute was an even stranger sight. And a larger one. Standing next to Chaiya, it was clear he'd make two of her—with enough brawn left over for a Pop Warner football team and three cheerleaders.

"Oh my!" Mrs. Mermann breathed.

That was a relief. Some of our more high-strung clients screamed at their first sight of Nightshade's ace detective.

Chaiya took a step forward and extended the cup. "You look like you need a drink," she urged.

I suspected it would have to be much stronger stuff than water for Mrs. Mermann to consider it.

The woman rose and gathered her purse to her chest like a shield. "I, oh dear, I . . . I really must be going."

Always considerate, Knute stepped into the room and well away from the door so Mrs. Mermann could make good her escape.

"I'll call you, Mrs. Mermann!" I called after her.

"I'm thinking that went well," Knute teased after Mrs. Mermann had fled. He lowered himself into the only chair in the room capable of accommodating his girth. It was a massive oaken number that Uncle Eddie, with his slightly warped sense of humor, had had custom-made to resemble an electric chair, complete with wired helmet.

Chaiya gave me the water. "This was for you, anyway," she said. "And two aspirin."

"Thank you!"

"We're running out," she cautioned. She didn't add, "We've all had a headache since you took over," but the downward curl of her burgundy-lined lips implied it.

I swallowed the tablets on my way back to Uncle Eddie's chair. I didn't feel at home there, but I hoped that at least the desk would catch me when I slumped forward in discouragement.

Chaiya looked through the open door into the front office. "Delano's here."

"Hey, Kayak," the man said, tapping the top of her head with a manila folder as he loped through the door.

If pressed, I'd guess Delano is in his late twenties, but I don't know for sure since the guy *seems* ageless. He has the grace of a Russian ballet dancer, the personality of a class clown, and the looks of a red-haired Robinson Crusoe. (And, as far as I've ever heard, he has only the one name. I have no idea how he deposits his paychecks.)

Chaiya made a grab for his long ponytail as he passed, but missed. "When are you going to let me do something with that mane of yours?"

Delano grasped an antique Windsor chair, then flipped it around and straddled it. "See me after you graduate from that bee-oo-tee school of yours, Care Bear." He raised long, tapered fingers to scratch at his bushy beard. "On the other hand, why mess with perfection?" He winked at me and nodded hello to Knute. "So, we ready to work here or what?"

"A couple of things before you start," Chaiya said. "Sammy, your mom called. Aunt Judy wants to know if you can take Arjay to his orthodontic appointment before work tomorrow. Oh, wait," she corrected herself. "Is it tomorrow or the next day?" (As a night sleeper herself, Chaiya sometimes has a hard time keeping track of my family's bizarre schedule.) "Anyway, I wrote down the date and the time."

"That's great, Chaiya," I said. "Thanks."

"One more thing. She says Wendela was up on the roof again tonight."

I cringed.

"They had to call the fire department this time," Chaiya continued. "She wouldn't let go of the satellite dish. Aunt Judy says she pointed it toward Venus and now they can't get the game-show channel. You know what those old folks are like without Bob Barker and Alex Trebek."

I did know. It would be a bad day indeed at Shady Acres without Bob and Alex. I knew I should never have asked Mom to keep Wendela yet again. I couldn't have taken my other, older roommate with me on the stakeouts the previous two nights, but she could have come to Nightshade on the third night and worked on her needlepoint while I obsessed.

Chaiya continued. "Aunt Judy says that as much as they all love her, Wendela's getting worse and creating a numismatic of herself."

"A nuisance," Delano supplied before I could figure it out for myself.

(One thing you need to know about Chaiya is that she never misses an installment of "It Pays to Increase Your Word Power" in *Reader's Digest,* but she seldom bothers to make sure her shiny new vocabulary words make sense in context.)

"Anyway," she concluded, "your mother says she's afraid you're going to have to industrialize Wendela again."

"I understand," I said, knowing I'd give up my job at Nightshade to work at Shady Acres if that's what it took to keep from having to reinstitutionalize Wendela. "I'll call my mother." To prove my good intentions—and to get rid of my cousin—I snatched up a pencil and dutifully noted the message on a piece of paper. "Anything else?"

"Isn't that enough?"

"Yes," I said, trying to keep my shoulders from sagging. "That's more than enough. Thanks."

"I need to leave early tonight," Chaiya said, heading for the door. "I have a test tomorrow on cuts and shapes, and I still need to find a volunteer." She cast a long look at Delano. "You sure you—"

"I'm sure, Cupcake," he said. "Stalk your victims elsewhere."

Chaiya considered Knute's mass of gray wool for less than half a second, knowing she might be able to cut it—with pruning sheers—but giving it shape was probably impossible. "Okay, then." She closed the door behind her.

"So, um, well . . . hi, guys!" I said by way of opening our nightly meeting. Uncle Eddie always opens with a quote from one of the many classics on his shelf—something uplifting and thoughtful and apt for the tasks at hand. I scribbled another note to myself to look up a quote for tomorrow. Surely somebody had waxed poetic about situations similar to ours. (Was it Lord Nelson who said something about not abandoning a sinking ship?)

Neither man replied to my greeting. They were too busy trying not to laugh out loud at the sight of me in Eddie's chair.

"Delano," I began. "What about the Crowell case?"

He raised the folder. "We found him."

"Already? That's great!"

I could scarcely contain my joy. The nineteen-year-old subject of Delano's missing-person case had been gone for little more than a week. The police wouldn't look for him because he was an adult and there was no sign of foul play. The guy had sold his car and cleaned out his mission fund before slipping out in the middle of the night. He'd taken his parents' car, which turned up just north of the Mexico border. It was abandoned with the keys in the ignition and a note telling his mother not to worry, that he'd found his "true mission in life." His parents had hired us to find him.

I leaned forward. "Then he's okay?"

"By all accounts," Delano said. A wide grin appeared beneath his rusty Brillo pad of a beard. "My contact says he looks about as happy as anybody has a right to."

"Thank goodness," I said. I couldn't wait to make the call that would mean so much to his parents. His father was a stake president and a good friend of my dad's. I reached for the Rolodex thinking I'd place the call before we moved on to the next case. "Where'd you find him?"

"A nudist colony in Rocky Point," Delano said. "It's a new cult that lives on the beach and worships sand crabs."

I dropped the Rolodex. It landed on its side, and white cards spilled across the blotter. I ignored them. I felt my mouth fall open, but I couldn't force any sound out of it.

"To each his own," Knute observed.

"You want to see the kid's picture?" Delano asked, extending the folder. The grin on his wolfish face told me this was the most fun he'd ever had at work.

"No!" I cried. I clasped a hand over my mouth and took a deep breath through my nose before trying the response again. "I mean, no thanks, Delano. Not . . . not right now." I managed to get an elbow on the desk in time for the palm of my hand to catch my falling forehead. I rested it there as I said, "I'll call his parents."

Someday. Maybe. Unless I could first find a cult of my own—a fully clad one—to join.

"Knute," I sighed. "Please tell me you have good news."

"It depends on how you look at it," he said. "I finished up the Longman case."

I waited for him to tell me how to look at it.

"I read the accident reports and went out to the scene," Knute began. "Took all the measurements—traffic flow, roadway markings, control signals—the pictures are all in the file."

I nodded. There's no more thorough investigator in the business than Knute. Nor is there one who takes longer to get to the bottom line.

"I talked to the witnesses," he continued. "Chaiya's typing up my notes tonight."

And tomorrow night, I thought. *And the night after that and probably the night after that.*

"Then I went to the weather service," Knute added.

Where, I suspected, he'd determined not only the weather at the time, but the position of the sun and the velocity of the wind. Heck, he probably noted down the dew point. "Uh, huh," I said, wishing he was finished but knowing he wasn't.

"I went over the municipal records for the timing of the traffic lights and—"

My arm went to sleep and fell onto the desktop. "Knute, please! Just give us the punch line."

The big man nodded. "The thing is, Sam, Mr. Longman lied to us and to the insurance company. The accident was his fault." Knute leaned forward and tossed the file onto Eddie's desk. "He ain't insured. He ain't hurt, and he sure—"

"Ain't going to pay our bill," I finished for him.

"That about covers it."

I let out the air from my lungs (it only *sounded* like a sigh) and moved the pencil across the paper yet again. "I'll call him."

I felt my face sink toward the desk. Just before my nose impacted with the blotter, the buzzer went off on the intercom. "You've got somebody else here to see you," Chaiya said. "He doesn't have an appointment, but he says he's lord of something or other, so maybe that's important enough for you to let him in."

I looked at the two men who sat across from me. They shrugged.

"He's here about his mommy," Chaiya added.

"You mean his mother?" I asked.

"No, wait," Chaiya said. "My mistake. He's here about his *mummy.*"

This time I didn't respond.

"His mummy," Chaiya repeated. "You know, Sammy. A mummy's one of those old, dead people wrapped in bandages and stashed in a sabbatical."

Delano grinned.

"No, wait," Chaiya said. I heard another voice over the intercom but couldn't make out the words. "Lord Herbert says it's in a *sarcophagus,*" Chaiya said. "My mistake." When I still didn't respond (mostly because I couldn't), she said impatiently, "Do I send him in or not?"

When my brain still refused to send a "speak" command to my mouth, Delano leaned forward and said, "What have we got to lose?"

If I'd known the answer to that question, I would never in a million, trillion years have raised my head from Uncle Eddie's desk long enough to press the button on the intercom and say, "Send him in."

ACROSS
9   *Made up of the best of varied sources; Uncle Eddie's office*
54 *What Knute and the Jolly Green Giant are*
DOWN
1   *Man-made object orbiting Earth; Wendela's favorite dish?*

Chapter 3

"Lord Herbert Graeme," Delano said, still amused by Chaiya's over-the-intercom introduction of our newest client. "You're bringing Nightshade Investigation up in the world, Sam."

I ignored his jibe and stared at the door, waiting for it to open. If asked to predict the looks of the new client, I would probably have described a tall, patrician gentleman clad in a natty tweed jacket, white oxford shirt, and gray woolen pants. But when the door opened, I knew I'd been reading too much Agatha Christie and not enough Roald Dahl.

Lord Herbert Graeme was five and a half feet tall and bareheaded, but he still looked for all the world like a yard gnome. His yellow cardigan bulged over his stomach in front but did nothing to conceal the ill-fitted green trousers in back. His shirt was red, and his polka-dot bow tie, just visible beneath his wild, snowy beard, was clipped on askew. Peering out from a tangle of bushy brows, his eyes were small and bright and a truer blue than even the cerulean stripes in his suspenders.

From behind his back Chaiya pointed to him and grinned. Her silent message was clear: *Have you ever seen such a snappy dresser?* I knew my cousin's idea of heaven would be piecing together an ensemble from this man's wardrobe.

Lord Graeme turned back to Chaiya and tipped an imaginary hat. "Thank you, dear Ophelia."

Huh?

Remembering my manners at last, I rose, circled the desk, and extended my hand. "Hello, um, Lord Graeme. I'm Samantha Shade. Welcome to Nightshade."

He didn't miss my hesitation over his title. He smiled warmly and waved a pudgy hand in the air. "A minor lord, my dear," he said. "It is an old title, passed down for many generations before falling upon me." He took my hand and kissed it. "Fair Hero. Charmed, I'm sure." Releasing my fingers, he added, "You may call me Lord Herbert. Lord Graeme, alas, doesn't fit me as well as it has others." He turned toward Delano and Knute.

With his back to me, I couldn't see the expression on his face when he saw the men, but he didn't bolt from the room. Judging by his posture, he wasn't even startled.

"My associates," I said. "Mr. Belanoff and Mr. Delano."

"Just Delano," the younger man said, extending a hairy arm to shake hands with the lord.

"A pleasure, Sir Romulus," Lord Graeme said. When Knute rose, the lord looked up admiringly and added, "'O, it is excellent to have a giant's strength.'" He shook Knute's hand while looking him squarely in the belt buckle. "It is an honor to make the acquaintance of mighty Orion." He turned back to me. "I am very pleased at what I see, Miss Shade. I believe Nightshade will do quite well for my purposes."

What purposes?

Mummies and classical name-calling aside, this man's unexpected appearance in our office was odd. We almost never have a stranger come to us without a referral. That isn't surprising. As much as I love this office and my co-workers, I'm not blind to our idiosyncrasies. The first impression Nightshade gives most people is that they've stepped into a couple of *Nick at Night* TV shows run amok. (Think what might happen if *Munsters* met *Rockford Files,* and you have Nightshade in a nutshell.) With Uncle Eddie being the only truly normal person in the office, most unexpected newcomers take one brief, horrified look around, then flee for their lives.

On the other hand, Lord Herbert was a guy who needed help with a mummy. Who better to consult for that than a group that calls itself Nightshade?

"How can we help you, Lord Herbert?" I asked, pulling back the brocade chair for him. When he was seated, I lowered myself onto the edge of the desk. Knute and Delano leaned forward. Even Chaiya stuck around to see what Lord Herbert had to say. She perched atop a wooden unicorn that had graced the carousel in Encanto Park a century or so before. I cleared my throat. "You say it's something about a mummy? How . . . intriguing."

"Ah, yes!" Lord Herbert exclaimed. "Intriguing indeed. It is perhaps *the* most intriguing find to come from the land of the pharaohs. That's why I've held onto him as long as I have. My little mummy is the last holding in what was once a vast and priceless private museum." He folded his hands across his ample stomach. "It has been in the Graeme family for generations. It must, it simply *must,* pass into the right hands now."

"You're selling it?" I guessed aloud.

"Oh, no! No, no, *no!*" Lord Herbert cried. "*Sell* Hermes? Never! None of my treasures have been *sold.*" For a moment I thought he might run from the room after all, but he eventually settled back into the chair. "I'm sorry, my dear," he said. "Kindly forgive my outburst. You couldn't know."

"Lord Herbert is a philatelist," Chaiya announced from atop the unicorn. "I read an article about him in the *Smithsonian* magazine." When she saw that not one of us believed she'd ever *seen* a *Smithsonian* magazine let alone *read* it, she added, "A lady at the beauty college had it open while I was doing her perm. Perms are so boring!"

Delano's eyes shifted from Chaiya to Lord Herbert. Clearly he was trying to establish a connection between philately and mummies. "You also trade in rare stamps?" he began.

"I'm afraid not," Lord Herbert responded slowly, confused himself. "I've collected many things in my time, but stamps, no."

"A philanthropist!" I exclaimed, pleased to have come up with Chaiya's meaning before Delano. "She means to say you're a philanthropist!"

Delano frowned to indicate he should have known it first.

Lord Herbert cleared his throat modestly. "So they say. But what I truly am is the last in a long line of curators. For centuries the Graemes have maintained a collection of antiquities without peer. Since I am, alas, the last to bear the name, it has been incumbent upon me to see that each parchment, each vase, each sketch goes where it will be best preserved, protected, and cherished. My little mummy, though, I have saved for last. Now I fear his time, too, has come to depart my care." He reached into the pocket of his cardigan and produced a brittle picture that he presented to me with the look of a proud grandparent. "I call him Hermes—the Little Messenger."

I squinted down at the fuzzy photo. It showed a younger, beardless Lord Herbert standing beside a sarcophagus that wasn't quite as tall or wide as he was himself. "It's so small," I observed aloud. "Does it hold a woman? A child?" I passed the picture to Chaiya who glanced at it and handed it to Delano.

When Lord Herbert smiled, his cheeks plumped and his blue eyes twinkled. I couldn't help but smile back at him. I suspected nobody could. "It holds a secret," he said. "Quite possibly the secret of the ages."

My smile disappeared. "You want us to solve the mystery of the ages?"

He laughed. "Oh no, my dear! We'll leave that for those who have both the desire and the expertise. I merely want you to be on hand tomorrow night to welcome the Little Messenger to my estate, to see to his safety during my gala dinner party, and to help ensure that he leaves in the right hands."

But why us? My eyes flew to Knute and Delano. If this thing was as valuable as he said it was, Nightshade was a rather unlikely place to solicit guards. He might as well ask us to solve the mystery of the ages. "Lord Herbert," I said, "why did you come to Nightshade Investigation?"

He held out his arms as if to embrace us all. "'Every why hath a wherefore,' my dear. Why *not* come to Nightshade?"

There were a few obvious answers to that question, but as acting CEO of the firm I hesitated to point them out.

"I mean," I said, "it seems to me you need professional security." I was thinking armed men with armored trucks and semiautomatic weapons. At least.

"That is precisely what I do *not* need," he said, as if he'd read my mind. "'For never anything can be amiss when simpleness and duty tender it.' What I need is *discretion.*"

Always up for a challenge—the more foolhardy the better—Delano scooted his chair forward. "Tell us what you have in mind, Lord Herbert."

The lord raised a finger. "Yes, cunning Romulus, that is *precisely* what I shall do."

I hoped "precisely" meant he'd explain it sans Shakespeare and mythology. Being an avid fan of crossword puzzles, I have a rather remarkable database of vocabulary and linguistic trivia in my head, but even I didn't know *precisely* what the lord was talking about—or even who he was talking to. My fingers itched to grab Uncle Eddie's *Bulfinch's Mythology* or *Bartlett's Familiar Quotations,* but I reached across the desk to retrieve only my notepaper and pencil. I might not have believed we should take the job, but I thought it would look more professional to take notes.

"First of all, Lord Herbert," I said with pencil poised, "did somebody refer you to us? I'd like to, um, thank them."

"The Delphic Oracle sent me," the man replied with a smile. "I had only to open her golden book of knowledge and set my finger to the spot."

I set my pencil to paper but had no idea what to write.

"He found us in the phone book," cunning Romulus (Delano) guessed.

Lord Herbert's smile widened. "Pure inspiration, those golden pages."

"Um, hmm." I made a quick note to myself to check Nightshade's ad first chance I got. What did it say, *We specialize in weird?* (Not that it would be wrong if it did.) "Well, then," I said, pressing on, "as Delano suggested, please tell us your plans. In American English."

I didn't really add that last line, but I should have.

"Precisely," Lord Herbert said. "'I, thus neglecting worldly ends, will dedicate all to closeness and the bettering of my mind.'"

Clearly, Lord Herbert had never stumbled upon the meaning of the word *precisely.* I sighed. "You mean . . ." My words trailed off. I had no idea what he meant. Since the pencil was useless for notes, I stuck it between my teeth to keep myself from saying what I was thinking.

"I plan to bequeath the last of the Graeme family's treasures to the most worthy of recipients," he explained in words I more or less understood. "And I will do so at my estate tomorrow night."

"And you're looking for security?" I said, removing the pencil from my mouth and hoping my gnawing on it had not left yellow paint chips between my teeth. "But not traditional security?"

"Precisely!"

From atop the unicorn Chaiya asked, "Who are you giving the Little Messenger to, Lord Herbert?"

He smiled. In fact, he never seemed to stop smiling. I thought of the tear-drenched Mrs. Mermann and the hearts I would break when I reported the results of Delano's "Case of the Missing Prospective Missionary." If nothing else, Lord Herbert would be a happy client for a change.

"With whom Hermes leaves the gala has yet to be determined," Lord Herbert told Chaiya. "I have, over the last few weeks, extended the most guarded of invitations to five renowned curators, foreign and domestic. I have also invited my sister and her son—though not even they have an inkling as to why the event is being held. Finally, I'll have a special guest whom I wish to remain anonymous."

The man had too many secrets. "For us to help you," I said, "we need to know everything you can tell us."

"And you *do!*" Lord Herbert exclaimed. "What else must you know?"

Clearly Delano could think of a detail or two. "Is, uh, Hermes at your estate right now?"

"Certainly not!" Lord Herbert said. "He is in a vacuum-sealed vault beneath the city. One cannot keep a centuries-old mummy lying around just anywhere, Romulus."

"Delano."

"Precisely."

To his credit, Delano persevered. "How will the mummy get to your estate?"

"He will come with the musicians. The violinist is a close, personal friend."

Delano shook his head, but I doubted the action helped to clear his brain very much.

I ventured, "You mean they're going to drive over together in a car?"

"Certainly not. I will send my limo for them."

"Don't you think it would be smarter to send an armored vehicle?" Delano asked.

"For a string quartet?" Lord Herbert chuckled. "Preposterous."

"For a mummy!" Delano said. "I'm assuming this thing you're talking about is the real deal. Worth a king's ransom."

"Your only error," Lord Herbert responded pleasantly, "is in the value you placed on the antiquity. No king could ransom Hermes if he is who I believe him to be. His worth to humanity, dear Romulus, is far beyond price as you calculate it."

Delano held out hands to me as if hoping I could pass him a little patience. Unfortunately, I was running a little short myself. "Aren't you worried the antiquity could be damaged, Lord Herbert?" I asked. "Or stolen?"

"Precisely!" He looked at me as though I had solved the mystery of the ages. Then he continued, "This is why I asked myself, 'Herbert, who would hijack a string quartet?' They are the most sublime entertainment, don't you agree?"

I ignored the question. "So you're planning to smuggle the sarcophagus onto your estate with a group of musicians." Before he could say, "Precisely," I added, "And you are certain nobody knows what you plan to do."

The lord nodded happily.

"But can you be absolutely sure of your vault keeper and the musicians? If one of them—"

"My secret is secure and my vault is better guarded than the gates of Mount Olympus," he interrupted. "As for my friend the violinist, he is Achates incarnate."

If only I'd known who Achates was.

"I could meet the musicians at the vault," Knute said while I eyed *Bullfinch's Mythology* again. "And ride to the estate with them and the mummy."

Lord Herbert clapped his hands. "Excellent, mighty Orion! I shall sleep soundly this night."

If we took this job, he'd be the *only* one who slept for the next thirty hours or so. I gnawed on the pencil for another second or two, then asked, "And at the estate? What security do you have there?"

Lord Herbert extended two pudgy hands, palms up. "My life, my Hermes, is in your fair hands. Tell me what you recommend."

"Armed guards," I said, heartened to think that if he

would listen to reason, we might be able to take the case after all. "Delano, Knute, and I will be there, of course—"

"And me!" Chaiya interrupted from atop the unicorn.

Lord Herbert smiled her way. "I would have it no other way, Polymnia."

"But you need more than the four of us," I cautioned. I couldn't believe I was thinking of doing this, but if I pulled this off—*when* I pulled this off—wouldn't I have something really impressive to report to Uncle Eddie the next time he called from Paris? I drew a deep breath and plunged in with both feet. "We'll take the job if you agree to an armed guard at each door and four more with the mummy at all times."

"A Roman legion?" Lord Herbert gasped. "Oh, no! We must keep this low-key. Understated. It must seem to be only a little dinner party among friends and associates. If the press were to get wind of his existence before Hermes is transported safely to his proper home . . ." The lord's words trailed off in a shudder of horror.

"He's got a point," Knute observed. "No use advertising for trouble."

I hesitated. I'd never known Knute to be wrong. On the other hand, I'd never known King Tut to travel around the country with only a string quartet for protection. Was the lord painfully discreet or mentally distracted?

When my molars began to ache from biting down on the pencil, I removed it from my mouth and said, "*Nobody* knows what you have planned for tomorrow's event? Not even the guests? You're absolutely *certain?*"

"Even the guests do not know why they come," Lord Herbert said. "They only know they were invited for dinner."

Yeah, but I bet they were salivating already. I mean, as curators, they must all read the *Smithsonian,* or at least know Lord Herbert. They would be hoping for a treasure of *some* sort to accompany the entrée. I looked Lord Herbert over from head to foot and wondered if he were insane or inspired. (Then I wondered just how fine the line was between the two.) Finally, I looked from Delano to Knute and asked, "What do you guys think? Should we take the case?"

Delano shrugged. "Dicey. But I'm up for it if you are."

Knute, I knew from his expression, had already told me what he thought. *No use advertising for trouble.* Besides, like Delano, he was always up for anything.

"*Two* armed guards," I told the odd, elderly man, hoping I sounded decisive and not pleading. "Plainclothes if you like, but I want them with the mummy every single second it's on your property." When the lord didn't object, I added, "We contract with off-duty officers from the Phoenix PD. I'll get you two of the best." I already had the men in mind. Between them they had more than fifty years of experience.

Lord Herbert smiled broadly into the face of my newfound enthusiasm.

"We need a guest list," I continued, turning to a fresh page on the notepad and, for once, using the pencil according to design. "And the names of the musicians." I turned to Knute. "Who else?"

"Servants. Caterers. Anybody who will be on the grounds when the mummy is."

I frowned in concern. "Can we get that many background checks run in time?"

"I can stay and help you with it," Chaiya volunteered. "I'm sure I'll find *somebody* to use for my test tomorrow." She looked at our new client's overabundance of white hair and observed happily, "You sure need a cut and shape!"

Clearly having no idea what the girl had in mind, the gnomish man nodded amiably.

Regardless of Lord Herbert's fate when next the sun rose, I was grateful to have use of my cousin's ten extra fingers. Still, I was asking the near impossible of our skeleton staff, and I knew it. "Knute?"

"No sweat, boss," he said with a grin. "Before morning we'll know more about them than their mothers do."

"Delano," I said, turning to the shaggier member of the team, "you'll go to the estate? And the vault? You'll have time to look at the limo? Check out—"

"Yep," he broke in. "Been there. Done that. Repeat."

"Okay," I said, standing. "Okay!" I extended a hand to Lord Herbert. "Thank you for the job, sir. You'll be glad you hired Nightshade."

"Why, dear lady," he beamed, "I already am!"

I smiled from him up to the framed portrait of Edward Shade that hung on the far wall. *Can you believe it, Uncle Eddie?* I asked the image silently. *The very first job I get on my own is to protect an honest-to-gosh Egyptian mummy.*

Lord Herbert's words began to come back to me, and my smile faded a millimeter at a time.

The most intriguing find to come from the land of the pharaohs, he had said. *No king could ransom Hermes if he is who I believe him to be . . .*

I leaned back against the desk. *That sarcophagus holds a secret.* The words echoed in my head. *Quite possibly the secret of the ages.*

A lump rose in my throat. I tried to swallow, but the lump didn't move.

"Oh, Uncle Eddie!" I whispered to the picture. "What am I getting us into *this* time?"

ACROSS
   13 *Small yard statuary; What Lord Herbert resembles*
DOWN
   17 *One of the mythical founders of Rome who was raised by wolves; What Lord Herbert calls Delano*

Chapter 4

"Where *are* those policemen?" I asked Chaiya for the sixteenth time in fifteen minutes. I didn't expect her to know the answer, of course, but that didn't stop me from asking the question.

We stood at the service entrance to Lord Herbert's magnificent estate, situated atop one of the most rugged and exclusive addresses in the Valley of the Sun—Mummy Mountain. (How ironic is *that?*) Hours before, Delano had pointed out with satisfaction that there was nothing but barren desert between Graeme Manor's front gate and the highway below. Lord Herbert was a man who liked privacy. Even the turnoff to his home was made to look more like a path for desert bighorn sheep than the entrance to an estate. The likelihood of surprise visitors was almost nil.

That was good. What was bad was that while we had an isolated fortress, we didn't have any troops with which to defend it. The two officers we'd hired were supposed to arrive at 7:15— a half hour before the mummy, and ninety minutes before the guests. I looked at my watch. It was 7:15 exactly. "They're late."

"Maybe they were deterred," Chaiya guessed. At the look on my face she tried again. "Oh, wait. My mistake. I mean *detoured.*"

"There's only one road—" I began, then caught myself as Chaiya's meaning became clear. "You mean *detained.*" I looked again at my watch, but it was only thirty seconds later. "They'd better not be deterred, detoured, *or* detained much longer." I turned to Chaiya. "Who did you get again?"

If only our regular guys had been available I wouldn't have worried, but Lord Herbert had chosen the busiest night of the year for his event. *Phantom* was being revived at Gammage, the Coyotes were on ice against the Blackhawks, some rock group had attracted 30,000 teenagers to the America West Arena, and John Williams was the guest conductor at Symphony Hall. In short, every man, woman, and canine in the Phoenix metro area who carried a badge and wasn't on active duty was somewhere downtown directing traffic, sniffing for drugs, or keeping an eye on the crowds. We'd had to take the leftovers.

"Don't worry," Chaiya said. "My friend says they're good. Especially Officer Casey."

I knew both Chaiya and her friend at Phoenix PD. To them, "good" meant "good-looking." I watched my cousin adjust her dress and tried not to roll my eyes. She wore a purple velveteen number studded with rhinestones. I couldn't guess where she got it, but surmised it had been hanging on a rack since the days of disco, patiently awaiting Chaiya—or a blind woman. With her tight braids undone, her raven locks were wild and kinky.

"How do I look?" she asked anxiously.

"You look like a skinny, diamond-encrusted eggplant with black ramen noodles on top."

Okay, I didn't say that. I told her the same thing I'd told her the last ten times she'd asked. "You look very pretty, Chaiya."

She smiled. "You do too. In fact, you look stunning."

Despite my best efforts to stifle them, near homonyms for *stunning* ran through my head. Because I'm sensitive about my height—or lack thereof—*stunted, stubby,* and *stumpy* came to mind. I looked down at my basic black dress in concern. "Are you saying this makes me look short? I mean shorter?"

Chaiya laughed. "It pays to increase your word power, Sammy. I'm saying you look gorgeous."

Gorgonic?

I commanded my mind to stop analyzing Chaiya's vocabulary and looked again at my watch. Then I glanced behind me to check on Wendela. Then I spun around and looked closer at the empty chair where I had recently placed Wendela and her needlework. It really *was* empty. I looked around the service entrance. Finally, I panicked.

"She's gone!" I told Chaiya. "I told her to sit right there. I told her not to move. She promised me she wouldn't move. She . . . oh my gosh!" I stepped out the door and looked up toward the roof three stories above my head. Thankfully, Wendela wasn't up there. At least, she wasn't up there yet.

"It's okay, Sammy," Chaiya said, grasping my elbow as if to keep me from dissolving into a puddle of nerves that might soil her purple silk shoes. "She's with Lord Herbert."

I've never fainted in all my life, but I thought this might be a good time to start. This was my first contracted job as interim head of Nightshade—the most important night of my whole life—and I'd had to bring Wendela. (Bring her, leave her at our apartment in a straitjacket, or drop her off at the state mental hospital on the way to work.) I couldn't impose on my mother to Wendela-sit even one more night—my father had made that clear. Besides, she *was* my responsibility. I'd already risked everything for her and there was no turning back. Most of the time I didn't want to turn back. *But tonight?*

"Oh, Chaiya!" I cried.

"Chill," Chaiya said calmly. "It's all good. While you were going over the floor plans with Knute, Lord Herbert came in and I introduced him to Wendela. He insisted on showing her around his house. He's even having a place set for her at dinner."

My stomach clenched. I was going to be sick, and then I was going to faint, and then I might just die. "He can't do that!"

Let me explain. Despite her lovely exterior, Wendela is less a lovely, mature woman than she is an animate grab bag. When you open the bag it's impossible to say what will come out, but it will almost certainly be bizarre. That's why I had to keep her hidden safely away in the kitchen. And it wasn't like she would mind. Wendela is content wherever she is. Mostly. Except when she has one of her "night spells." Then she feels compelled to scale trellises, trees, billboards—whatever's handy as long as it's high. What if she had a spell at Lord Herbert's? And even if she didn't have a spell and managed to keep her feet on the ground, what would keep her from opening her mouth?

"Wendela can't converse with those people!" I exclaimed. "They're scholars and diplomats. What will they think?"

Chaiya shrugged. "Who cares what people think, Sammy?"

Everybody cares! I wanted to scream. *Everybody but you and Wendela!*

"Lord Herbert doesn't care," Chaiya said. "It's his party."

I held up my hands in surrender and was appalled to see how badly they shook. I clasped them together and turned toward the door. "I have to find her." Skirting the cook on my way through the kitchen, I added, "If those policemen aren't here in five minutes I want you to call the station and raise—"

"Here they come."

A small, older-model car turned the corner of the estate. If I'd given it more than half a backward glance I might have noted it looked familiar. As it was, the only thing that hit me was a wave of relief.

"Radio Delano," I said. "Tell him they're here, and then keep them right here to wait for the mummy." Chaiya was already readjusting her dress and shaking her head as if to further tangle her hair. "I'll be back as soon as I've found Wendela."

I waited to make sure Chaiya stopped primping long enough to pull the tiny two-way radio from her beaded purse. "My radio is on," I said as I reached the far side of the kitchen. "Call me if you need anything."

But don't need anything, I begged silently. *Please, please don't need anything.*

It was ten minutes before I found Wendela, but I was grateful it hadn't taken me longer. (The Pentagon is smaller than Lord Herbert's house.) I finally found them in the study—a more-or-less isolated room with a single door. It was painted soft beige and was devoid of both windows and decoration. A dozen plush chairs were arranged in a semicircle around a raised dais in the center of the room. A spotlight recessed in the ceiling cast a muted golden glow onto a plain, padded stand that must have been custom-designed to hold the sarcophagus. The only other furnishings were four music stands and a like number of straight-backed chairs that awaited the arrival of the musicians. Clearly, all was in place for the mummified guest of honor.

"Has he come?" Lord Herbert asked, rising from his chair when I skidded into the room. His white hair was now cleanly cut over the collar of his rumpled tuxedo, and his beard had been perfectly shaped by Chaiya.

At least there's hope for her career, I thought with a twinge of envy.

"Oh, my!" the elderly man sighed. "It's been so long since I've seen my Hermes!" He held out a hand for Wendela. "My dear, he's here."

Before I could correct the lord's misunderstanding, Wendela extended her slender hand and smiled up at him. As it had the first moment I saw her, it struck me what a classic beauty this woman was. With her large eyes, delicate features, and luxurious blond tresses—hair that showed but a few silver streaks though she must be in her mid-seventies—Wendela looked like a fairy queen who had tumbled carelessly from between the pages of a tale by the Brothers Grimm.

Lord Herbert took the hand gingerly, raised the lady to her feet, and kissed her palm. She was several inches taller than the gnomish lord, even in the satin slippers she wore with her ankle-length gown. (Don't blame me. I'd almost cleaned out D.I. trying to nudge Wendela's wardrobe from the twelfth century into the twenty-first, but all the jeans, slacks, and modern dresses I took home to her had yet to touch Wendela's creamy skin. Instead, she wore simple, flowing gowns of her own design and construction, as if she had just stepped away from a Renaissance festival and expected to be called back momentarily.)

Lord Herbert approached with the lady on his arm. "Are they bringing him in now?"

"The mummy isn't here yet," I explained. "But the security officers are. Finally."

Lord Herbert sighed again, but this time in resignation. "Another few moments, Wendela, dear. I suppose we must be patient." To me he said, "We *will* have a few moments alone with Hermes before the guests arrive?"

Time. Guests. Mummy. Wendela. Stress.

I shook myself, hoping Lord Herbert wouldn't think I was having a seizure. (I hoped I *wasn't* having a seizure.) Ignoring his question, I took Wendela's other arm, gently but firmly. "I've been looking all over for you. You promised me you'd stay in the kitchen. Where's your needlework?"

"I promised?" Wendela murmured, her violet eyes limpid. "Forgive me, Samantha."

"No, fair Samantha, it is me you must forgive," Lord Herbert said. "I captured this lovely lady and dragged her away against her wishes."

"Anyway," I said, "I need to get Wendela back to the kitchen before the mummy comes."

Although I tugged, Lord Herbert would not relinquish Wendela's other elbow. Instead he tugged back. "She is 'all the comfort I pray the gods will diet me with,'" he said. "Could you be so cruel as to take her from me?"

I didn't have time for this, but what could I do? I couldn't leave Wendela. I couldn't use her slender arms to play tug-of-war with an aged, rumpled Romeo. And I certainly couldn't come right out and tell the lord his new crush was even loonier than *he* was.

"Wendela must be with me tonight to see to the care of Hermes," Lord Herbert continued. "Her arrival is a gift from the gods." He leaned close and lowered his voice. "I hear that she and Hermes may in fact be family."

"Wendela!" I cried, horrified, but unsure what I was objecting to.

Family? Why add a new story line now? Why tonight? Why to Lord Herbert? I wanted to look into her head to see if her mind was getting worse. Could it possibly *get* any worse?

Wendela had maintained from our first meeting at the mental hospital that she'd come to Phoenix from the stars and would return someday, trailing clouds of glory. That she had Wordsworth confused with Asimov was apparent; the mystery was where she *had* come from. No matter who asked her, or how important her answer was to her future, Wendela would say only that she came from the stars. At least she *had* said that—right up until tonight when she'd apparently told Lord Herbert she hailed from ancient Egypt.

What a change of venue. But I wasn't quite as alarmed when I had a chance to think it through. I mean, is ancient Thebes any less likely a birthplace than Orion? Besides, if she decided she was Cleopatra, maybe she'd stop climbing trellises to watch for spaceships. Then my mom and I could fix her up with a private little palace at Shady Acres and she'd finally be happy.

A girl can dream, can't she?

"That's very, um, interesting, isn't it?" I said to Lord Herbert. "But—"

The tiny two-way radio on my chest beeped, interrupting my words. (With no pocket in my dress and a tendency to mislay a purse within the first ten minutes of picking it up, I'd resorted to using a narrow, black satin ribbon to hang the device around my neck. I released Wendela's arm to reach for the radio and pressed a button.

"We're at the gate," Knute said through the device. "Smooth sailing all the way."

I let out a sigh of relief. "The guards are waiting at the back entrance," I told him. "Delano?"

"Present," the man chimed in from who knew where.

"Hermes is here!" Lord Herbert exclaimed. "At last, Wendela, my dear! At last!"

I bit my lower lip, having nothing more to lose by the nervous habit since I'd chewed off the last vestiges of lipstick hours before. Looking at Wendela, my mind raced. I was out of time and options, both at once.

Maybe Chaiya was right about Wendela, I decided (with only desperation to guide me). With Lord Herbert already displaying the eccentricity that only the rich get away with outside of an asylum, what could Wendela hurt? Assuming, that is, she kept both feet on the ground at all times.

"Do you want to stay with Lord Herbert?" I asked.

"Oh, yes!" Wendela exclaimed.

"And that's all right with you, Lord Herbert?"

"'I hold her as a thing ensky'd and sainted.'"

"Don't get her started thinking about the sky," I warned him. Then I took both Wendela's hands in mine and looked deep into her eyes. If only I could be sure there was somebody inside that pretty head to pay attention to me. "You'll stay right here with Lord Herbert?" I urged. "You won't go outside, no matter what?"

"Yes?" Wendela said. "No?"

That was good enough.

"Keep her with you, Lord Herbert," I pleaded. "I'll be right back with Hermes."

"An assignment for which to perish," he said. "Be fleet of foot, Samantha! Bring us our Hermes!"

"Maybe you should use some of that money of yours to hire a dialogue coach."

I didn't say that, of course. I didn't say anything. Instead, I was as fleet-footed as possible without running in the halls, and I found my way back to the kitchen with only a couple of wrong turns.

Chaiya met me at the door. "They're inedible!" she whispered. "I have dibs on Officer Casey."

"Whatever," I said, hoping the policemen were incredible instead of unpalatable, and that Chaiya referred to their professionalism rather than their biceps. Even with their backs turned to me, I could see as I approached that it was likely their biceps that impressed her. But the way the one guy filled the coat of his formal wear *did* inspire some confidence in me as well. (At least it inspired *something* because my heart beat faster for sure.)

"Good evening, gentlemen," I said. "You're late."

When they turned, my jaw almost hit the floor. I knew those men; I just didn't know *how* I knew them. Then, in the next gasp, I did.

"You!" the broad-shouldered officer and I said at the same moment.

The other policeman stepped forward and extended his hand, grinning. "I wondered if you'd remember us, Miss Shade."

I didn't raise my hand because I couldn't be sure what I'd do with it—shake hands with him, cover my mouth to stifle a scream, or slap his partner. This was the officer (Monroe, wasn't it?) that I'd given my statement to on the stakeout a couple of nights before. Sure, it was a coincidence to run into him again, but not impossible. Chaiya *had* called the Phoenix PD after all. What was impossible was the man at his side—the tall, good-looking creep who'd propositioned the child and stolen my camera. He was the reason I couldn't get Uncle Eddie's camera back. He was the reason I was in such hot water with Mrs. Mermann. And he was here.

"Why aren't you in jail?" (And I really did say it this time.)

"Robert Monroe," the slighter man continued, as if I hadn't spoken. "Nice to see you again. This is my partner, Thomas Casey." His grin widened. "Thom's an undercover cop, but he's off duty for a few days until a certain civilian's assault charge goes before the board of review."

I crossed my arms over my chest. *Undercover cop?* It was too much to process in too little time, so I took the easy way out. "You're fired."

Thom shook his head. "Don't bother, lady. I quit." He scowled at his partner as he turned to leave. "Very funny, Bob. You outdid yourself this time."

"Yeah," Monroe chuckled. "I thought so too." They were already out the door.

"Wait!" Chaiya cried. "Don't let them go, Sammy!"

I turned away, only to see Delano leaning in the doorway. "That's not bad advice," he said. "Unless you can be in two places at once, Sam, we don't have anybody else to mummysit."

"We'll call—"

"Who? Even if you found somebody—and you won't with everything going on tonight—it'll take two or three hours to get them up here." Delano motioned out the door with his thumb. "And you've got about one minute before the royal Egyptian stiff arrives." He shrugged. "You're the one who wanted armed guards, Sammy. What are you gonna do if those men leave—hang a revolver around your neck with the radio?"

"Okay," I hissed. "I get it. Tell them they can stay."

"I'm not the one who fired them."

A dozen retorts crossed my mind, but in the end I knew better than to argue with Delano. I turned and ran back to the open door. "You can stay," I called after the officers.

Thom Casey had already opened his car door. "Thanks, but no thanks."

"You're not fired!" I said. "And I'll . . . I'll sue if you quit at the last minute for no reason!" He shook his head, and I was furious. "I have a good attorney, mister! Mick Farrell. Maybe you've heard of him." I didn't mention how unlikely it was that Mick would take a call from me after the way I'd screwed up Mrs. Mermann's case.

"It's your call," Bob said when Casey hesitated. "I only took the job because I figured she owes you. Besides, it's not me the cap's gonna rag on if she shows up at the precinct again to complain."

I saw by the way Casey stiffened that Monroe's threat was better than the one I'd come up with. "I will complain!" I told Casey. "I'll march in there tomorrow morning and tell him how you walked out on me. How you walked out on *Lord Herbert Graeme*. I'll—"

Casey slammed his car door closed just as a long, black Hummer limo rounded the corner and pulled to a stop.

"Good choice," I said, turning to go back into the manor before Casey saw me slump in relief. "Knute's in the car," I said over my shoulder. "He'll tell you what to do."

If only Knute would tell ME *what to do,* I thought on my way back to the study. *Or even tell me what it is I've already done.* It was as if I could feel Thom Casey's hostile gray eyes looking through me as I walked back down the hall. If there was one thing I didn't need on this night of nights, it was to have to deal with him again—whoever he was.

ACROSS

    16 In Greek mythology, the winged messenger of the gods;
       Lord Herbert's mummy

DOWN

    41 Ancient land of pharaohs, pyramids, and puzzles

Chapter 5

So this is Hermes.

I stood near Officer Monroe in the doorway of the study and watched the reunion unfold between man and mummy. (Believe me when I tell you that the prodigal son was received with less enthusiasm.) Lord Herbert had met Knute and Officer Casey and supervised every careful step they took until the pint-sized sarcophagus was in its place of honor on the dais. Then Knute beat a hasty retreat from the lord's florid exclamations of delight and took his post at the end of the hallway that led only to this and two other rooms. Casey remained at the mummy's side. It was clear he was trying to be professional, but he wasn't having much success. The officer's eyes kept straying to the Lord of the Manor and the Lady of the Lake on his arm.

Even I couldn't blame him for that. They were quite a sight.

And I couldn't fault Casey for not doing his job, either. When he first came in he'd scanned the bare walls and ceilings as if to memorize every inch. Now, as his partner leaned against the door frame flirting with me, Casey stood alert and at attention. He looked ready for anything, even though the room was empty save for Wendela, the owner of the antiquity, and those employed to protect it. When Casey caught me staring at him, I looked down in chagrin.

"He's always like that," Monroe said.

"Excuse me?"

"Dudley Do-Right." Monroe motioned toward Thom with his chin. "That's what we call him down at the station."

"Why?"

"Isn't it obvious?"

I didn't know if it was or not. The guy was an enigma. "He's your partner, did you say?"

"Yeah. We were assigned together right after we finished training. We did some patrol work as rookies, then landed in vice." Looking at his partner, he grinned. "Casey doesn't look like he could pull off an undercover gig outside of Disneyland, does he?"

I shook my head, but it was mostly at the dawning realization that Knute had been right. I'd only *thought* I knew what I was doing on that stakeout. Instead of righting wrong I'd interfered with an undercover cop and maybe blown his cover. I'd—

"He's a Mormon boy," Monroe said, breaking into my thoughts. "A real gentleman and scholar." It was hard to tell from the guy's ironic tone which of those three things he thought was most distasteful. "He's trying to prove himself, but Casey's not cut out for police work, no matter what his old man thinks."

I drew a breath. "So you were working on Wednesday when I . . ."

"*I* was," Monroe said. "Casey was off duty. That's what landed him in the soup. That and your charges, of course."

Then he is *a creep*, I thought with relief. (I just hate when Knute can tell me, "I told you so.") That must be why Monroe said Casey wasn't cut out for police work, and why he sounded so ironic when he called his partner a gentleman.

I couldn't wait to tell Knute I'd told him so, and to add that I'd done an even better deed than I'd first imagined—I'd busted a bad cop. I cast the two-faced "Mormon boy" my best glare, but he missed it because he was looking at the sarcophagus.

And I could see why. Now that Lord Herbert had ceased to embrace it and had sat down with Wendela—apparently to chat with the mummy—I was able to get my first real look at it myself.

The ancient coffin stood about five feet tall and was maybe three feet wide. It was beautifully carved and set with semi-precious stones. The top third probably represented the person interred therein, but the bottom was carved with hieroglyphics. At least I assumed they were hieroglyphics since they looked a lot like what you see on the frontispiece of the Book of Abraham. (Or scribbled notes from Chaiya. Her handwriting looks a whole lot like reformed Egyptian too.) Among the figures of dogs and beetles and ministering Egyptians was something like the equations found on chalkboards of trigonometry teachers. All in all, it was weird and a little creepy.

But the weirdest thing was the top. Although Hermes wore a headpiece like all the best-dressed mummies on the covers of *National Geographic,* the face beneath the headdress was different from anything I'd seen. I took a step closer to better see the face and the long, delicate arms crossed over a narrow chest. Within its hands were a rod and a triangular something I didn't recognize. I blinked when it seemed to me the mummy's amber eyes returned my stare. But looking again, I decided my first impression was wrong. Hermes wasn't creepy. He was intriguing. Whoever this mummy was, I wished I knew his story. I wished I knew if the wise and wistful expression on his face had been the art of the coffin makers or a replication of how he had looked in life.

"How do you like our Little Messenger?" Lord Herbert asked, turning and extending a hand to urge me closer.

"I like him," I said. "He's simply . . . amazing."

"*Isn't* he?" Lord Herbert beamed and squeezed Wendela's hand. "'A breath thou art,'" he told her. "'Servile to all the skyey influences.'" He looked deep into her eyes. "Do you know him, my dear?"

I caught my breath at the aptness of the lord's words. If ever anybody was "servile to skyey influences," it was Wendela. From the corner of my eye I saw Officer Casey's eyes widen as he too looked at Wendela. It made me angry that a person like him would dare to look at her, let alone stare at her the way he was now.

Wendela didn't notice any of us. Her eyes sparkled with tears. "Oh, Herbert! He looks so sad!"

This, thankfully, didn't answer the question. Before she could elaborate, or Lord Herbert could press, a woman's voice echoed down the hall—apparently in response to something Knute had said to her.

"I will go where I please!" the stranger shrieked. "Who are *you* to tell me where I will and will not go in my brother's home? You, you . . . monster!"

There were more adjectives spewed Knute's way, but they weren't the kind I listen to, let alone list.

Lord Herbert shook his head. "'Here will be an old abusing of God's patience and the king's English.'"

"*The Merry Wives of Windsor*," Officer Casey said under his breath.

"Precisely!" the lord exclaimed, clearly pleased. He clasped the officer's arm as he turned to me. "Samantha, my dove, for the second time tonight you have surprised me with yet another kindred spirit. First Wendela, and now young Nestor, the epitome of wisdom and justice."

Lord Herbert might have known his mythology and Shakespeare, but he was a lousy judge of character. Of all the people to clasp to his bosom, he'd chosen a lunar moth and an asp. I might have told him as much—at least where Casey was concerned—if the voice in the hall hadn't grown louder as it drew closer. Clearly this woman didn't share her brother's good-natured temperament—or his vocabulary. Most of the words she screeched at Knute continued to be of the four-letter variety.

Officer Monroe leaned out the door to look, but that was all. "The big guy oughtta toss her back down the hall," he observed. "He looks like he could do it."

The big guy, I knew, was too professional and too kind to do any such thing. "Lord Herbert?" I said, seeking his wishes.

"My sister," he sighed. "'A little more than kin, and less than kind.' I suppose I must go to greet her. It won't do for her to come upon Hermes prematurely." He released Casey's arm to extend the elbow to Wendela. "My dear? Shall we retire to the lounge to endure my sister and await my guests?"

Wendela stood and slipped her slender white hand into the crook of Herbert's arm, but her eyes were still on the sarcophagus. "Yes, Herbert."

I started to follow, but first turned back to Casey. "Don't move," I said. Then, so only he could hear, I added, "If you mess this up in *any* way for me, Casey, I'll have your badge *and* your hide."

"Yes, ma'am," he said.

I didn't know if the tone I heard in his voice was sycophancy (crossword-puzzle dictionary definition: "smooth talk") or sarcasm, but I suspected the latter. I turned and walked away, but in my mind's eye I could still see the dimple that winked into his right cheek when he set his lips into a grim, determined line.

***

"Herbert!" Hedda Mead said sharply. "What is this about?"

Clearly the other guests in the dining room wondered the same thing, but were too polite to ask. Either that or they were intuitive enough to know they might have something to gain by answering Lord Herbert's enigmatic invitation, but were keeping their curiosity in check for fear of losing the prize before they knew what it was. Almost in unison, they raised silver spoonfuls of bouillabaisse to their lips and exchanged furtive glances across the candlelit table. The only ones who seemed to enjoy the soup were Lord Herbert, Wendela, and Chaiya. My cousin had finagled herself a seat next to the youngish, almost-handsome curator of a small but prestigious museum in Naples. He was, I knew from the background checks of the day before, unmarried. Apparently Chaiya knew it too.

I looked down both sides of the long table. There were eleven of us in all, but from what I could tell, the only thing we had in common was membership in the species Homo sapiens. (And that might not be true if one believed Wendela's claims of descent.)

At my left was a distinguished gentleman from the Smithsonian Institution. Of the curators, he knew Lord Herbert best. At my right, unfortunately, was Harrison Mead, the lord's only heir apparent. It had taken me less than five minutes to understand why Herbert had so carefully parceled out the Graeme treasures to worthy institutions. Like his mother, Harrison was arrogant and ill-tempered. Unlike his mother, he was silent and glassy-eyed. Still, I felt bad for the poor woman on his right, a middle-aged representative of the British Royal Museum. Although Harrison said no more to her than he did to me, his left elbow kept impacting uncomfortably with her right one while they ate. If Harrison noticed his rudeness, he didn't care to apologize for it.

The last two "contestants" in Lord Herbert's bizarre game sat across from me. They were an attaché to the ambassador of Egypt, and a wild card. It hadn't escaped my attention that not only had Lord Herbert left the man off our list of people to check out in advance, he'd failed to introduce the fifty-ish, balding man to anyone at the table. He'd never even called him by name—actual or mythological.

For his part, the mystery man was quiet, speaking only when spoken to and then briefly. I didn't think he was part of the antiquities crowd. He wore a suit rather than a tuxedo, and even that was ill fitting and threadbare at the elbows. He didn't know which fork to use for the shrimp cocktail or which spoon to pick up for the soup. I didn't think he knew why he'd been invited here any more than the others did, but he seemed much less concerned about the peculiar circumstances. Overall, he impressed me as a man who was used to waiting and watching and not getting what he wanted. At the moment, he watched Wendela and that made me uncomfortable. I was almost glad when Hedda slapped her spoon down into her soup, splattering the poor attaché at her side. At least it took the mystery man's attention away from Wendela.

"Herbert!" Hedda screeched. "Answer me!"

All eyes turned to the head of the table where Lord Herbert seemed to have already forgotten his sister's question.

"She wants to know why you've invited them here, Herbert," Wendela said.

My eyes widened at the realization that Wendela's mind seemed to be within her head for a change. After more than an hour, she still seemed to behave like a normal person. Better than a normal person; Wendela was charming. It was too good to be true. And then in the next sentence it wasn't.

"She wants you to tell them about Hermes," Wendela continued. "About your Little Messenger who came from the stars."

I coughed bouillabaisse into my linen napkin. When I recovered, I glanced around the table. Maybe it was all right after all. As cryptic as her words were, Wendela's remark made as much sense to the scholars as Herbert's continuing off-the-wall Shakespearean quotes. Only Hedda and the guy in the suit seemed affected. The color of Hedda's eyes deepened in anger while the mystery man's lightened in interest.

"A messenger from the stars?" he said. "Do tell."

"Don't tell!" I cried. Feeling every eye in the room move to me, I stammered, "I mean . . ." What did I mean?

Moreover, what did Wendela mean? And where was inspiration when one needed it?

In this case, it came from the most unexpected source.

"She means it's Lord Herbert's surprise, Wendela," Chaiya said. "Don't spoil it for him."

"Oh!" Wendela cried. "Forgive me, Herbert."

He smiled. "Nothing to forgive, my dear. You are merely as anxious as I to introduce our guest of honor to my friends."

"Friends, my foot!" Hedda said. "You don't know these people, Herbert!"

"I know every one of them," he replied serenely. Then his bright blue eyes moved to the man in the ugly suit. "If only by reputation."

Reputation for what? More than anything, the enigmatic guest looked like a stereotypical used-car salesman.

"I must admit, Lord Herbert," the Smithsonian curate said, laying down his spoon, "my curiosity is piqued. I am here because your kind invitation said I 'must' come, but," he exchanged a look with the woman from England, "I do wonder if perhaps you are stringing us along."

Lord Herbert looked stung. "Stringing you along? My dear Professor Northcutt, surely—" He cut himself off in midthought and pushed his chair back from the table. Then he pulled the napkin from the collar of his starched shirt and patted it to his lips before rising.

"I had thought to save the introduction of Hermes for after dessert," he said. "But I see that our rack of lamb and Yorkshire pudding might well be ruined by our anticipation." To the serving maid he said, "Extend to the cook my apology, will you, my dear? And implore her to keep this sumptuous repast warm." To the assemblage at the table he concluded, "Shall we retire to the study between courses?"

I almost knocked over my chair trying to get out of it quickly enough to precede the group into the hall and notify Knute and Delano by radio of the change in plans.

Fortunately, I am naturally fleet of foot, so I arrived at the hallway well before Lord Herbert and his guests. Knute had just left the study to return to his post.

"Is everything all right?" I asked as we met.

"It's as quiet as a tomb in there."

I smiled thinly at the pun. "Delano?"

"He's still prowling around outside," Knute said. "Nothing to report." As I let out a sigh of relief, he asked, "Is the lord serving fast food? I didn't expect them for another hour or better."

"A change in plans," I said, using an index finger to massage a newly developing sore spot on my temple. "Lord Herbert's sister's been impossible, and with all his guests expecting treasure beyond their wildest imagination, everyone's a little antsy." At the sound of approaching voices, I glanced nervously up the hall. "Is the quartet in place?"

"You in charge of entertainment, too, Sam?"

"I just want everything to be perfect."

"It is perfect." He reached past me to press a button on the wall that activated the manorwide intercom. Chamber music wafted over the speakers and Knute smiled. "See there? The musicians are playing. The guards are standing at attention. Doggone it if I don't think the mummy's smiling."

Although I massaged the sore spot a little more vigorously at the thought of the guards—or one of the guards—I looked up at my friend in appreciation. "You're the best."

"That's what they tell me."

Judging by the increasing volume of the voices coming toward us, Lord Herbert's group would arrive any moment. "Okay," I said. "This is it. Good luck to us."

I hurried down the corridor to the study doorway. Both officers now stood at Hermes's side. Seeing me look in, Monroe grinned and Casey frowned. I shifted my gaze toward the tuxedo-clad musicians and tried to focus on their soothing music. In a few moments the scholars— Egyptologists all—would arrive, perhaps to confirm Lord

Herbert's belief that his little Hermes was the most important thing to ever come from the land of the pharaohs.

I stiffened at the thought of what this evening could mean to the worlds of art and science—and what it could mean to me. I was standing right there, right then, in charge of what could turn out to be the greatest archeological discovery of the twenty-first century.

I reached behind my back to grip the door frame. I'm pretty sure if I hadn't used my arms to reinforce my faltering knees, the temporary head of Nightshade Investigation, Inc., would have slid to the floor in a heap of terror and black silk.

ACROSS
   27 Teutonic name meaning "wanderer"; Woman of the
      Welkin (welkin: arbor of heaven; stars)
DOWN
   19 Private Utah (Idaho, Hawaii) university; Thom Casey's
      alma mater

Chapter 6

It had been twenty minutes since the group entered the study, but not one of the chairs Lord Herbert offered his guests had been put to use.

My powers of deduction felt as extraneous as the furniture. Although I'd watched the group closely and strained to hear every word they said, I had yet to determine the consensus on Hermes—or if there was a consensus. After the first few moments of startled exclamation, they had mostly stood and stared. The only one who spoke was Lord Herbert, and he might as well have recited a Shakespearean soliloquy for all the sense he made.

In fact, I wondered if perhaps he *was* reciting Shakespeare. The part about 'God's journeyman' sounded vaguely familiar. I glanced at Thom Casey and suspected he would know—not that I would ever ask him. Thus far, he hadn't missed a single one of the vague references Lord Herbert had cast his way.

Talk about a classic creep, I thought.

On the other hand, Casey didn't miss much, period. While his partner chatted with Chaiya (whose plan to attract Thom's attention by playing hard-to-get seemed doomed to failure), his eyes were on the only two people in the room besides the musicians and me who were not gathered around the mummy.

I followed his gaze. Hedda Mead spoke to her son—quietly for once—in the corner. When the woman's eyes moved to her brother they narrowed in suspicion at what Lord Herbert planned to do next.

I looked back at the group and wished one of them—any one of them—would say something to give me a clue as to what that mummy was worth. The first one to pick up on my psychic vibes was the stranger, but considering the profanity he used, I was sorry I'd heard his thoughts verbalized. After the admiring obscenities, he said, "I didn't believe it when you first called me, Lord Herbert. I tell you, I didn't believe it for one minute."

Something in the timbre of the man's voice seemed familiar. I thought for a second I knew him. Then I dismissed the thought as silly. Nothing about the man looked familiar, and he certainly seemed like the kind of person that, once met, was never forgotten.

Lord Herbert beamed. "Do you believe it now, sir?"

The man laughed and collapsed onto a chair. "Do *you?*"

Lord Herbert's eyes twinkled. "'There are more things in heaven and earth, Horatio, than are dreamt of in your philosophy.'" He chuckled. "Well, not *your* philosophy, of course. I speak of the others." He turned and took Wendela's hand as he asked the scholars, "What think you magi from the land of Osiris?"

I held my breath, but nobody wanted to be the first to speak. They exchanged furtive glances and held their tongues.

At last Northcutt cleared his throat. "Where—?" he began. Then he paused and began again. "That is to say, when—?"

"How—?" the Egyptian attaché interrupted.

"Who—?" the British curator broke in.

"Precisely!" Lord Herbert exclaimed. "You must know more! May I prevail upon you to be seated?" Like obedient school children, the four men and one woman quickly took their seats. "Hedda?"

His sister had moved closer, her recalcitrant son a step behind. They took chairs on the end of the row and glared up at Herbert.

Lord Herbert gallantly seated Wendela and then straightened to face his audience. I moved closer until I stood beside Officer Casey. (As distasteful as it was, this was the only spot left where I could both see and hear the proceedings.)

"The mummified remains of this . . . person," Lord Herbert began, "fell under the care and protection of the Graeme family some six generations before my birth. As all of you know who have so kindly listened to the Graeme genealogies, Lord Horatio Graeme was an intrepid explorer, adventurer, and aficionado of the arcane. That his wanderings took him many times to the Valley of the Kings is well documented. On one of those expeditions—this would be near the end of the eighteenth century, if I am not mistaken—the desert crypts in the domain of the Sphinx herself opened to his mind a riddle worthy of Oedipus. That riddle, lovely ladies and gallant gentlemen, you see before you tonight."

"The hieroglyphics," the Egyptian, Adib, ventured when it seemed nobody else would speak. "Have they been translated?"

"No," Lord Herbert replied to a murmur of surprise and disapproval.

"Has the mummy been scanned?" the Englishwoman, Mrs. Carroll, asked.

"No."

It was all Northcutt could do to stay in his seat. "But surely, Lord Herbert, a man of your education and experience knows—"

"Even a man of my limited education and hard-won experience knows when a time is right and when it is not," Lord Herbert told his friend gently. He looked at Wendela and smiled.

"A virgin discovery," the man from Naples breathed. "Unheard of!" He moved to the edge of his chair in youthful enthusiasm. "What will you do with it, Lord Herbert?"

"Sell it, of course!" Hedda exclaimed. "Why else would he bring you ninnies all the way out here?" She looked at the assembled group disdainfully, as though she suspected they had neglected to bring their checkbooks, or, if they had brought them, that the balances therein would be too miniscule to consider.

Apparently she was right about their budgets. The curators looked from the priceless antiquity to their empty laps, and their collective sigh was audible from where I stood.

"There is no doubt that a thing of this . . . uniqueness . . . should be returned at once to its native land," Adib said with more hope than confidence.

Lord Herbert ran a hand through his beard and winked at the only man not in formal attire. "His native land," he said. "Can we, dear friends, learned friends, determine where that land might be?"

"It's clearly Egyptian!" the attaché said. "See the markings. Consider the workmanship. A schoolboy could tell you that sarcophagus came from Egypt!"

"I do not doubt the origin of the sarcophagus, Adib," Lord Herbert said. "Not for a moment do I doubt it."

"Then—"

"You think the mummy inside is a child from . . . Greece perhaps?" Mrs. Carroll ventured. "A prodigy in science and mathematics who had gone to Egypt to study astronomy?"

I wondered if Mrs. Carroll was naturally conciliatory or if her womanly intuition told her that the better one played Lord Herbert's game, the more likely one was to take home the prize.

Jane Carroll continued, "Is that why you call it the Little Messenger, Lord Herbert? Is there something about the sarcophagus, or the journals handed down by Lord Horatio perhaps, which leads you to believe a foreigner is interred therein?"

"You mean an alien?" the man in the suit asked with a grin.

"All right," she said patiently. "An alien, if you prefer. A non-Egyptian, to be perfectly clear."

"Scans might tell us," the man from Naples said with excitement. He, too, had something to gain by calling into question the origin of the mummy. "A child of a Roman citizen, possibly." His eyes lighted when he thought of his Italian museum. "That could be it!"

"The sarcophagus is all wrong for the Roman period!" Adib objected. "It is earlier. Much earlier." He turned to Northcutt. "Don't you agree, professor?"

"I'm not sure," the older man said slowly. "Perhaps later, I think—judging only by the portrayal of the deceased. Does it look human to you?"

The man in the suit leaned forward, and Lord Herbert's grip on Wendela's hand tightened.

"What are you saying?" Mrs. Carroll asked.

"Only that while its size would lead one to suppose it to be a child," Northcutt said, "its face strikes me as odd."

"A birth defect," the British woman said. "Not at all uncommon in those days. It would account for the premature death. We've a holding in our collection that was stricken with—"

"I've seen it, Jane," Northcutt interrupted. "Scans will determine if that is the case here, but I'm saying there might be another possibility. Consider the nineteenth or twentieth dynasty of the New Kingdom, say 1075 BC."

I watched the proverbial lightbulbs appear over the scholars' heads and wished I had one of my own to turn on. Although the guy in the suit also frowned at his exclusion from the mental loop, Wendela nodded along. (Of course, that probably didn't mean anything. Wendela agrees with almost anyone about almost anything.) I didn't look at Thom Casey to see if he understood, because I knew that if he did, it would only make me hate him more.

"A fascinating period," Mrs. Carroll mused. She leaned forward to examine Hermes more carefully. "But see the artifacts in its hands, Richard. Why would they have chosen those objects—symbols of science and mathematics—if this was a mummified baboon?"

"A baboon?" I choked, mortified when I realized I'd said it aloud.

"Not uncommon, my dear," Lord Herbert told me. He clearly had anticipated the conversation taking this turn. "There was a time when the Egyptians mummified baboons, cats—"

"Were they running out of people, or what?"

This time I *didn't* say it out loud. I merely looked at Hermes, but he didn't look like a baboon. On the other hand, he didn't look like a child, either. He didn't look like anything I recognized. Or did he? There was something about him that was familiar, but I couldn't for the life of me decide what it was.

Hedda rose. "A *baboon,* Herbert? *You* are the only baboon I see here!"

"It would not be without value," Northcutt said quickly, as if to shield his friend from a coming storm. The other curators nodded hastily in agreement.

"The sarcophagus," Adib said, "is without peer. It is—" At last, he realized his assurances of the antiquity's value might be the very words that could remove it from his grasp. He closed his mouth. None of the other curators were foolish enough to open theirs.

"He's not a baboon," Wendela said. Her hand slipped from Lord Herbert's, and she rose and moved toward the dais in a swift, fluid motion.

I saw Officer Casey tense, but he waited for me to respond. I moved toward the dais as the scholars gasped their shock. Before I could intercept Wendela, she dropped gracefully to the feet of the Little Messenger and reached up to caress his face.

"He's not a baboon," she repeated in a soft, melodic voice. "But he doesn't mind you being mistaken, professor. He's been called worse and he's very forgiving of us. All of them are. They have been since the beginning. That is why they were willing to come to us in the first place. To teach. To lead. To set us on our way."

I froze, but I wasn't the only one. Even the musicians stopped playing. I think every person in the room ceased to breathe as we followed the path of Wendela's fingers up the elongated, hollow cheek, around the spherical amber eyes, across the wide forehead, and back down the cheek to the small, thin lips above the tiny, pointed chin. Her fingers were pink against Hermes's bronzed, jade face. There was one thing particularly unmistakable about his visage. Unlike the pharaohs and Egyptian aristocracy, unlike baboons, unlike Greek or Roman children afflicted with birth defects, Hermes was *green*.

That's when I knew what Lord Herbert hadn't said. We all knew. At one time or another we'd all seen a variation of the face etched on the sarcophagus. Ever since Roswell—and probably before—it had graced the covers of tabloids and books and been magnified on the silver screen.

I knew I should reach for Wendela, but I felt as immobile as the figure in the sarcophagus. Although no rational thoughts came to mind, a title from one of Ray Bradbury's Martian stories crept into my brain: *Dark They Were and Golden-Eyed.* Dark, Hermes was, and golden-eyed. Despite myself, I shivered.

"Precisely!" Lord Herbert said to break the stunned silence.

"Preposterous!" Northcutt replied when at last he found his voice.

Only one of the two men could be right, but I was simply too surprised and too engrossed in looking at Wendela and the Little Messenger to know which of them it was.

ACROSS
    57 Me and Chaiya: "We _____ family!"
    *61 One modern technique to determine contents of sealed
       sarcophagi*
DOWN
    8 Foreign; Strange; Extraterrestrial

Chapter 7

"Shall we return to our repast?" Lord Herbert suggested to his guests. "I do hate to keep a well-prepared rack of lamb waiting." He extended a hand for Wendela, who blew a farewell kiss to Hermes as she rose from the dais like a queen.

Queen of the Uncanny, I thought, but fondly. How could I help but love and admire a woman so totally without guile and inhibition? How could anyone? If a thought came to Wendela's head, she said it. If an impulse came to her heart, she followed it. If she believed she was in the presence of a mummified extraterrestrial, she admitted it—let the consequences fall where they may.

And there were consequences falling everywhere. The air was so thick with consequence I was surprised any of us could move through it. But move we did. One by one, the professor, the curators, the diplomat, and the stranger rose to trail Lord Herbert from the room as if he might lead them next to the Holy Grail. Not that they'd believe any cup he handed them *was* the Grail, of course. But neither would one of them risk being out of Lord Herbert's presence. They didn't have to know what was in that sarcophagus—child, baboon, or E.T.—to know that winning it for their institution would be the coup of their career.

For her part, Hedda Mead seemed equally determined to see that if that glorious mummy was worth a thousand times its weight in gold, she got the gold and Lord Herbert got the glory.

Already she had hold of the arm of the young man from Naples. (Perhaps since he wore the nicest clothes, she presumed he also had the largest budget.) Her son, Harrison, skulked along behind. Clearly, he resented his mother. Resented his uncle. Resented Hermes most of all. Harrison Mead impressed me as the type of man who wanted the spotlight focused on him, not on a few pieces of rag and bone in an old stone box. (I phrased that badly. I should have said that Harrison Mead *didn't* impress me. He didn't impress me at all.)

Chaiya paused at the door. "Aren't you coming, Sammy?"

I hesitated, weighing the possible consequences of leaving Wendela alone with the group against the possible consequences of returning to that dining room. "No," I said finally. "I'm . . . I'm not hungry." It was true. Though I'd eaten almost nothing, I already had a nasty case of indigestion. Rack of lamb was the last thing I thought I could face. "Please give Lord Herbert my apology. And Chaiya," I called before she could leave. "Keep an eye on Wendela." (It was rather like putting Tweedledum in charge of Tweedledee, but I was a desperate woman.)

Chaiya's carefully tweezed eyebrows rose. "Like she could do anything stranger than carousing a mummy? That thing is positively aberrant!"

"She means, um, caressing a mummy," I told the officers after Chaiya left. "And she thinks it's abhorrent."

Thom said, "Maybe she meant what she said."

I frowned. Who was he to correct me? If I didn't know what *aberrant* meant, surely Chaiya didn't.

"Aberrant means differing from normal," Casey continued as if his font of knowledge was full to the brim and I clearly needed some of it to splash over onto me. "That mummy's not normal."

Now that he mentioned it, I did recognize the word. "I know what it means," I said. "Aberrant is the kind of behavior grown men display when they proposition little girls."

Bob Monroe snickered and I winked at him. (That would prove to be a mistake, but it would be another twenty minutes or so before I realized it.)

"Listen, lady," Casey said. "I think it's about time you—"

"I think it is too," I said coldly and stalked toward the door. "Time I leave, that is." As much as I hated lamb, I liked it better than wolf. Maybe I'd take my chances in the dining room after all.

"A little excitement down your way?" Knute asked as I approached. "The way those people talked as they went past, you'd think Lord Herbert had introduced them to Cleopatra."

"It was stranger than that," I replied, sinking down onto the low couch at his side. Knute looked uncomfortable on the plush antique furniture, but I felt like Goldilocks in Baby Bear's bed. The sofa was soft and low and just right. I kicked off my heels and tucked them under the furniture, wondering what it was about high heels that made my head throb. "What would you say if I told you Lord Herbert hired us to protect the mummified remains of an extraterrestrial?" I waited for the incredulity to register on Knute's face, but it never did. Of course, it took a lot to surprise Knute. A *whole* lot, if this couldn't do it.

"That depends on how you told me," he said. "Are you saying Lord Herbert hired us to protect what *he* believes to be an alien?"

"Yes. I think that's 'precisely' what he believes."

Knute let out a low whistle. "Then I'd say this job is something to tell the grandchildren about."

"Are you married, Knute?" I asked in surprise.

(It's embarrassing to admit how little I know about the two men I work with, but it would take a better detective than me to uncover much of Knute's or Delano's lives, let alone dig up anything about their past.)

"No," he said. "I meant your grandchildren."

He shifted position and the divan groaned. I began to worry about my Goldilocks analogy. What would Lord Herbert think if we broke his settee to bits?

"Anyway," Knute said, "I like Lord Herbert."

"I like him too," I said, wondering now what it was about the eccentric that attracted me. (But I didn't wonder very long. As a psychology major I knew better than to examine the question too carefully.)

"That said," Knute continued, "if you told me *you* believe we're babysitting an extraterrestrial, I'd say that maybe you and Wendela are getting a little too close."

"You should have seen her, Knute. She seems to really love that thing."

"It's probably been a long time since she's been to a family reunion."

I didn't know whether to laugh or cry. It was funny, but it was also sad. Poor Wendela was as out of place in the world as if she *had* been born on Saturn. I'd never seen her in a place where she looked like she belonged—until tonight.

"When did you last talk to Delano?" I asked. Not only did I want to take my mind off Wendela, but I knew I should get it back where it belonged—the job at hand. That supplied enough to be concerned over to keep even a worrywart like me occupied through five courses of Lord Herbert's feast.

"About five minutes ago," Knute said. "No, seven," he amended, checking his watch as if the two minutes mattered to anybody but him. "I let him know the folks were back on their way to the dining room. He says everything's quiet."

"Too quiet?"

"Just quiet."

"Where is he?"

"It's Delano," Knute reminded me. "Who knows where he is."

Nobody knew. It was one of the things that made him so good at his job.

Knute nudged me. "Quit worrying, Sam. There's nothing to worry about. This job's a piece of cake."

"Fruitcake."

He smiled. "You'd know best about that."

He meant my degree. At least I hoped that's what he meant.

In the absence of a good wooden pencil, I chewed my lower lip to give my mouth something to do while my mind obsessed. There were more things to worry about than the mummy. Topping the list was my worry over the attraction I felt toward Thom Casey. It was just wrong—especially given the fact I was a superhero and he was a scumbag. "What else is the matter?" Knute asked. Because he knew me so well, he didn't wait for a response. "It's those two guys Chaiya hired, isn't it?"

"No," I said. "Yes." I looked up at him not knowing what to say or even what to think. Thom Casey was undeniably handsome and smart, but that wasn't what impressed me. What caught my attention was the way he took the rather off-beat Herbert and Wendela (not to mention the Nightshade staff) in stride, and how professional—and even kind—he was being about this whole assignment given our previous confrontation. Wasn't forgiveness an odd quality to find in a miscreant?

"I don't like the one guy much," Knute said when I didn't respond.

Finally, the voice of reason.

"He's too much of a smart aleck."

Huh? I'd spent way too much time observing Thom Casey, and still I'd missed the smart-aleck facet of his multiple personalities.

"But it's not Monroe you're thinking about, is it?" Knute said. "The one you're worrying about is Casey." He settled back against the settee. "You shouldn't feel guilty, Sam. It's not your fault. You had no way to know."

Guilty? Me? I motioned for time-out. "Who are you talking about?"

"Thom Casey," he said. "Who are you obsessing about?"

"Thom Casey. But—"

"I talked to him while you were at dinner," Knute interrupted. "He's understandably unhappy about what happened the other night, but I don't think he'll hold a grudge. Thom's a decent enough guy, even if he did graduate from BYU." He winked at me, but his teasing smile faded at the indignant look on my face. "It's *not* your fault, Sam," he insisted. "You didn't know he's a cop."

"He wasn't *working* Tuesday night," I said. Obviously, the scumbag had lied to Knute. "Monroe says he was off duty."

"Yeah. Too bad it went down the way it did. Heck of a coincidence both his partner and his boss were in the neighborhood."

"*Too bad?*" I cried. This wasn't like Knute. The Knute I knew should want to break the guy in half. I blinked several times, but it didn't help any since it was my ears, not my eyes, that were malfunctioning. "He's a pervert and you say it's too bad he didn't get away with it?"

"Come again?"

"His partner told me he wasn't working that night," I repeated. "He—"

"He was breaking the rules," Knute admitted. "Sure, the area an officer works undercover in is out of bounds when he's off duty, but the runaway girl you saw him with was talking to him, Sam. Listening to him. He didn't want to chance a night without contact or he might have lost her for good. I'd have risked my job if that's what it took to get a kid off the streets. Wouldn't you?"

I couldn't answer the question. I wasn't sure I understood it even. Monroe's words swirled around in my head. I'd thought . . .

Or had I just assumed?

Before I could finish sorting it out, Knute continued, "Thom had just gotten her to agree to letting him take her in when you showed up." When I still didn't speak—because I still couldn't—he concluded, "But you didn't know that. It looked different."

The pieces fell into place all at once. When Monroe called his partner Dudley Do-Right he wasn't being ironic; he was being a smart aleck like Knute said. He thought I would agree that one little runaway wasn't worth Casey's career. And I *had* agreed. At least it must have seemed to Monroe—and Casey—like I had.

"Are you okay?" the big guy asked me.

"I thought . . ." I said. "I mean, I didn't think." I left it at that since it was true. I *hadn't* thought. Why think when I could do what I do best—mind other people's business and jump to conclusions? I swallowed. "*Please* tell me the girl is safe despite me chasing her away."

When Knute wouldn't meet my eyes, he didn't have to answer. "It wasn't your fault," he said again.

I felt like I was talking to a telephone answering machine. No matter what I said, I would get the same message. But the message was wrong. It *was* my fault. I felt terrible. Worse than terrible.

"I'll find her," I said, rising. I'd forgotten Wendela. I'd dismissed Lord Herbert and his Martian mummy. All I could think about was the waiflike runaway with the huge, frightened eyes. Because of me she was still alone on some of the scariest streets in Phoenix. Thom Casey would have taken care of her if I hadn't made his boss drag him off in handcuffs to protect his cover.

Knute took my elbow and pulled me back onto the couch. "She'll turn up."

Dead, I thought. *Worse than dead.* I was going to cry. "I have to find her," I repeated, struggling to get out of his grasp.

Knute wouldn't let go of my arm. "Casey spent most of last night and all of the day before looking for her. She's disappeared." He touched my stricken face. "I'm sorry, Sam," he said softly. "I thought you knew. I thought Thom told you."

Like I had given him a chance to tell me anything—that night or since. Besides, his partner was the chatty one. To Monroe this job was a lark. Casey was too concerned with protecting a rare Egyptian antiquity to worry about defending himself to me.

That, or he didn't think I was worth an explanation.

"I'll apologize to Casey now," I said, resigned to the fact that I couldn't undo any more damage than that. (Or at least that I couldn't undo it at that moment.) But I didn't move. I merely stood and stared down the hallway toward the study. Surely corridors that lead down death row are shorter and less forbidding than that one appeared.

ACROSS
   11 Where Lord Herbert's mummy came from? (four words for "unearthly")
DOWN
   30 Giant, philosopher, saint, ace detective, and (sometimes) the most annoying man I know

Chapter 8

Knute rose when I did, but while I looked down the corridor toward the study, where Thom Casey stood guard, he looked the other way, across the grand hall in the center of the manor. He nudged me before I could get up the nerve to take the first step toward the chamber of doom.

I turned in time to see Hedda Mead exit the dining room. After a furtive glance over her shoulder, she tiptoed across the polished parquet floor to peek into another room. In her hand was a piece of notepaper.

"I can smell her perfume from here," Knute said.

"I think that's brimstone," I replied, watching the unpleasant woman move on to the next room and look into it. I wondered whether she was looking for some*one* or some*thing*. I stepped into the hall. "May I help you, Mrs. Mead?"

Hedda jumped and then whirled in my direction. When she saw who it was, she said angrily, "You may not! This is my brother's home you . . . you . . . whoever you are!"

After what I'd heard her call Knute, I'd braced for worse. I pasted on a smile. "I'm sorry I startled you. You seemed to be looking for . . . something . . . and I thought I might be able to help you find it."

Hedda huffed. "Are you implying I'm a common prowler?"

"Of course not," I said. "I only—"

"Forgot your place," the woman interrupted imperiously. She moved to the next door. "I know my way around this manor, young lady. I am simply . . . I am on my way to the powder room. If you don't mind."

"Of course not," I said. Far be it from me to interfere with something like that.

"That's the library," Knute interjected as she moved toward another door. "The powder room's the third door on your left."

"I *know* that."

Judging by her scowl, either she didn't know it or she didn't expect Knute to know it and call her on it. Hedda stalked to the room Knute had named and slammed the door behind her.

I took a deep breath and turned back toward the study, ready to face the music. But before I could take a step, the string quartet exited my destination, led by Bob Monroe.

"The crowd is at the food trough," Monroe said as they approached. "Casey's in there with E.T., and you and Giganto are out here for backup, so we're going outside for a smoke. Any problem with that?"

None that I was going to mention. If it gave me a chance to apologize to Thom Casey without a sardonic audience, I would support them chain-smoking themselves into early graves.

The group crossed to the front doors and went out, but still I hesitated.

"No time like the present," Knute said, urging me forward.

"You're right," I said. "I'm—" Before I could say what I was, another of Lord Herbert's guests entered the hall from the dining room. It was the "used-car salesman." I watched him look around the hall, but before he took a step in any direction, he saw us. At first he seemed embarrassed, then he shrugged and approached amiably. "You folks happen to know where the lord keeps his facilities?"

"See that corridor?" Knute asked, pointing a different direction than the one in which he'd sent Hedda. "Rest room's fifth door on the right."

Did he memorize the house plans or what? I wondered in admiration.

"You know who that is?" Knute asked when the man was out of earshot.

"No," I confessed. "Lord Herbert hasn't introduced him."

"I don't think he wants anybody to know who he is."

"But you know?"

"I thought I recognized his voice," Knute said. "So I used the remote access on my PDA to see if I was right. That guy's mug matches the picture on his website right down to the ugly suit and the red carnation in the lapel."

"I thought I recognized his voice too," I said. "But I couldn't place it."

"Think *doo-doo, doo-doo*," Knute said. He'd mimicked the show-opening sound for the old black-and-white *Twilight Zone* episodes we watched on slow nights.

But I still didn't get it. "Rod Serling's better looking."

"And less living." Knute pointed a finger toward the ceiling, gave me another second or two to catch on, then said, "'Stay tuned. Stay awake. Stay alert . . .'"

"'Things are looking up!'" I supplied automatically.

So I have heard that voice before, I reminded myself sheepishly, *but only four or five times a week.* Good old Wick Barlow's voice had been a long-standing companion on stakeouts. The UFOlogist's nationally syndicated show is good company in the middle of the night; while I can think of lots of uncomplimentary names to call it, "boring" isn't one of them. (Besides, I have to admit that since I do live with Wendela, if there ever is something going on "up there," I figure I ought to be among the first to hear about it.)

"Small world," Knute said.

"In a big universe," I added, again quoting Barlow. "Huh. A real celebrity. Maybe I ought to ask him to autograph my car radio before he leaves town."

"Leaves?" Knute asked. "The way he was talking to Wendela on the way back to dinner, I think he's going to be around for quite some time. They never did solve the mystery of those strange lights over Phoenix, you know. He says he's thinking of reopening an investigation."

I knew about the lights, of course. Virtually everybody who lived in Arizona in March of '97 knows about the lights. For more than a week the bizarre phenomena made Phoenix almost as famous as Roswell. The stories have mostly faded away into cyberspace by now, but once in a while you still have to dodge huge, satellite-equipped vans on I-17 since a few of the most determined UFO-seekers have never left the state. (Of course, they've never found any flying saucers or little green men, either.)

I was afraid to ask, but I had to know. "What did Wendela tell him?"

"She told him that she came to Phoenix with the lights."

And it might have been true, at least in a manner of speaking. For sure that was the same night the police found her wandering the streets and took her to the psychiatric ward of the county hospital. Sweet, gentle Wendela had been institutionalized from that night until just before I left my internship at the state facility where she was a "lifer."

"Don't sweat it, Sam," Knute said. "Wendela doesn't know any more about those lights than I do. Barlow probably figured that out for himself before they got back to the dining room."

I wasn't so sure. From what I'd heard, people didn't have to be credible to make it onto Barlow's show—they just had to be as delusional as he was. In that way Wendela qualified in spades.

"Besides," Knute continued, "don't you think he'll be talking about a certain extraterrestrial mummy for the rest of his career? When would he squeeze in a show about Wendela?"

"You might be right," I conceded slowly. When Barlow next hit the airwaves, Hermes would be the hottest topic there and in cyberspace. At least he would until Professor Northcutt established there were baboon remains inside the sarcophagus, or Jane Carroll proved it was a mummified, misshapen child.

"Don't borrow trouble," Knute advised. "One crisis at a time, Sam. Why don't you go talk to Thom Casey now? Then, if Barlow's still sniffing around Wendela after dinner, I'll help you read him the riot act."

"Right," I said and turned again toward the study.

"Whoa," Knute said as if I'd galloped away. (I hadn't even moved until I turned around to see what he was "whoa-ing" about.)

Hedda had exited the powder room and turned back toward the dining room, but she was looking at the piece of paper in her hands as she folded it carefully. In another moment she would collide with the Egyptian attaché who had just left the dining room and was now punching enough numbers in his cell phone to reach Cairo.

"Watch—" Knute called. "Out," he finished with a wince as the two met head-on.

Instinctively, I raised my palms to cover my ears. While Hedda cursed, the Egyptian apologized profusely. Finally, he escaped into one of the rooms to finish his call while Hedda glowered after him. When I was sure the area was once again G-rated, I lowered my hands.

Wick Barlow exited the far corridor. He motioned toward the front door and said, "I'm going out for a little fresh air."

I didn't know how fresh the air would be around the smokers, but I nodded. Probably, I thought, he wanted to check the sky—just in case. As he so often said, his line of work depended on seeing things you only see when you're outside looking up. (If then.)

As the front door closed behind Barlow, Harrison Mead entered the hall. He saw us immediately and scowled. "Going to the john."

Knute pointed right and then left. "Take your pick." To me he said, "Looks like the lord better serve a Pepto-Bismol mousse for dessert. There are more people out here looking for rest rooms than in there eating Mary's little lamb."

He was right. If anybody else came out into the hall, I'd have to call Officer Casey to direct traffic. I watched unhappily as the lord's nephew chose the rest room out of sight down the corridor. Maybe it was time to call in reinforcements. "Delano's outside, right?"

"Outside," Knute said. "Inside. Around, for sure."

"Right." Delano was where he was, and nothing I could say into the radio would alter what he'd already decided to do. I'd have to rely on his good judgment and hope for the best. "The *only* way into that study is down this hallway, right?"

"It's the only way I know of," Knute said.

Then it was a safe bet. Knute probably knew the manor better than Lord Herbert. Still, I chewed my lower lip as Mrs. Mead approached. (There is one perk to being an obsessive worrier. I will never need collagen injections; my lips tend to look permanently pouty from the abuse they get from my teeth.)

The stout woman was probably a foot and a half shorter than Knute, but she was still intimidating when she poked a bejeweled finger into the proximity of his belly button. "I do not like this!" she said. "I do not like this *at all.*"

Frankly, I didn't like it much either.

"I want to speak to your employer, sir, and I want to speak to him now."

"You're looking at her," Knute responded with a grin. "Samantha Shade of Nightshade."

Suddenly, I liked this even less.

"Nightshade?" Hedda repeated as though saying it gave her a toothache. "What kind of a name is that?"

"It's a family name," I said. Before the woman could berate my ancestry, I added, "And I assure you Mrs. Mead, everything is fine. The mummy is secure."

"You have people wandering *everywhere!*"

"Yes," I admitted. "And I wish they would all go back to the dining room." *Starting with you.* "But I can't very well chain Lord Herbert's guests to the table." *As much as I want to.*

"You are insubordinate," Hedda decided, even though I'd only said half of what had come to mind. "You are inexperienced and insufferable." The woman obviously had word power beyond the four-letter variety when she chose to wield it. "I will speak to my *brother* about your incompetence."

"Oh, gosh. That's like tattling to the Tooth Fairy that I forgot to floss."

Okay, you probably already know I didn't say that. I said, "Yes, ma'am." It was a good answer in that it got Hedda to spin on her heels and stomp back toward the dining room instead of ripping my hair out by the roots.

"What do you suppose is on that piece of paper she keeps looking at?" I asked Knute when she was gone.

"Profanities she doesn't want to forget," he guessed. "Or maybe a roster of people she plans to have bumped off." He winked. "You're at the top."

I grinned despite myself. "Or maybe it's a shopping list for bat wings and eye of newt."

Our repartee was short-lived. Knute said, "You were going to talk to Casey, remember?"

"Uh, yes." But before I could turn that direction yet again, doors reopened and one by one all the people who I'd feared were "missing in action" began to file back toward the rooms they were supposed to be inhabiting. All except for Lord Herbert's nephew. Hadn't Harrison been a long time using the rest room?

"Maybe you should go check on Harrison," I told Knute. "I'll wait here to see that nobody goes down the hall."

"Right, boss," he said.

I smiled after him. There wasn't a hint of derision in his voice when he called me "boss." On the other hand, I wasn't off the hook when it came to derision. The smart aleck had just stopped in front of me and leaned against the wall with a slow, lazy grin. I felt my smile turn upside down and regretted my earlier winking at Monroe almost as much as I regretted accepting this assignment.

"Hello beautiful boss lady," he said.

I took a step back from the strong smell of tobacco on his breath.

He grinned. "You're not afraid of me, are you?"

"No!" I said louder than was necessary.

"Glad to hear it." He closed the gap between us. "I've got tomorrow night off. What say we get together?"

"*I* work tomorrow night."

He shrugged as if my job—or possibly work in general—was of little or no consequence. "Meet me at seven for drinks, then. You can decide from there if you want to spend the night working with weirdos or playing with me."

I glanced over my shoulder, hoping Knute would return. No luck. Then I looked down the hall. It was also too much to hope that Thom Casey would exit the room at that moment. I was on my own with Monroe.

"I have to take my little brother to the dentist before work," I said. "His appointment's at seven." The lame-sounding excuse had the benefit of being true.

"Come on," Bob said. "No kid goes to the dentist at night."

"My brother does." I didn't add that my eleven-year-old brother goes to the dentist, the doctor, the zoo, and almost everyplace else at night. I don't mention Arjay's genetic affliction to very many people, and certainly never to a stranger who's propositioning me.

"Saturday night, then," Monroe persisted.

"Sorry, no." Despite myself, I was still looking hopefully down the hall toward the study.

"Don't tell me Casey's more your type."

"No," I said quickly, but not truthfully. "I just don't date much."

The "not dating" part was also true, if you're keeping track. I spend most of my free time with Wendela. How many men do you suppose want to take out me *and* her? For sure it doesn't happen more than once, and those dates are usually short-lived—when and if we get past introductions at the door. At any rate, once was more often than I wanted to see Officer Monroe socially.

"You haven't dated the right man," he said and reached for my waist. To say I was stunned is an understatement. "Let me show you—"

Before I could remember a tae kwon do move (Thom Casey's right, I *am* slow), a deep voice from the end of the hall said, "Monroe, what say you hold up your end of an assignment for a change?"

At first I imagined I saw hatred flicker across the man's face at the sound of his partner's voice, but in the next second I decided it was my imagination because he grinned broadly. "I keep trying to tell Casey that all work and no play makes Dudley a very dull guy," he said loud enough for Thom to hear. Quietly he said to me, "We'll pick this up later, boss lady."

"Only if 'later' is the morning of the First Resurrection."

Yes, I said it out loud, but I said it softly enough that he didn't hear it as he walked away. Watching him saunter down the hall, I amended it to later still, figuring that Monroe wouldn't be up early that morning, even if I somehow manage to earn a wake-up call myself.

"He's not in the bathroom," Knute reported a couple of minutes later, having returned from his mission to check on Harrison's whereabouts.

"Where did he go?" I asked.

Knute shrugged his huge shoulders. "It's a big house, Sam," he said. "Easy to get lost in. I radioed Delano and told him to be on the lookout in case he went outside."

"There's no other way into that study?"

Fortunately for me, Knute is the most patient mortal currently taking his turn on earth. "No," he said. "As I've told you before, Sam, there's no other way in. No other way out except that one door. The mummy might as well be in a vault."

I nodded but knew I wouldn't be satisfied until I saw the antiquity safe and sound for myself. I took a purposeful stride toward the study, but froze in midstep as I remembered that Bob Monroe and Thom Casey were down there in the same room at the same time. It was just too much to face on an empty stomach—or any other time. Figuring that I'd just as soon eat lamb and make small talk with Hedda as face those two men, I turned back toward the dining room.

But it was too late for that, too. Dinner was over, or, judging by the pitch and fervor of the voices entering the hall, it had been called off. Most of the guests had left their appetites and impeccable manners in the study with Hermes and were anxious to return there. Only Lord Herbert and Wendela looked serene. (But I suspected they could have strolled hand in hand through the fields of Gettysburg in the summer of 1863 and not noticed the difference of opinion going on around them.)

"Oh, dear," I said under my breath to Knute. "This looks bad."

Ever the optimist, he responded, "Don't worry, Sam. How bad can it be?"

In another thirty minutes we would know.

ACROSS

4 *Abbr. for mysterious lights in Phoenix sky in March 1997?*

25 *Lord Herbert's sister?; "Wicked ____ of the West"*

DOWN

31 *Teacher/lecturer/museum devotee*

Chapter 9

Even I know enough Greek mythology to recognize harpies when I see them, Lord Herbert's learned guests looked to me like modern-day equivalents as they stood once again before the mummy, bickering and pointing fingers. Although these people of science and the arts could not agree on who or what Hermes was, they were united in their belief that the mummy belonged to them more than it did Lord Herbert—no matter how honorably it had come to him. According to them, it should be removed from Graeme Manor immediately and examined at length.

It seemed that everybody except Lord Herbert wanted to exploit Hermes for their own scholarship, prestige, or—in the case of Hedda Mead and her son—the price it would bring on the lucrative antiquities market. Well, not Wendela, of course. She clearly remembered that the sarcophagus contained the remains of a real person, albeit a very, very old one. She sat on the edge of the dais as if to shield the mummy from the ugliness around him by her own slight form. When the debaters paused as one to take a breath, I heard her soft reassurances that all would be well and that Hermes would find a good home. I hoped she was right.

Officer Casey stood beside Lord Herbert, frowning as the man's guests disgraced themselves. The lord was calmer and much more pleasant than I'd have been in the same situation. (Come to think of it, he was much calmer and more pleasant in his situation than I was in mine.) It looked almost as if he had decided to move aside and award the prize to whomever was left standing when the fight ended and the dust had cleared.

The only two people in the room oblivious to the mummy were Chaiya and Bob Monroe. Chaiya was talking animatedly to him, but her eyes kept moving toward Thom. Thom was again looking at Wendela, and Bob was looking at me. It was strange and uncomfortable all the way around.

"'Infinite riches in a little room,'" I heard Thom observe quietly to Lord Herbert a few minutes later.

"Christopher Marlowe!" Lord Herbert exclaimed. "Act One of *Malta*, if I'm not mistaken." He smiled. "'Now will I show myself to have more of the serpent than the dove; that is, more knave than fool.'"

"Act Two," Casey said.

Who reads Marlowe these days, let alone memorizes him? I didn't give it much thought because I was too busy trying to decipher what Lord Herbert meant by the serpent and dove thing. Fortunately, deductions were unnecessary because his next action explained everything. He meant that despite appearances to the contrary, he had made up his mind.

"Pardon me, my friends," he said, holding up his hands for silence. (He might as well have tried to part the Salt River while he was at it, for all the good the gesture did.) "If you will allow me a moment—" he tried to continue.

If anything, the volume increased, possibly because Hedda climbed up on a chair like a country auctioneer and bellowed, "It's about time, Herbert! Let's cut to the chase. What am I bid for this . . . thing?"

"Hedda!" Lord Herbert cried in dismay. Getting no response, he turned to his nephew. "Will you see to your mother, Harrison?"

Clearly, the young man who had returned from who-knew-where and was even more glassy-eyed than usual could see to nothing that didn't benefit himself more concretely.

"Mr. Barlow, sir?" the lord continued.

The UFOlogist stood at the foot of Mrs. Mead's chair, matching her off-color language word for word as they loudly debated the ethics of selling the remains of what might be an intergalactic caller to the highest bidder among earthlings.

Lord Herbert shook his head sadly and held out a hand to another quarter. "Jane, darling?"

Jane Darling had hold of the Egyptian attaché's cravat to better get across her point that her royal museum already possessed more valuable mummies than Egypt would ever unearth in their giant sandbox, and was thus the only fitting place for Hermes.

Lord Herbert looked as if he might cry. "My dear, dear Northcutt."

Dear Northcutt was much too near calling the curator from Naples to a duel (pistols *or* antique swords) to hear his old friend's entreaty.

Thom Casey raised a finger and thumb to his lips and produced a whistle that was probably heard by everyone this side of the Milky Way. "Thank you," he said quietly when the folks in the room turned toward him, slack jawed. "I believe Lord Herbert has something to say."

"Thank you, Thomas," Lord Herbert said. He looked dazed, and his fingers were held to his hearing aid. Although I feared the elderly gentleman might now be completely deaf, in a moment or two he recovered. "'Infinite riches in a little room,'" he repeated. "We are, I fear, none of us ourselves just now." He smiled at Wendela. "Except for you, my dear."

Lord Herbert's bright blue eyes scanned the remainder of his invited guests and family but found nobody else unaffected by greed and ambition. "'Between two hawks, which lies the higher pitch; Between two dogs, which hath the deeper mouth; Between two blades, which bears the better temper; Between two horses, which doth bear him best . . . I have perhaps some shallow spirit of judgment; But in these nice sharp quillets . . . Good faith, I am no wiser than a daw.'"

"*King Henry the Sixth*," Casey said to nobody in particular.

"Lord Herbert—" Northcutt began.

Before the words were out, the others began to talk over him. Thom raised his fingers to his lips. Seeing the gesture, everyone in the room grew still.

"I assure you I see your point, my friend," the lord said to Northcutt. "And yours, madam," he promised Mrs. Carroll in the next breath. "And yours, sir, and yours and, of course, yours," he told the Egyptian, the Italian, and the radio host in turn. He turned to his sister, "And I am *trying* to see your point, Hedda love."

His sister reddened and opened her mouth, but she closed it again when Thom Casey took half a step forward.

That is one man who's good to have around, I thought. The thought made me flush. Or perhaps it was hot in the room. (Yes, that was it. It really was quite warm.)

"I see the situation very clearly, in fact," Lord Herbert said. "And I can give you ten reasons why my Little Messenger should be entrusted to each of your stewardships. Unfortunately, with there being only one mummy, there can be but one recipient."

Nobody spoke this time. Nobody looked as though they were capable of speech.

"After long and careful deliberation," Lord Herbert continued, "taking into account your strengths and weaknesses as I know them and relying upon the words of the immortal Bard to guide me, I have decided."

Because Lord Herbert did nothing without high drama, he left his guests looking like a school of stunned goldfish while he walked across the room to the quartet. There he whispered into the ear of the violinist. The man nodded, raised his bow, and the group began to play.

"Mozart," Lord Herbert said, returning to the front of the room. "Music of the spheres for a momentous announcement." He smiled from one person to the next, but his eyes lingered the longest on his old friend Northcutt, and there was behind them the hint of a smile.

The Smithsonian, I thought, my heart beating faster. *He's going to give it to Professor Northcutt.*

I was glad. If the decision had been mine I'd have chosen the Smithsonian . . . or possibly the Royal Museum in memory of Herbert's British ancestor who had first discovered Hermes and saved him from vandals.

Apparently, I wasn't the only one who thought I knew where the mummy would go. The man from Naples exchanged looks with the attaché from Egypt, and they glowered together at Lord Herbert. On the other side of the arc, although he had surely been a long shot from the start, Wick Barlow looked as if he'd just lost the million-dollar lottery by one lousy number. Of all people to turn to, he looked at Hedda, and I could have sworn he winked at his recent nemesis. For her part, Hedda looked meaningfully at her son standing in the corner. He met her gaze and scowled, but he did slouch across the room to stand beside her in the half circle around his uncle.

As the music rose toward crescendo, I knew Lord Herbert had orchestrated this announcement—literally. He held out a hand to Wendela, who kissed the mummy and then left it with tears in her eyes. When she stood beside him, Lord Herbert clasped his hands over his ample belly. "I have decided," he began again.

It was all he said. In the next moment the spotlights over the dais went out, plunging the room into blackness. The moment after that there was a thud and then another, followed by a scream and the rise of panicked voices.

I fumbled for the radio around my neck and wished fervently I'd been smart enough to hang a flashlight there as well. Uncle Eddie would have brought a flashlight. I couldn't berate myself enough for being so unprepared and unprofessional.

I pushed one button and then another, willing the stupid radio to work. All around me voices called out in alarm, and I was repeatedly jostled as the guests bumped into each other like frightened cattle.

"Please!" I called out. "Will you all stand still?"

Why wasn't Officer Casey helping me? What was Monroe doing? Where were Knute and Delano?

It was impossible to tell one voice from another. There was a sound I couldn't identify followed by another thud. The voices rose anxiously.

"Stay calm!" I cried, but I sounded hysterical myself and I knew it. "Knute!" I called into the radio, hoping I had pressed the right button at last.

"On my way!" he said. "The power's out all over the manor. Delano's working on it."

I wasn't reassured. Delano is a lot of things, but an electrician isn't one of them. On the other hand, I'd have bet my next six paychecks that he and Knute had flashlights.

"Please hurry, Knute!" I gasped into the radio. "It's a madhouse. Stay at the door when you get there. Make sure nobody leaves the room."

"Almost there," Knute said. His breath was labored, so I knew he was running as fast as he could. Despite his advanced years, with those long legs he should arrive any second.

There was a strange reverberation. I tried to move toward the origin but ran into at least two people trying to move away from it.

"Freeze!" I ordered in my most authoritative squeak. "Whoever you are, wherever you are, just freeze!"

"Do it!" Monroe echoed in a stronger voice. "Do it now."

Thank goodness he had at last come to my aid, but where was Thom Casey?

"We have a generator," I heard Lord Herbert call out. His voice sounded strained and anxious and out of breath. "It should be on in just a moment. If only we can—"

Whatever it is he would have proposed, these people couldn't do it. They drowned out the rest of his sentence with exclamations of their own.

But at least I breathed easier knowing Lord Herbert was safe. My next thought was of the mummy.

So many people had bumped and pushed against me, I no longer knew if I faced the dais or the door. "Knute!"

"Here, Sam!" he said. "I'm at the door." A flashlight beam confirmed it.

"Stay there!" With my bearings now established, I turned in the direction of the mummy and stumbled forward. Although people cried out, at least they moved when I pushed them out of the way. But there was something on the floor between me and the sarcophagus. Somebody, I mean. He didn't move when I fell over him.

"I'm so sorry," I told Thom as I climbed over his body to get to the mummy in my charge. "Call 911!" I yelled to Knute.

"Already have," he responded. The beam of his flashlight swept the room toward the dais, but there were too many people between us for its light to do me much good. "You okay, Sam?"

"Yes," I gasped. "It's Officer Casey. I don't know. I think—" What I thought was that the warm, sticky substance I'd felt on his head must be blood, but I couldn't bring myself to say it out loud.

I finally reached the dais and crawled onto it in relief. Reaching forward I was able to touch the cool, metal base of the stand. My fingers moved upward—then fell between the padded bars of the frame. I waved them back and forth frantically, but there was nothing there to touch.

The sarcophagus was gone.

ACROSS
  *32 Institution, museum, magazine; Professor Northcutt's
       domain*
DOWN
  *38 My odds at the end of this chapter of someday
       becoming CEO of Nightshade Investigation, Inc.*

Chapter 10

They say that in moments of extreme duress it is not uncommon to see your life pass before your eyes. In the few seconds I sat on that dais in the dark, I saw every one of my twenty-three years go by—and the rise and fall of Egypt besides. When the emergency generator finally kicked in and the spotlight came back on, dimmer but welcome, I blinked my vision into focus.

The mummy wasn't knocked aside or toppled over. It was gone.

Everybody looked where I did, and there was a collective gasp.

I glanced around. People frozen in place by the light looked as though they'd been playing swinging statues. Chairs were overturned. Thom Casey lay facedown on the floor but was already moving. Wendela was at his side, waving her hands over his back and apparently moaning for him since he was silent. Knute's large frame filled the doorway. Everything else looked pretty much as it had when the lights went out—everything except the dais which was now devoid of a certain priceless Egyptian antiquity.

I took a head count as I moved back toward Thom. Everyone was present and accounted for. Everyone except Hermes, and his disappearance was simply impossible. The lights had been out for three or four minutes at most. Nobody but Superman could have gotten that mummy out of the room, hidden it, and then returned in that short of a time. For sure nobody in this room looked like Superman—with the possible exception of Thom, whose muscles bulged as he pushed himself up from the floor.

My mind raced as I reached to help him. Who had hit him, and with what? What had happened next? The thief couldn't have passed the mummy to an accomplice outside the door because Knute would have seen the other person enter the hall before the lights went out. Wouldn't he?

Knute must have been thinking the same thing. He leaned out from the doorway, looking back the way he'd come. "There are only three rooms off this hall," he told me. "Take care of Casey. I'll check the other two."

I nodded while my mind continued to process the data. There were no windows in the study. There were no other doors. The walls were painted rather than paneled, so the possibility of a secret passageway seemed remote at best. Besides, who would know about a passageway besides Lord Herbert?

When Thom shook off my helping hand, I turned toward Lord Graeme and my heart sank. Despite the confusion, the poor, elderly man hadn't moved six inches from where he'd stood to announce his decision. He looked pale and drawn, and the hand he raised to his chest shook. I left Thom to take Herbert's arm and urge him toward a chair, fearing that when he had a heart attack that, too, would be my fault.

As the lord sank into the chair, staring blankly at the dais, the lights went out again. But this time it was more of a blink because they came back on again a second later at full strength. When the air conditioner clicked on as well, I knew Delano was a better electrician than I'd given him credit for.

"Sammy?" Delano's low growl came from the radio around my neck. "Everything okay in there? Somebody flicked off the main switch at the fuse box."

"Nothing's okay," I said, grasping the silken cord around my neck as if it were a lifeline. "The mummy's gone, Delano, and—"

"Police are on the way," he said. "But it'll be another twenty minutes, maybe more."

"No police!" Lord Herbert cried out in a strangled voice. He reached for my hand and pulled me toward him. "You promised me, Samantha. The publicity . . . the notoriety . . ."

He couldn't continue, but I got the point. He'd made it quite clear the night before in Uncle Eddie's office.

The guests got the point too. They looked from Lord Herbert to me, to one another, and back again. Then they all began to protest at once. Clearly, a police investigation was the last thing any of these notable foreigners wanted.

I was speechless. I *had* promised. But I'd also promised to protect the mummy.

"Lord Herbert," Thom said, grasping the back of a chair to pull himself up. "I understand your concern, but you need a forensics team and—"

"I will not stand for this!" the Egyptian attaché interrupted. "I have diplomatic immunity. Your investigation will have to proceed without *me.*" He turned toward the door.

I suddenly found my voice. "Don't move," I told him. He was one of the ones who had left the dinner party. Who had he been talking to on that cell phone, anyway? "Officer Monroe, take the door, please."

The sound Jane Carroll let out led me to believe she may have been responsible for most of the screaming. "Lord Herbert!" she cried. "The reputation of the Royal Museum is impeccable. I will not have it sullied by—" She interrupted herself with a nervous wave of her hands and turned away. "This is inexcusable. Insufferable."

Northcutt took up where she left off. "To have invited us here without proper security was not only ill-advised, Herbert," he said, "it was unconscionable."

"I am incensed that you would infer that one of us might be capable of larceny!" the Italian curator injected.

"Wow," Chaiya said from her spot near the quartet. "These people have really increased their word power!"

Except for Hedda Mead, of course. She flew at Lord Herbert in a fury. The gist of the profanity was that she considered her brother an idiot and Nightshade Investigation something worse.

Superheroes do not cry, I reminded myself, trying not to remember that Flash Gordon would never have lost the mummy in the first place.

Thom had struggled to his feet and stood beside Lord Herbert's chair, grasping the top for support. The lord looked up at him imploringly. "Everything they say is true, Thomas," he said. "Must we . . . might we dispense with . . . ?"

Thom shook his bleeding head. "You need the police, Lord Herbert."

"You *are* the police." The lord crossed his arms over his ample belly. "Your investigation is the *only* one I will allow, Thomas. I will not file a report. This is private property. Hermes is private property—uninsured, I might add—and these people are my guests. They are my friends."

And at least one of them was a thief. I waited for Casey to talk some sense into the man. Clearly, the stunning loss had deranged Lord Herbert's mind.

Thom spoke quietly to Lord Herbert for a few more minutes. "Call the dispatcher," he told Bob Monroe at last. "Tell them it was a mistake and to call back the squad cars." Clearly, the stunning blow had deranged *his* mind. Before I could protest, he added, "And get the crime kit from my car, would you?"

Bob didn't move.

Casey expelled a breath. "Sorry. I don't mean to order you around, Monroe. I'd get it myself, but I don't want to bleed on any more of Lord Herbert's carpets than I already have."

Bob's expression changed instantly to a genial grin. "Sure, partner," he said. "On my way. Anything else?"

Casey shook his head and winced at the pain. "A couple of aspirin, maybe."

"The ambulance will be here in a few minutes," I assured Thom, then included Lord Herbert in my worried glance. There were beads of perspiration on the older man's forehead, and his hand was once again over his chest. The tightness in my own chest, and the pain throbbing in my temples, made me wonder if I might be having a stroke myself. This was the first assignment I'd contracted, and not only had I lost a priceless antiquity, wounded a Phoenix police officer, and possibly killed my client, but—judging by the debate raging all around—I might also have ignited an international incident. I wouldn't have to call Uncle Eddie to report the fiasco. He'd see it on the news in Paris.

"I don't need an ambulance," Casey and Lord Herbert said together.

I ignored them. If they didn't need the ambulance, I probably did.

Thom checked Lord Herbert's pulse. "Cancel the ambulance, too," he called after Bob. "The fewer people we have parading through here destroying evidence, the better." Then he bent over Lord Herbert. "Do you have nitro?"

"Yes, yes," the lord said, patting his pockets. "Somewhere, I . . ." He found the vial and placed a little white tablet under his tongue. "I shall be fine, Thomas. It's only—" He looked at me but didn't continue. He didn't have to. I knew what he was too polite to say: *It's only the incompetence of the girl I hired that's giving me heart failure.* He turned instead to Wendela. "Are you all right, my dear?"

"Yes, Herbert," she said, but she didn't look it. She looked almost as bad as Lord Herbert. In trying to help Thom she'd gotten his blood on her dress and her hands and was rubbing at her palms now as though she'd just been cast as Lady Macbeth.

Professor Northcutt separated himself from the group and stepped forward. Herbert looked up at him. "So sorry, old man," he said.

If you'd seen the hangdog look on Northcutt's face, you'd think it was he who had lost the mummy. But perhaps, in a sense, he had, since he was almost certainly Lord Herbert's choice of guardian. "Please forgive my rash words," the professor said, extending his hand to his old friend. "I have not been myself this evening. And at the turn of events . . ." His words trailed off and he looked sadly at the empty dais. "Tragic," he sighed. "Utterly tragic."

"It's unbelievable," Mrs. Carroll added quietly. "There simply wasn't *time* for someone to steal it. And a sarcophagus can't vanish into thin air."

And yet it had.

Now that the group had recovered from their shock and fear, the accusations had died down and the guests stood soberly around Lord Herbert.

"This I do not understand," the Egyptian attaché said.

"Nor I," the Italian added, staring up at the high ceiling as if expecting to see a giant spiderweb with Hermes wrapped up in the silk.

Barlow looked up with him. "I don't think the aliens came back for him," he said. "If that's what you're thinking."

"That is not what I think!" the curator exclaimed.

Before another skirmish could break out, Thom inserted, "We won't undertake an official investigation in deference to your positions and in compliance with Lord Herbert's wishes, but you'll understand if we ask you a few questions privately and individually. And before you leave the manor tonight, your vehicles will be searched, of course. Finally, I'd like a set of fingerprints from each of you." He held up a hand to silence the objections before they began. "If you are who you say you are, you have nothing to lose and everything to gain. After all, your prints will already be in the international register." He glanced at Barlow, Wendela, and the Meads. "With a few exceptions."

My heart stopped. Then it raced. Then I don't know what it did. What was I going to do? I couldn't let Thom Casey take Wendela's prints. If he did, he might find out her secret. *My* secret. If that happened, not only would I never get my private detective's license, I might end up celebrating every birthday from my twenty-fourth to my fiftieth in prison.

"I won't stand for it!" Hedda exclaimed. "I will not be treated as a common criminal within my brother's home!"

With a leader to rally around, the mob mentality reasserted itself.

I knew I should support Thom. *I* was supposed to be in charge, and here he was doing both our jobs. But I was also the only one in the room that I knew for sure was guilty of committing a crime—albeit one with extenuating circumstances—and he was a law enforcement officer. I had everything to lose—and Wendela had more. I simply couldn't open my mouth. I could scarcely breathe. Never in my wildest nightmares had I dreamed that taking this case and bringing Wendela along could lead to *this*.

To my astonishment, Lord Herbert agreed with his sister that the guests should not be fingerprinted. To my greater astonishment, Thom folded. "Fine," he said. "If Lord Herbert demures, who am I to insist? After all, it isn't *my* priceless mummy that's gone missing."

But he was the one who'd bled for it, I thought guiltily. Clearly, Thom Casey was the only one the thief thought he or she needed to get out of the way. Though he was ignoring it, blood ran down behind his ear and soaked the collar of his shirt and coat. I knew I should have insisted the paramedics come. I wondered if I should call them back. Then I wondered if I was wondering for the right reasons. After all, if I got him out of there right then, he couldn't probe into Wendela's past, even accidentally.

Thom looked over everybody's heads at Knute, who had returned to the doorway. At a motion from the big man, we both walked over to meet him.

Thom waved off Knute's questions about his head before he could ask them. "I'm fine. You find anything?"

"The room one door over was open," Knute said in a low voice. "But it was locked earlier this evening before anybody got here. I checked it myself. Twice."

"Was the mummy there?" I asked. (Yes, it was a senseless question. Being struck dumb would be the very least of my problems at that moment.)

"No," Knute said. "And the room is almost bare. It's a conservatory, I think. About the only thing in it besides a few chairs and a whole lot of plants is a grand piano. Anyway, it's got a pair of French doors that open onto a back garden and—"

"The doors were open!" I guessed. "That's how they got Hermes out! The accomplice came in that way and met the thief at the door before you got there, Knute."

"It might be possible," Knute said. The way he said it didn't indicate he had much confidence in my theory.

"But?" Thom asked, voicing my question.

"But I didn't see anybody inside, and Delano didn't see anybody outside. Delano doesn't miss much."

Neither does Knute, but that clearly didn't hold much weight with the policeman. "It's a big house and he's one guy," Thom said. "No way Delano could be everywhere at once."

"No, but he was nearby and he didn't hear anything," Knute said. "Delano hears everything." Before Casey could protest again, he added, "Besides, that scenario would take at least three people from the get-go—one to snatch the mummy, one to meet the snatcher at the door, and a third to flip the switch that turned off all the lights. Does that wash? It's too coordinated. I mean, these people didn't come here planning to steal a mummy. None of them knew about it beforehand. Lord Herbert didn't tell them why they were here until after they arrived."

Leave it to Knute to think it through.

"Maybe they didn't know what Herbert had," Thom argued, "but they sure as heck knew he had something. They're all smart enough to figure out he might have saved the greatest of his donations for the last." He frowned, and I tried not to admire the dimple in his cheek. "And they're not the only ones here, you know. Caterers, servers, cleaning staff, the limo drivers who drove the guests in. There must be more than a dozen people outside this room right now who could have been in on a heist."

"Nineteen," Knute supplied. "Including the live-in employees Lord Herbert has on staff."

"We checked the staff out ahead of time," I pointed out for Thom's benefit. I couldn't bear for him to think I was inept—even if I was. "They've worked for Lord Herbert since he retired to Arizona."

Thom shrugged. "Maybe one of them is ready to retire himself and is looking for a nest egg."

I sighed. It was possible. Moreover, it was reasonable. Considering the accomplice must have known the location of the fuse box, perhaps it was even likely. "But nobody's left the grounds," I said, hoping it was true.

"Nobody we know of," Knute pointed out.

"If it was an inside job, they're more likely to hide the sarcophagus than try to take it out tonight," Casey said. His eyes moved as if he could see the vastness of the estate through the walls. He shook his head. "It'd take a whole team to cover this place top to bottom. Two teams. More. You've got to convince him to call the cops, Miss Nightshade."

I ignored the name assassination since I didn't know if he was being sarcastic or merely ignorant of the fact that the company is Nightshade and I am Shade. "Me?"

"Hey, you're the boss," Thom said. "I only work here." He raised his hand to the back of his head. "And I should have known how stupid that was when I first arrived and saw *you* again."

I didn't know whether to apologize or retort, so I did neither.

While Delano continued to prowl the perimeter, Knute and Thom spoke to the guests one by one. Meanwhile, I wasted valuable time urging Lord Herbert to send for more help. Despite my own precarious position, I simply had to give him the best chance to recover Hermes. I owed him that much. I owed Nightshade and Uncle Eddie that much. After more minutes of him continuously and adamantly refusing reinforcements, I was both relieved and dismayed.

I'd just rejoined Knute and Thom when Bob Monroe returned with what looked like a small suitcase and a tackle box. It was about time. No, it was way past time. I figured he must have stopped for a smoke, a bathroom break, and to proposition both the upstairs and downstairs maids.

Thom scowled at the first-aid kit. "I don't need that," he said.

I started to object, but Monroe interrupted me. "You wouldn't believe how hardheaded he is. It'd take more than the back of a chair to break that thick skull of his."

"How'd you know it was a chair?" Thom asked.

Bob grinned and tapped his temple. "Superior powers of deduction, my dear Casey. That's why I'm gonna beat you out of that detective spot, remember?"

Thom frowned, but said only, "You can make good use of your superior reasoning tonight. Miss Nightshade says Lord Herbert still insists on a do-it-ourselves job."

"Shade," I said. "My name is Samantha Shade."

Thom didn't care. He looked at the guests and musicians. "I don't think we can keep them here," he said, "especially without Lord Herbert's cooperation. You want to escort them out and check their cars, Monroe, or shall I?"

His partner looked at his watch and turned to me. "I'm not saying the company's not good, pretty lady, but this isn't the job I signed up for."

"You signed us on to guard a mummy," Thom told him. "Since we didn't do a very good job of it, and Lord Herbert won't call in the guys from the crime lab, we're going to have to handle the police investigation ourselves."

"It's not your fault," I began, then caught myself. What was I doing? I couldn't afford to give them an easy out.

But it was too late. "She's right," Bob said. "It's not our fault. They're the ones who were unprepared. We did our bit. We showed up to guard a mummy. Mummy's gone. Job's over." One corner of his lips turned up. "Besides, partner, I still have a *real* job to show up for tomorrow, even if you don't."

I felt the blood rise to my cheeks as I remembered I was the reason Casey had lost that job.

"Go, then," Thom said. "Take my car. I'll call a cab."

"I'll give you a lift home," Knute said to Casey. He glowered at Monroe as though there was something he'd like to give him too—a kick in the pants.

"No hard feelings, right?" Monroe said to me. "I'd still like to show you a good time some night."

I took a step back.

He chuckled as he turned toward the door. "That won't be the first priceless thing you lost tonight."

I didn't watch him leave. Instead I gazed from the empty dais to Wendela to Thom Casey and finally down at my feet. Although I'd seen all the old monster movies with my brother Arjay (and a few of the newer ones as well), I'd never actually believed in the paranormal or fantastical, but now I began to wonder. There *was* a full moon hanging over Mummy Mountain. If anybody had ever been zapped by a mummy's curse, well, I was willing to bet it was me.

ACROSS

29 Accept or agree; What I probably shouldn't do when asked to take on bizarre cases

45 Word to describe mummy, runaway, and (once) Wendela; Obscured; Missing

DOWN

5 Formal argumentation from Barlow; Evidence sought by Thom

Chapter 11

"Delano and I checked every vehicle," Knute reported an hour later. "We looked in every compartment and under the chassis. That mummy didn't leave this mountain by car, van, or limo."

"You mean it hasn't left yet," I said, still massaging the sore spot on my temple. (At the rate I was going, it wouldn't be long before I bored a hole through to my brain.)

"Yeah," Knute allowed, lowering himself onto the chair next to mine in the study. "But Delano says nothing's leaving while he's here."

As if even Delano could keep an eye on twenty acres.

Lord Herbert and Wendela sat side by side on the edge of the dais, exchanging looks from time to time, but not speaking unless spoken to. I'd spent the time my associates were seeing to the guests' departure going over every square inch of wall—just in case. Lord Herbert said he'd never heard of a secret passageway in the study, and apparently he was right. Or if he wasn't right, I couldn't prove him wrong.

Realizing how much I'd slumped, I struggled to pull myself upright when Thom and Chaiya came back into the room. That Lord Herbert had essentially asked him to take charge of the investigation didn't offend me. In fact, I was grateful for it. With most of my mind occupied by guilt, there were too few synapses left for pride or offense.

"I've got full sets from everybody who was in the dining room," Thom reported.

"I assented," Chaiya said happily.

Thom cleared his throat. "She *assisted*."

"I told him where everybody sat at dinner."

At last the significance of what they had been doing reached my brain and almost overloaded it. Just when I'd thought Wendela was safe, Thom and Chaiya had been in the dining room lifting fingerprints. That's why he'd let the subject drop so fast when the guests objected to being printed. He'd known that with dinner ending midcourse, the maid wouldn't have known whether or not to clear the table, so she had left it alone.

And I should have known it. I should have . . . what? Obstructed justice for my own guilty reasons?

"I'll get somebody at the precinct to run the prints," Thom told Knute.

The big man frowned at the expression on my face. "Something wrong, Sam?"

"Of course not," I said. It was the truth. *Everything* was wrong. I sank down in my chair thinking I'd probably slump now for the rest of my life. I'd already apologized to Lord Herbert, but it wasn't enough. I had yet to apologize to Thom for the other night, and that wouldn't be enough, either. And that wasn't even the worst of it. I could *never* apologize to Wendela if they sent her back to the asylum. Thoughts of the girl on the street, the mummy, and Wendela's secrets being revealed when Thom ran the prints spun around in my head and made me too dizzy to think.

I must have looked almost as bad as I felt because Lord Herbert leaned forward.

"This isn't your fault, Samantha, my dove," he said. "Nobody blames you, my dear. Certainly *I* don't."

Hedda Mead's cold eyes told another story, but I didn't care what she thought. She and her surly, spacey son topped my list of suspects for a number of reasons. They were the only ones who might know the manor besides Lord Herbert—and the only ones who might have a key to the conservatory. They were least likely to benefit from Herbert's plans to donate Hermes anywhere. They'd both been AWOL from dinner. Finally, they were the ones for whom it would be easy to hide the mummy now in order to smuggle it out later. As Lord Herbert's relatives, Hedda and Harrison could stay as long as they liked and come and go when they pleased.

As confident as I felt in my reasoning, I didn't know what to do about it. It was like being trapped in an old *Columbo* episode on A&E. In the first ten minutes you know who committed the crime and why; then you spend the next seventy minutes watching Lt. Columbo bring the overconfident perpetrator to justice. I had the crime, the motive, and the overconfident suspects. What I didn't have was Columbo—or even the last act of a screenplay to tell me how this would turn out.

"Okay," Knute said to Thom as he rose. "Shall we see what prints we can lift from the conservatory?"

"As soon as I figure out who clobbered me," Thom said. He looked around, startled to see the chairs once again upright, perfectly aligned, and practically polished.

As his surprise registered with my brain, I drew in a breath. *Wendela.* While I'd been looking for a secret passageway between the study and the kitchen (or the study and anywhere else in Graeme Manor), Wendela had been straightening up the room. It didn't strike me at the time— cleaning and climbing are two things that come naturally to Wendela. But I realized in a flash that she'd not only muddled or erased all the fingerprints, she'd so thoroughly cleaned Thom's blood from the chair with her long, chiffon scarf that it would take a forensics expert to tell which chair had been used in the assault in the first place. In other words, she'd compromised a crime scene, and she'd done it right under my nose.

Thom's eyes moved from the bloody sash in Wendela's hand to my ashen face.

"I'm sorry," I said for probably the fiftieth time that hour. "I wasn't paying attention. Wendela thought she was helping by cleaning up."

"Helping who?" Casey asked with a raised eyebrow.

Even Knute looked disappointed by my latest gaffe.

"Did I do something wrong?" Wendela asked with her lower lip aquiver.

"Of course not!" Lord Herbert exclaimed. "You and Hedda were only being helpful. I thank you both."

That's right! I thought. Hedda *had* helped to right and rearrange the chairs. Since consideration wasn't a trait one would associate with Lord Herbert's witchy sister, I filed it away as another piece of incriminating evidence. Her son, Harrison, hadn't helped—or seemed the least concerned about the loss of the mummy. After giving churlish answers to Thom's questions, he'd slunk from the room to who-knew-where. I could only hope he wouldn't be able to elude Delano if he tried to leave the manor with a twelve-thousand-year-old mummy tucked under his shirt.

That Casey considered saying something to me before he turned to Knute and said, "Let's lift the prints from the conservatory," was obvious. I wondered why he didn't just say what he thought of me and get it over with. I wondered when he finally *would* tell me what a menace to society he thought I was.

As the two men left the room, I knew I had to pull myself together. The mummy was missing, but it wasn't necessarily *lost*. Not yet. If my suspicions about Hedda and Harrison were correct, it was still hidden somewhere on the premises. I had to make sure it stayed there until I could find it.

"Lord Herbert," I said, "I want to post 24-hour guards at the gate to make sure the mummy doesn't leave your property. At my expense, of course."

And I did mean *my* expense. Since Uncle Eddie paid his freelance workers almost as much as he paid me, and since I'd need three shifts per day, I hastily calculated that every day I *couldn't* come up with the mummy would cost me three days' salary. The way things looked now, Uncle Eddie couldn't fire me when he got home. He could *never* fire me. He'd have to let me work gratis for the next six decades just to pay back what I'd owe. And if I never found the mummy . . . I couldn't do the math. No matter how much minimum wage might be in the hereafter, eternity wouldn't be half enough time to earn enough to pay Lord Herbert back for trusting me.

"Guards," the elderly man mused. "Outside the manor, certainly." I was already prepared to counter his objections, but I didn't have to. "Whatever you say, my dear."

After setting Chaiya to the task of arranging a schedule and calling in the first guard, I began to mentally tally up my net worth. Including the piggy bank full of dimes I'd been saving for a rainy day (they almost never happen in Phoenix, so my bank is full), I figured I was worth . . . less than the parlor chair upon which I sat.

And worthless was certainly how I felt.

***

By the time the first guard arrived to relieve Delano, Hedda had retired to her suite while Knute, Delano, Thom, Chaiya, and I had split up to look in every room, closet, cabinet, and crevice of Graeme Manor. There were "treasures" everywhere. We found an elephant's-foot umbrella stand that had purportedly belonged to Rudyard Kipling, two petrified oranges Lord Graeme II had supposedly plucked in Florida while searching for the fountain of youth (Lord Herbert didn't know if he had found it, but suspected not since the man had long ago gone the way of the world), and a coonskin cap that the lord insisted had seen active duty with Davy

Crocket (or was it Daniel Boone?) We didn't, however, find a mummy.

Lord Herbert grasped the petrified raccoon tail in one hand and Wendela's fingers in the other. He hadn't moved from the dais in all that time, and I wondered if by now he *could* move. The poor man was visibly shaken. A rivulet of perspiration ran down his sallow face, and he seemed to have difficulty focusing.

"Lord Herbert?" I said softly. "May I help you up?"

The lord didn't reply. He didn't even look at me. I was glad of the latter because I knew it would kill me to see the look in his eyes. It would be better if he were angry over the loss of the antiquity. Better even if he were incensed and threatening a lawsuit. It was the stunned silence I found almost impossible to bear.

"Lord Herbert?"

Meanwhile, Thom had dropped to his knees on the other side of the dais. I didn't know what he was doing, but if he was praying, I was ready to join him. At that point it seemed like our only hope.

"Knute," Thom said. "Look at this."

The big man joined him with me on his heels. Even Lord Herbert turned.

"The carpet fibers?" Knute asked at last.

"Yes. See there?" Thom looked up. "Have they always been that way?"

Knute rubbed his chin. "Dunno. Sam?"

Before I could confess that I hadn't given the floor a second glance before or after the theft, Thom was running his fingers along the base of the dais.

"I—" the lord said, but nothing more. He listed toward Wendela. The next moment he slumped into her lap, unconscious.

Thom was on his feet and around the dais before I could swallow. "Call an ambulance."

While Wendela hummed soothingly, Thom removed Lord Herbert's bow tie, unbuttoned his vest and shirt, and loosened his cummerbund.

To my horror, the elderly man's chest didn't move.

"He's breathing," Thom told Knute, who relayed the information by cell phone to the 911 dispatcher. "But it's shallow." He pressed his ear to Lord Herbert's chest. "The heartbeat's rapid and a little irregular, but seems otherwise strong."

"Is it a heart attack?" I gasped.

"I don't know," Thom said. To Knute he said, "How long before those paramedics get here?"

"Not long," Knute replied. "The dispatcher says they were on their way back to the station from another call, so they're only a few minutes away."

The next few minutes were the longest "not long" I hoped to ever endure. Knute went to meet the paramedics to show them the way to the study. Thom sent Chaiya to alert Mrs. Mead of her brother's collapse while he remained bent over the lord ready to perform CPR if it became necessary. My self-appointed assignment was to do something about Wendela. If only I knew what.

"Lord Herbert will be all right," I said again, managing to pry his head from her lap just as the paramedics rushed in the door.

"Of course he will be," Wendela agreed.

"It's probably just angina brought on because he's distraught over losing the mummy," I continued.

"Hermes isn't lost," Wendela said. "Hermes was never lost in all his life. How could he be lost now?"

I pulled her up and dragged her to the side of the room, grateful that Thom and Knute were too preoccupied with the paramedics to overhear. "What do you mean he isn't lost?" I whispered. "Wendela, do you know where the mummy is?"

"Why, no, Samantha. Do you?" She looked down at me with that Mona Lisa smile of hers, and I frowned. I'd never known Wendela to lie, but I'd never known her to make much sense, either.

"What *do* you know about the mummy?" I asked.

"He came from the stars," Wendela began, looking wistfully over my shoulder toward the door.

I knew that look. I knew also that if I turned my back on Wendela for even a moment, the fire department's next task would be to get her down from the highest point of Lord Herbert's estate. I tightened my grip on her hands.

The older woman bent to kiss the top of my head. "Don't worry, Samantha. Your face puckers unattractively when you worry."

I tried to relax my puckered facial muscles as I glanced reflexively toward Thom. He was looking at us with his eyes slightly narrowed as if to bring us into better focus. When I met his eye, he looked down at Lord Herbert instead, but the expression stayed the same. I wondered what had made Officer Casey so suspicious of us all.

I was still trying to dismiss the uneasy feeling when Knute approached a few minutes later. "They think he's okay," the big man reported. "But they're going to transport him as a precaution because of his age and symptoms."

"May we go with him?" Wendela asked at once.

I hadn't yet made up my mind where to go, or even if I should leave the scene of the crime. As it turned out, I didn't have to decide because in the next moment Hedda swept into the room like Mary, Queen of Scots. (Or maybe she was more like *Queen Mary*, the ocean liner.)

She said only two words—"Get out!"—but they were enough because her tone of voice and the look on her face said the rest.

I wasn't sure who all was included in the imperious banishment—surely not the paramedics who already had Lord Herbert on a stretcher?—but I knew beyond doubt everybody associated with Nightshade was included. I wasn't surprised when instead of turning to me, Knute consulted Thom.

Thom's eyes made a slow pass around the room. At last they came to rest on the empty dais and stayed there. "I think we've reached a dead end for now," he told Knute.

"Isn't there something else we can do?" I asked.

Thom shrugged. "I don't know what. This is private property and Lord Herbert won't file a report. With him incapacitated, his sister's running the show."

Knute agreed.

"No!" I cried. I didn't miss the smug look on Hedda's face as she watched her brother being carried from the room. If Hedda had orchestrated it herself, Lord Herbert's collapse couldn't have been better timed. Could something that serendipitous also be a coincidence?

"What if she planned this?" I said without thinking. "What if she poisoned him? What if—?" I caught myself as Hedda's expression changed from smug to smoldering. I'd crossed the line and I knew it.

"Come on, Sam," Knute said, taking my arm to pull me toward the door.

First Mrs. Mead called for her attorneys, then she called for my head. (Forget the *Queen Mary*. She was most like the Queen of Hearts. I, unfortunately, was Alice.)

Thom stepped forward to ensure our safe retreat. As we crossed the threshold I heard Hedda insist to the young policeman that she wanted to press charges against me personally for slander and that she would sue Nightshade for fraud, incompetence, malfeasance and some other things my word power wasn't powerful enough to translate into plain, everyday threats. At that moment I not only believed Hedda would do it, I believed Thom Casey would probably act as a corroborating witness against me.

The only thing I didn't know was if there was any way out of this rabbit-hole-from-heck I'd fallen into.

ACROSS

    *34 Fictional (TV) detective who makes crime solving look
a lot easier than it really is*

DOWN

    *14 Soon; Approaching; Now my career seemed ____ its
end*

    *21 Locate; What we couldn't do with regards to a certain
priceless Egyptian antiquity*

Chapter 12

"When the going gets tough, the tough go to Purple Cow," I told Arjay as I turned onto Indian School Road to head for my favorite ice-cream parlor. Located a block away from Nightshade, it's usually the most convenient place to satisfy a hot-fudge sundae attack. Usually, but not that night. That Friday evening I'd been chauffeuring my little brother to and from the orthodontist, so Purple Cow was several miles out of the way from the route that led to Shady Acres and my parents' home next door.

Besides being off course, I was behind schedule. It was nine o'clock and I was already an hour late for work—and in no hurry to get there. With the cases I touched degenerating into disaster, I pretty much figured every minute I spent away from Uncle Eddie's business was time in which I did him a favor.

Arjay grinned at my suggestion. Not only did he love Purple Cow, he wasn't in any hurry either since going home meant going to school—a return to the home school classes he takes mostly via the Internet under the watchful eyes of our parents. "Then can we go to a movie?"

That was pushing it, especially since our mother had her usual residents *and* Wendela to worry about. Still, the temptation was strong and I was weak. "What's playing?" I asked, thinking we could pick up Wendela and make it a threesome.

Before Arjay could consult my cell phone for movie listings, it rang. "It's Chaiya," he reported after answering it. "It sounds like she's mad at you."

My face puckered (probably unattractively) as I wondered what in the world I'd done to offend my cousin. I'd given her first use of the bathroom when we got home from Graeme Manor early this morning, and I hadn't seen or spoken to her since. She was still asleep when I got up—early by anybody's standards (except maybe worm-hunting birds and newspaper delivery people). I would have slept until midafternoon as usual—I work until 5:00 A.M., remember—but I had a busy day. First I took Wendela to the hospital to see Lord Graeme before he was released. Then I swung by the Phoenix PD to right at least one of my many wrongs—and to get back my camera if I could. (I couldn't.) But nothing I had done had anything to do with my cousin.

"Chaiya wants to know what time you'll be in tonight," Arjay reported. He listened for a minute. "No, *my mistake*," he said in a perfect imitation. "Chaiya says 'the hottie from Phoenix PD' wants to know what time you'll be in tonight. *Her* hottie," he added at a prompt from Chaiya. "She says she put in dibs on him and doesn't appreciate you trying to steal him."

I rolled my eyes. Arjay was delighting in this as only an eleven-year-old could. Still, my heart beat a little faster at the thought of Thom Casey wanting to see me. I wished I knew if the emotion causing the accelerated pulse was anticipation or dread.

"What does he want?"

"Sam wants to know what he wants," Arjay told Chaiya. He listened then relayed, "Chaiya says she's not a profiteer." He moved the phone away from his mouth and added, "I think she means she's not a prophetess."

I sighed. "Tell her we're making a quick pit stop before I drop you off and pick up Wendela. I'll be in after that." *Maybe.*

"Samantha needs a hot-fudge sundae," Arjay reported, giving more information than was necessary. "And then we might go to a movie." Arjay was a better prophet than Chaiya, or else he knew me better. He listened for another few moments then said firmly, "Sam says she'll be there when she gets there, Chaiya. Mind your own business." He turned off the phone and said to me, "You can say things like that to lackeys when you're the boss."

"Only if you don't live with the lackey," I told him with a frown.

But Arjay had cinched my playing hooky and he knew it. Now I was definitely going to a movie instead of into the office because I didn't dare show up at work until Chaiya left. It was bad that she apparently had delusions of me flirting with Casey. It was worse to imagine how she'd interpret Arjay's implication that my "CEO-hood" was going to my head. By working only the second half of the night, I would miss Chaiya at Nightshade plus be sound asleep before she got up in the morning to go to beauty school. One great thing about Chaiya is that she rarely holds a grudge. I knew if I could avoid her for another twenty-four hours, she'd have forgotten Arjay's "mind your own business" crack.

But she probably wouldn't have forgotten that Thom had come by Nightshade asking for me. Thom Casey wasn't as forgettable as most things. At least I hadn't been able to get him off my mind all day, even after going to the police station to retract my statement and drop the charges.

I drove the rest of the way to the ice-cream parlor, ignoring Arjay as he rattled off movie listings, reviews, and off-the-wall recommendations he'd received from his legion of e-pals. Frankly, I didn't care what we saw. When you're only going to a movie to hide out, it doesn't matter much what's playing in the lair.

Since it was Friday night, Purple Cow was packed. I found a parking spot in a far corner of the lot and followed

Arjay to the door, where I stopped in my tracks. What was up with the lights? Two of the long fluorescent bulbs had been replaced, and the rest had been washed. Sure, Arjay wasn't his only customer, but Rick, the owner, might still have been more thoughtful. Dang the downtown renovation project anyway. I'd liked this place better when it was more of a dive than a trendy hangout.

"It's okay, Sam," Arjay said before I could voice a concern or pull him back into the darker outdoors. He pulled a light meter about the size of a pocket calculator from his jacket pocket and consulted it. "It's not too bad."

"The corner, then," I decided. The light there wasn't fluorescent and therefore not as broad-spectrum. "But get out your goggles anyway. I'll order."

"I'll have the Whammer," Arjay said cheerfully as he pulled the special UV-blocking glasses from another pocket and removed his hat just long enough to put them on.

"As if I didn't know."

I watched Arjay make his way through the crowd toward a small table in back. Since it was mid-October, having almost every square inch of his body covered didn't attract too much attention, but a few people did look up in surprise at the skinny kid with the Panama hat, white gloves, and frog eyes. If Arjay noticed their stares, his only reaction was to smile broadly, showing off the new Day-Glo orange bands in his braces. Those people who continued to look at him fared worse. Arjay wasn't shy about stopping at their tables to show them his brochure of magazine subscriptions—his latest scheme to raise money for Camp Sundown. Watching him make yet another sale to a startled, if intrigued, stranger, I wished for the umpteenth time I'd been sent to mortality with a fraction of my adopted brother's good attitude and unfailing chutzpah.

As I inched forward at the end of a long line of customers, a tall, uniformed officer approached. I looked up at him in surprise. "Thom? I mean, Officer Casey? I mean . . ." What did I mean? And why, all of a sudden, couldn't I think? "You're in uniform!"

"When you dropped the assault charges, the board settled on a reprimand and reassigned me to patrol," he said.

He didn't look as pleased to have a job again as I thought he should. "You don't have to thank me," I began.

His eyebrow rose. "You think I came here to thank you for undoing something you shouldn't have done in the first place?"

"I thought—"

"No, you didn't," he interrupted. "You *assumed*. If you'd listened—"

"If you'd *told* me—"

"If you'd given me a chance to—"

"If you hadn't taken my camera—"

"If you hadn't taken my picture—"

"If you hadn't—"

Thom held up a hand to stop the war of the words. "Never mind." He indicated with his eyes that we had become a focus of attention for everybody within a thirty-foot radius. "Thank you for doing the right thing," he said. "Finally."

I felt the color rise to my cheeks. "You're welcome."

The line shortened considerably as a group of teens claimed their yellow plastic order ticket and sat down to await their ice cream. I moved forward. Casey moved with me. "Did Chaiya tell you I was here?" I asked when he wouldn't go away.

"No," he said. "She barely spoke to me. She told me to come back in about an hour, then she rushed out."

I almost smiled at the puzzlement on his face. Obviously, Chaiya made even less sense to him than she did to the rest of us.

"But Knute overheard her telephone conversation with you," Thom continued. "He told me you were here."

Before I could ask what he wanted with me, it was my turn to order. "What can I get you?" I asked Thom. "I owe you at least a dish of ice cream after everything you did last night." My eyes rose to his head, but he was too tall for me to see how bad the wound beneath his thick hair was.

"No, thanks," he said. "I'm on duty." He glanced around. "Both Nightshade and this place are on my new beat." The way he said it indicated that he didn't consider that a good thing.

In fact, it was a terrible thing. He was *on duty?* My mind raced, but my body became suddenly immobile. If Casey had tracked me down while on duty, it must be official business. That could only mean he'd already run the fingerprints and found out about Wendela.

The girl behind the counter asked for my order.

"Go ahead," Thom said when I didn't respond.

Talk about compassion. He was going to let me one last hot-fudge sundae before he had me sent to prison. Maybe he'd also be kind enough to call Knute to come pick up Arjay before I was hauled off in handcuffs. I'd hate for my little brother to be left here all alone until my father could arrive from the lab and . . .

My father! I knew then Thom wouldn't have a chance to arrest me. The heart that had been thudding against my ribs stopped beating altogether. In another minute I would die and be out of the reach of the law. The earthly law, that is. As for the hereafter, I'd always heard we're judged by the intent of our hearts. I hoped it was true.

I grasped the counter to try to bolster my puttylike knees. Why had I been so stupid? I should have known I wouldn't get away with it. Now that it was too late, other ways I might have "chosen the right" six months before swirled through my head.

Thom took a firm, authoritative grip on my elbow.

And why did it have to be this man who finally hunted me down? Couldn't it have been anybody *but* him?

"Miss Shade?" Thom said.

This is it, I thought as I waited for Casey to tell me I had the right to remain silent. (Not that I had any option besides silent. With fear constricting my throat, I couldn't have confessed *or* professed my innocence—even if I'd known which one to go for.)

"Are you all right?" he asked.

Despite myself, I looked up at Thom to see if he'd asked just so he could laugh in my face. I blinked twice. If there was anything in those soft gray eyes besides concern I didn't see it.

"Are you all right?" he repeated. "I thought for a second there you were going to faint."

"I . . . I'm fine," I managed.

He DOESN'T know! I realized in a flash. He couldn't know and still look at me so kindly. I needed a save and I needed it fast. I said the only thing that came to mind. "I . . . I'm just . . . hungry."

"Then why don't you order?" the teenager behind the counter suggested.

I took a deep breath and ordered Arjay's Whammer along with a scoop of plain vanilla yogurt I knew I'd never be able to force past my still-chattering teeth.

The girl pushed a placard across the counter. "It'll only be a minute. Put this on the table for your server."

I nodded but didn't pick up the piece of plastic. For the first time in my life I felt like a superhero—Elastic Girl. I was afraid to let go of the counter for fear I'd fold into a mound of Silly Putty at Thom's feet.

He picked the placard up for me without releasing my elbow. "Is that your brother over there?" he asked.

"Yes," I said without turning to see where he'd pointed. Instead I stared down at my hands. They were still clutching the countertop as if superglued into place.

Thom applied just enough drag to move me backward a foot or so. Miraculously, my arms didn't stretch, and my fingers slid from the Formica countertop to fall limply at my sides.

"When was the last time you ate?" he asked as he steered me toward the table where Arjay sat, watching in interest.

"About an hour ago," I said, forgetting that I'd just attributed my vertigo to hunger. (Frankly, I'm a terrible liar. People like me should never commit felonies or be asked if somebody's tight new jeans make their thighs look fat.)

If Thom noticed my slip of tongue he didn't call me on it. He just pulled out a chair and let me dissolve onto it while he remained standing.

Arjay extended a gloved hand. "Hi there!" he said. "I'm Arjay Shade. You must be the hottie."

"Arjay!" I cried. (There are certain things that can startle a girl from a stupor. Mortification is one of them.)

"I'm Officer Casey," Thom said, shaking Arjay's hand.

"My sister told me how you lost the mummy last night," my brother said.

"He doesn't mean you lost it," I inserted hastily, wondering if this could get any worse. "He means . . ." They both waited for me to finish the sentence, but I didn't have the energy. Hoping to remain mostly upright a few minutes more, I rested my elbows on the table and dropped my chin into the palms of my hand. "Why do you want to see me?" I asked weakly, wondering why Thom Casey would *ever* want to see me again if not to arrest me.

He reached into his pocket to retrieve Uncle Eddie's small, digital camera and set it on the table in front of me. "I want to return this."

I bolted upright. "Thank you!" I cried, reaching for it. At least the Mermann case would turn out okay. Even if Thom eventually discovered Wendela's secret and sent me to jail, I'd always be grateful to him for first helping me save face in front of Uncle Eddie and his pal Mick Farrel. Besides, perhaps Mick would represent me when I needed a good attorney—which could be any day now. "You don't know how much this means to me!"

"You're welcome," Thom said, turning to leave. "Good night." He was almost to the door by the time I had looked at the first few pictures displayed on the camera's small viewscreen.

"Wait!" I called across the room to him. "These aren't my pictures!"

For the second time, I'd attracted the attention of almost everybody in the place. Thom wasn't smiling when he walked back to our table. This time he pulled out a chair and sat down. "Now what's the problem?"

"These aren't my pictures!" I repeated, trying to keep the hysteria out of my voice as I flipped from one frame to the next. Casey's eyebrows rose. "Have you looked at them?" I demanded.

"Yes," he said thinly. "I saw them the night they stuffed me in the back of a patrol car. After my boss took the handcuffs off me, of course."

I ignored his sarcasm. "Then you *know* they're not my pictures!"

Thom took the camera and held it up to view the first of the remaining twelve shots stored in the camera's memory chip. "It's Van Buren," he said. He pushed a button to advance to the next shot. "Same place. Same time." He looked at a third and then lowered the camera. "I don't know what you're talking about. They're all pictures of some rich guy in a silver car either picking up a hooker or trying to buy drugs. That's the same disgusting thing I saw the first time I looked at them."

"'Some guy?'" I repeated. "Don't you know who that man is?"

"No," Thom said. "But I know it's the same guy in the same car talking to the same girl."

"It's the same car," I said, not sure I believed what I was saying myself. "But it's not the same license plate. I memorized it so I'd be sure to get it right." I shook my head as if to clear it. "And it's not the same girl, either. This one is younger." Leaning close so only he could hear, I added, "Most importantly, it's not the same guy—though it looks a lot like him. My pictures were of Sid Mermann. *Councilman* Mermann." When Thom didn't respond I said, "Somebody erased my pictures and staged these with a stand-in."

Thom was dubious. "Councilman Mermann? Did you include that in your statement?"

"Of course not!" I said. "I work for his wife, and we keep our cases strictly confidential."

At least we did until then, I realized, kicking myself under the table.

Thom shook his head. "These are your pictures. That camera hasn't left the station. You shot the wrong guy. It wouldn't be—"

"The first mistake I ever made?" I asked, anxious to say it myself before he could. I leaned across the table, desperate to make him believe me. If he didn't, nobody else would. "Thom, I swear these aren't the same pictures. Please look at them one more time. You must be able to see *something* different."

I was certain he would lay the camera down and walk away. When he raised it and once again peered carefully at the next several pictures on the tiny screen, I held my breath, crossed my fingers, and said two prayers.

"I'm sorry," he said after more than a minute, "but . . ."

When no more words were forthcoming, I released the breath I'd been holding into a sigh of resignation. "But you don't see anything."

He didn't reply. Instead he kept staring until he was sure. "My gosh," was all he said. When at last he set the camera on the table and met my eyes, my heart soared. "Those aren't the same pictures," he said slowly. "Even as indistinct as the shot is, I would have seen Taryn in the background if she'd been in the first set. I'm sure of it."

Under the circumstances, I took little pleasure in the corroboration. "Is Taryn the runaway you were talking to the night I . . . interrupted?" I asked. I hated to say the name or broach the subject because my guilt at frightening off the poor girl was still so raw it gave me nightmares. (Or daymares since that's when I sleep.)

Thom nodded.

"I'm sorry."

"I am too." His eyes were on the digital camera, but he didn't reach for it again.

"What do we do now?" I asked. It was the same thing I'd asked him about the missing mummy twenty-some hours before.

His answer was the same, too. "I don't know," he said. "I just don't know."

ACROSS

62 *Where Arjay and thousands of other children learn*
   algebra

DOWN

48 *"When the going gets tough, the tough go for ice ____"*

52 *Mathematician with a "beautiful mind" rather like*
   Wendela's; Author of "I never saw a purple cow . . ."
   poem

Chapter 13

The ice cream had been delivered to our table by the time Thom made up his mind. He pushed the camera toward me and said, "Take this to Nightshade as soon as you can and make copies of all those pictures." He stood. "Make at least three sets. I have to get back out on the street, but I'll drop by later to pick one up. Leave one at the office."

"And the third?"

"Take it home." He considered. "Better yet, send it home with Knute."

I was almost afraid to touch the camera now. It seemed dangerous since Thom didn't want to take it back to the police station. Wasn't that the logical place to start looking for answers to this newest mystery?

"What do you think it means?" I asked. When he looked at Arjay I added, "It's okay. He won't say anything."

"I don't know what it means," Thom said at last. "I only know two things. First, I know somebody must have found out whose pictures you had on that camera."

"And second?"

"I know there's no record of it ever leaving the locker I put it in," he said. "I signed it in and I signed it out. According to the docket, nobody else even looked at it."

But somebody *had* looked at it—looked at it and then went to a lot of effort creating shots that were near duplicates of my own. It didn't make sense. The only thing I knew for sure was that nobody would believe me if I showed up at the precinct complaining of tampering. Nobody but Thom Casey, that is—the man they probably assumed was the last person on earth who'd be willing to help me after what I'd done to him. "I'll go straight from here to Nightshade."

Thom watched Arjay devour his Whammer with gusto. "Take your brother home first," he suggested. "It's getting late."

"I'm nocturnal," Arjay informed the policeman. Caramel ran down his chin. "That means I'm most active at night."

Thom nodded, but he'd turned to me as if for a rebuttal or punch line.

"It's true," I said. "Nine P.M. is still morning for Arjay. I brought him here after his specially arranged orthodontist appointment. Our mother will kill me when she finds out I let him eat ice cream for breakfast."

"Next we're going to a 'morning' movie," Arjay announced happily.

"Next you're going home to your classes and I'm going to work," I corrected him. I glanced up at Thom and almost smiled. He had no idea what was going on with us.

"I've got XP," Arjay said, tapping his spoon to his goggles as if they explained everything. "Just like a vampire, sunlight will kill me. Splat!" He slapped his spoon into strawberry sauce for special effect.

I watched Thom's eyes widen as they moved from my little brother's unconventional goggles and getup to take in my all-black ensemble. I could almost watch the wheels turning behind his eyes as he realized he'd never seen me dressed in any other color.

"*I'm* not a vampire," I said with a grin. "I only dress like one." Thom was still nodding, and I knew if I didn't get an explanation out soon, I wouldn't be able to talk because I'd be laughing too hard at the expression on his face. "Arjay was born with a rare genetic condition called xeroderma pigmentosum. Exposure to ultraviolet rays from sunlight and other sources *is* deadly to him."

"Yeah," Arjay said, setting aside his ice cream for a moment to lapse into his well-rehearsed professorial mode. "Sunlight is bad for everybody's DNA, but people like you have enzymes that strip out the damaged nucleotide strands and replace them with healthy DNA. I don't have those enzymes, so exposure to broad-spectrum light can give me skin cancer—and cause all kinds of other problems."

Thom had finally stopped nodding.

"Last year, about a thousand Americans were struck by lightning," Arjay continued matter-of-factly, "but fewer than a hundred were born with XP." He grinned. "That makes me rarer than a giant panda." When he stuck out his now-glove-less hand, it was apparent that it was almost as white as a panda's paw from lack of sunlight. "You can shake my hand again if you want to."

I swatted at my little brother's fingers with a smile. "If you don't start watching your smart mouth, you're not going to be rare, you're going to be extinct."

While Thom processed the information he'd just heard, Arjay stuck the hand into a jacket pocket and came up with a slick, colorful brochure. "Want to buy a magazine subscription?" he asked. "Every sale I make helps fund Camp Sundown. That's a camp for kids like me. And werewolves," he added, contorting his chocolate-covered lips into a wolfish grin.

Thom accepted the brochure Arjay pressed forward, but didn't respond for several more seconds. (People never know what to say in the face of something as mind-numbing as Arjay's affliction—or his warped sense of humor. Thom did better than most.) "Sounds like a fun place," he said at last. "There weren't any werewolves where I went to camp, only coyotes."

"You can take the flyer with you," Arjay said magnanimously. "Bring me a check when you come to Nightshade to pick up the pictures. Buy as many magazines as you want."

"I will, thanks." Thom stuck the brochure in his uniform pocket. "Nice to meet you, Arjay. See you later, Miss Shade."

"Not if Chaiya sees you first," Arjay said with a grin.

If Thom heard the warning, he didn't turn back to ask what it meant. Minutes passed and I watched my brother begin an elaborate sculpture out of melting ice cream. I knew he was too full to eat another bite but unwilling to go home and face algebra. "Assuming Mom will look after Wendela for me a little while longer, do you want to come with me to Nightshade?" I asked.

Arjay dropped the spoon. "Yeah!"

I smiled and leaned across the table to give him a hug. I'd felt the very same way at eleven years old—and older. There'd never been a better place to be than Nightshade Investigation.

Until tonight, of course. Tonight there was still the irrational ire of Chaiya to face.

***

"Anything?" I asked Knute about an hour later.

It was impossible to read over his shoulder because of his size, so I had to settle for leaning around him in order to get even a glimpse of his computer screen. Arjay was in the next room counting his magazine money while he watched *Babylon 5* DVDs (from which comes my second and more meaningful motto: *Faith Manages*), and Chaiya was downloading and printing the digital pictures. But she was doing it only because I'd promised her Thom would be by for them later, and that his business with me was strictly business.

"Nothing," Knute said, exiting the last website. "But it's too early." He leaned back in his chair. "Besides, despite what Northcutt said, we probably don't know where all to look."

"How many places *are* there to sell a stolen mummy?" I asked. "Did you check eBay?"

Knute rolled his eyes, but he wouldn't look at me. "Yeah," he admitted at last. "I checked eBay."

"We're not going to find it, are we?" I asked in dismay. With Lord Herbert still "indisposed" and his sister guarding

the door to his estate more ferociously than any dragon, I'd
agreed with Knute and Delano that the best chance we had
to catch the thief was to backtrack from wherever the
mummy turned up. *If* it turned up.

Predictably, Professor Northcutt had been the most co-
operative of the "suspects." He'd even confessed that, like
almost everything else, the black market in antiquities thrived
on the World Wide Web. After swearing us to confidentiality,
he'd sent Nightshade a list of almost a dozen sites frequented
by not-always-aboveboard traders, and the passwords with
which to access them. I was amazed at what turned up. Amazed
and disgusted and daunted. It would take a whole league of
cyber Spider-Men to clean up the corruption on that web.

I sat back down in my chair and leaned my head back as
far as I could—in my best Marlene Pringle imitation.

Marlene is a resident at Shady Acres who does yogalike
contortions in her custom-designed wheelchair. Her favorite pose
is something she calls "bat contemplating paradise" where she
crosses her arms over her chest, releases the back of her chair and
leans so far backward that she's almost upside down. She claims it
makes the blood flow to her brain, thus causing it to work better.
Since she's the reigning chess champion at the Acres—and decidedly sharper than I am—I figure her exercises must have merit.
(I mean, even to people besides her chiropractor.)

"I don't know what to think, Knute," I said about the
time my face started to turn purple and my ears began to
buzz. (Marlene's "bat contemplating paradise" technique
works better for some people than it does for others.)

"About the mummy?"

"About anything!" I rolled my head forward again and
uncrossed my arms to catch myself before I passed out.
"You're the smartest person I know. Help me out here."

He tapped the keyboard. "I thought I was helping you out."

"I mean the pictures! It's too strange. Who would have
anything to gain by messing with my camera?"

"Councilman Mermann," Knute replied, stating the obvious first.

"Yes. But how would he know what was on my camera, or that the police had it?"

"He would know if somebody tipped him off that you'd staked him out the night before. He might have had you followed the next night. Not that I think you blew your cover," he added hastily. "We're just speculating, right?"

"Right," I said, but my stomach knotted in worry. I'd taken on more than one case I was too inexperienced to handle correctly.

"Or," Knute continued, "he'd have known if somebody at the station saw the pictures and tipped him off after the fact."

"Still," I said, "why go to all the effort of changing the license plates on the car and setting up new pictures? Surely whoever did it knew *I'd* notice the difference."

Even when I said it I knew it wasn't necessarily true. Not if they knew how inexperienced I was. Or how quick to jump to conclusions. Or how just plain ditzy I could be at times. I shook my head to dispel the depressing thought that I might as well wander the streets in a Super Klutz costume as try to save the world by becoming a private investigator.

Still, nothing about this thing with the camera made sense. I leaned toward Knute. "Why didn't they just erase the pictures and tell me it was an accident or 'police procedure' or something? I'd have believed them."

Knute took his time before responding. "Would you? If your pictures had been erased at the station, wouldn't you have carried on about it?"

"Possibly," I admitted. "Probably." (Knute knows me pretty well. Too well, in fact.)

"And maybe you'd have carried it far enough that the press would catch wind of it and make a certain councilman's life very uncomfortable," Knute continued. "But this way, with the pictures gone, it cuts you off at the knees. If you walk in with the story that the police replaced your pictures, you're most likely to look like *you* blew it—never had anything to start with—and are trying to save face before your client." He reached forward and patted my hand as he saw the truthfulness of his words sink in. "I'm sorry, Sam, but nobody's going to believe you without the goods. If you try to go public now with what you saw, Mermann will sue Nightshade for every penny Eddie ever made."

"Thom Casey believes me," I said. "That's two witnesses that the pictures were tampered with, right?"

This time it was even longer before Knute responded. "That's another thing I'm afraid of." I waited for him to continue. "Casey's the only one besides Mermann who obviously had something to gain by tampering with your pictures."

"You don't think—"

"No, but I think he'll be the only person Internal Affairs looks at." He stretched out his long legs. "Thom doesn't see it yet, but something's going on down there. Something bad. I thought at the time it was a pretty big coincidence for Casey's boss to show up when he did on Tuesday night. What're the chances in a city this size—especially when you factor in that the streets aren't routinely patrolled by police captains?"

"You think somebody set Thom up?"

"I think it's a possibility," Knute said. "They couldn't have figured on you being there, of course. That must have been an especially lucky break for them—and an especially unlucky break for Thom."

"But who?" I asked, trying to ignore the growing knot in my stomach. If there was anything I wanted to be in Thom Casey's life, an "especially unlucky break" wasn't it. "And why?"

Knute shrugged his massive shoulders. "That I can't tell you."

I shifted in my chair. I was uncomfortable in it, in my new position at Nightshade, and maybe even in my own skin. "So if I do go to the police, all I'll accomplish is getting Thom fired."

"That's my take."

"He doesn't seem to like being a patrolman," I said for what it was worth.

"He's ambitious," Knute said. "It runs in his family. He'd hoped to make detective."

"How do you know so much about him?" I asked, suddenly suspicious.

"We talked for a while," Knute said. "I drove him home last night. Remember?"

I did when he reminded me. Then I remembered Knute wouldn't have had to drive Thom home if his partner had stayed to help.

"Bob Monroe!" I said. "He said something about making detective before Thom. Maybe he set him up to eliminate the competition."

"Maybe," Knute said, but he didn't sound like he believed it.

Another mystery, I thought, instinctively slipping a wooden pencil in my mouth to gnaw on. I'd always thought I'd thrive on mysteries, but now that they were falling so thick and fast and affecting people I cared about—not that I *cared* about Thom Casey, exactly—I wasn't so sure I was in the right line of work.

ACROSS

    50 Abbr. of rare genetic affliction; Why Arjay will never
        sunbathe

DOWN

    26 Of or relating to night; What Arjay, me, lemurs, owls,
        and vampires are

Chapter 14

I whipped the car around the corner fast enough that Arjay's head impacted with the passenger-side window. "Sorry," I said. "Hold on. We're being followed."

It was after eleven and, at my mother's explicit request, I was finally taking my brother home and picking up Wendela. Wendela had been most of the way up the arbor toward the roof when good old Mr. Lamar, a retired NBA basketball official, had seen her and blown the whistle. Literally. Wendela and the satellite dish were safe for now, but I wasn't so sure about Arjay's well-being—not the way I was driving.

The creep chasing us had appeared outside Nightshade around ten. I don't know how he'd known I slipped Arjay down the back staircase to the employee's parking lot, but we hadn't gone a full block before he was on our tail. He'd stayed there ever since.

"Hold on!" I told my brother. "We've got to lose this guy."

Arjay turned around as far as his seat belt would allow. "Cool! A car chase!" His wide eyes sparkled with excitement at the sight of our pursuer. "That van's a monster, Sam. You can outrun it!"

I glanced in the rearview mirror. If we were being filmed by helicopter for the midnight news, our scene would more resemble a rhinoceros trailing a stinkbug than a bona fide car chase. My little black VW is the pride of my life, but it isn't all that fast. The van on our tail, on the other hand, had power to spare, but it was a behemoth. From his vantage point, Wick Barlow had probably seen us the second we exited the building.

I stepped on the gas and looked for an alley, a driveway—anything narrow enough to slow the wide van with the satellite dish on top and keep its driver from following us home to Wendela. Without a mummy to talk up, the UFOlogist was undoubtedly anxious to make Wendela the hottest topic out of Phoenix since the mysterious lights. And, with his broadcast beginning in less than an hour, he was probably as desperate as I was.

Ignoring a stoplight and narrowly missing an oncoming delivery truck, I cut another corner onto a one-way street. Unfortunately, I was going the wrong way on it. Before I could draw a breath I saw that in three seconds or less I was going to hit an approaching car head-on. The other driver was moving even faster than me, but his car had an advantage—besides being headed the right way, I mean. Because of the red-and-blue flashing lights on top, the rest of the traffic had stopped to let it pass.

I slammed on my brakes and swerved left at the same time the officer in the patrol car swerved right. I didn't feel a jolt, but I heard the sickening crash. I mean *crashes.* They seemed to go on forever, but I didn't open my eyes to see why.

"Wow!" Arjay exclaimed when at last the banging stopped. "That policeman just plowed through a whole row of garbage cans to keep from hitting us. Look at his car!"

I couldn't look. All I could do was squeeze my eyes closed and pray that the officer at the wheel was all right. After a minute—or an hour or a week—I heard Arjay open his door.

"Hey, Officer Casey!" he called out. "Choose which magazines you want yet?"

I tried to scrunch farther down in my seat. Maybe Thom wouldn't see me. Or maybe I'd sink right through the floorboard and the pavement and disappear forever into the sewer system. Either one would have worked for me.

"Are you all right?" Thom asked, pulling open my door after he'd checked out Arjay and seen he was uninjured. It was the second time he'd asked me that question that night and, incredibly, I'd been better the *first* time he'd inquired. (You remember, the time when I pretty much thought I was going to die.)

Still, I nodded and opened my eyes. Unable to look up at Thom, I stared at the curb instead. His patrol car looked like it had taken on a bulldozer, a wrecking ball, and two garbage trucks in a demolition derby—and come in fifth. I squeezed my eyes closed again. "That was my fault, wasn't it?" I whispered.

"Would you please step out of the car?" Thom said as another squad car rounded the corner. He pretty much pulled me to my feet, then said, "They're going to ask you to take a Breathalyzer test. Should you call a lawyer first?"

"No!" I said hastily. "I'm not drunk! I do these kinds of things sober."

Okay, so I didn't really say that last line, but I probably should have. Thom could have used the warning for later reference.

He sighed. "You're not going to tell me you're hungry again, I hope."

"No. I'm . . . I was just . . . just trying to get away from *him!*" I pointed down the street toward the corner where Barlow had pulled to a stop—on the correct side of the street. He looked like the epitome of a law-abiding motorist. I hated him even more than I had five minutes before.

The radio show host approached at a jog. "I saw the whole thing, Officer!" he told Thom with a grin. "That woman's a maniac."

"Funny thing," Thom replied just before I exploded. "I got a report of a large, white van pursuing a black Volkswagen at unlawful speeds. That van's driver wouldn't be anybody you know, would it?"

"No, sir."

"That's what I thought."

I was still sputtering when Thom turned back to me.

"Let me handle this, please. Save your remarks for the official report."

After telling Barlow to stay put, Thom turned his attention to the first policemen to arrive. They were followed closely by paramedics. "Check out the woman and the kid," he said to the latter. "But I think everybody's okay."

Thom's car was the one that had been through the trash compactor. If anybody here was hurt, it would be him. But like the night before, he didn't ask for so much as a Band-Aid. As one of the officers left to direct traffic around the crash and hold back the gawkers, Thom said to his other colleague, "Take her statement for me, would you? I know her. She's—"

I wondered what he'd have said if he hadn't noted me listening in. Would he have said I was the bane of his existence . . . or merely his worst nightmare come to life?

"I've moonlighted for her agency," Thom said, beginning a new sentence instead of finishing the last one. "I'll talk to the other guy."

I watched him take Wick Barlow back down the street toward his van before a medic armed with a flashlight and blood-pressure cuff accosted me. The flashlight brought me back to my senses. "Don't shine the light in his eyes!" I called to the paramedic who approached my little brother. "Arjay, show him your tags."

Obediently, Arjay pulled the chain holding two medical dog tags from beneath his shirt and extended them.

The next thirty minutes passed in a blur. I was in the middle of a statement to the officer when my cell phone rang. "That'll be my mother," I said, feeling like an incorrigible teenager caught out after curfew. "She'll worry if I don't answer."

And when I do answer, I thought in the next breath, *and tell her how I almost killed myself and Arjay trying to outrun a lunatic, then she'll be frantic.*

"Never mind," I told the policeman, leaving the phone where it lay. "She'll be happier if she doesn't talk to me."

About the time I'd responded to what I hoped was the last question, Wick Barlow's sonorous voice rose loud enough to be heard without benefit of the microphone in his hand. I turned at the same time as the policeman to see that Barlow had raised his satellite dish and opened up the side of the van to reveal a traveling studio. He'd already attracted a small crowd of street-wandering insomniacs. Standing at the fringes of the group was an ecstatic little boy under the watchful supervision of a very pained-looking police officer who'd just bought who-knew-how-many magazine subscriptions to help pay a sick kid's way to night camp.

"Welcome aboard, America!" Barlow intoned. "Are you ready to boldly go where . . ."

It must be midnight, I thought, tuning him out. *Prime time for UFOlogists, people like Arjay—and idiots like me.*

"Is that all?" I asked the policeman who was clearly more interested in Barlow now than he was in me. I'd already answered every one of his questions with more patience than I thought I'd ever possess. I'd even passed the Breathalyzer test with flying colors. (Wouldn't Thom be surprised by that?) "May I go?"

"No," he said. "Sorry. You'll have to wait for Casey. As the first officer on the scene, he'll issue the citations."

"Citations?" I said, aghast. "You mean *tickets?* But it wasn't my fault! I was just—"

Talk about being tuned out. The policeman was already down the street, anxious to trade places with Casey so he could better hear what Barlow had to say. Of course, the officer didn't yet know about the pint-sized supersalesman who would dog his every step until he bought at least one year's worth of *Better Homes and Cop Cars.*

I leaned against my car and lowered my eyes as Thom approached, but he walked past me to his own battered vehicle. I watched from beneath my lashes as he reached inside for a metal clipboard and pen. By the time he returned, my cheeks were burning from shame and dismay. A handful of tickets were probably the least of what I deserved, but much more than I thought I could handle.

"I didn't do anything wrong!" I protested. "Not really."

He was already writing. "You failed to yield to a traffic control device."

"You mean I ran the red light?" I bit my lip. "Well, only *kind of.* And it's the middle of the night."

"Laws tend to be in effect regardless of the hour."

"There was nobody coming—"

"You made an illegal turn onto a one-way street," Thom continued as if I hadn't spoken.

"I didn't realize—"

"You failed to control your vehicle, resulting in a significant loss of public property and a threat to life and limb of other motorists."

"*You* hit the garbage cans and wrecked the squad car," I said, but my heart wasn't in it. After all, I knew he'd risked his life to keep from hitting us head-on. I could see by the damage to his car and how far the impact had thrown the garbage cans just how bad a collision with my little Volkswagen would have been. I shuddered.

It was the only time he glanced up. In the next moment he was writing again. "You were traveling at a speed in excess of—"

"There were extenuating circumstances!" I interrupted. "Wick Barlow was trying to follow me home. He wants to use Wendela. I can't let that happen! She's . . . she doesn't understand. She . . . she . . ." I looked up at the handsome young officer and sighed. "*You* don't understand."

To his credit, Casey seemed to be listening. At least he'd stopped writing for a moment.

I took a deep breath. This was probably the only chance I'd ever get to make Thom Casey understand the larger picture—or at least to gauge how he would react if he ever discovered our secret for himself. I grasped his arm impulsively. "I *have* to protect Wendela, Thom. Aren't there times when a person's desire for a greater good outweighs the things she does to accomplish it?"

"I took an oath to uphold the law," he said slowly and as if he'd already given what I was about to say a lot of thought. "I can't look the other way when somebody breaks that law— no matter what her reasons or how good her intentions."

My hand slipped from his arm. There was the answer to my questions and the end of any hope I'd had for mercy outweighing justice in Thomas Casey's mind.

"How many tickets are you going to give me?" I asked, willing myself not to cry. If I'd broken as many motor-vehicle laws as I thought I had, surely my driver's license would be revoked, and then my job at Nightshade would be over. I'd never get my PI license and would be stuck emptying bedpans at Shady Acres—at least I would until Thom Casey finished investigating Wendela's background and sent the poor woman back to the state hospital and me to prison. If he couldn't overlook a little traffic offense, he certainly couldn't ignore kidnapping and obstruction of justice. I bit down hard on my lower lip, but it didn't keep it from quivering.

"I'm citing you for two violations," he said quietly. "You can clear the more serious one from your record in traffic school, and the lesser will result in only one point being charged to your license. In three years, even that will be gone." Before I got over my surprise, he added, "I didn't see you run the red light, Miss Shade. I merely assumed you had. And you're right about the property damage. That should go on my record, not yours."

Suddenly, despite his professional, no-nonsense manner, I wanted to confess everything to him and take my chances on his inherent compassion. But Thom didn't give me a chance.

"Sign this, please," he said, extending the clipboard.

There was so much I wanted to say, but I couldn't speak. I could scarcely see the words and numbers on the page under the grateful tears that welled in my eyes. I blinked rapidly to bring the paper—if not what had just happened—into focus. When I saw what he'd written, my conscience got the best of me and I whispered, "I was probably going faster than what you wrote down."

"Faster is a felony violation," he said. "Were you watching your speedometer?"

"No."

"And I didn't have radar on you, so that's my best estimate. If you want to challenge it before a judge, go ahead."

I looked up, but he wasn't smiling. I signed the tickets and handed back the clipboard. I couldn't help but look beyond him at his totaled vehicle. Once the other officers had finished taking pictures of the scene, a crew arrived to clean up the mess. One city employee now attached a cable to the squad car's chassis to pull it up on the tow truck, while a couple of others swept the debris off the street and righted the few trash cans that hadn't been demolished.

Thom followed my line of vision, and his dimples deepened with his frown.

I couldn't stand it. "You . . . you won't get in trouble for that, will you?" He shook his head, but I knew it was more resignation than denial. "Give me more tickets," I said impulsively. "This was my fault, not yours."

Thom glanced at me then with a look of appreciation that would have been worth the loss of both my driver's and

PI licenses. But in the next moment the expression changed and he shook his head. This time it did mean no. Cryptically, he said, "I tried, but it had to stop somewhere."

Before I could ask him what he'd tried and what had to stop—and why he looked and sounded so melancholy about it—he'd walked away.

ACROSS
> 28 *The kind of light Arjay prefers; The bulb in my head sometimes?*

DOWN
> 57 *Throb; With "head," it's what Thom must have had most of the time after he met me*

Chapter 15

"Chaiya," I said, trying to shake my cousin awake. "Go home and go to bed."

It was after three in the morning, and I was back at Nightshade after finally getting Arjay home and facing all the wrath my five-foot-two saint of a mother could muster. (It was quite a bit, all things considered—but nothing compared to what I'd hear when my six-foot patriarch of a father came home from his research lab and she told *him* how I'd endangered Arjay and myself by careening madly around corners and taking out squad cars.)

I'd confessed right off because my version was sure to be less dramatic than Arjay's—and not even a permanent brand of duct tape properly applied could have kept his mouth shut about the "car chase." It had been the most exciting six or eight minutes of his life, and each time he retold the tale to another Shady Acres resident, it became longer and more exciting still. By the time he finished embellishing, NASCAR legend Dale Earnhardt would have nothing on *my* driving. (Thank heaven—and thanks to Thom Casey—we didn't come to the same end.)

Chaiya didn't stir. I looked at her lying there on her back on the antique chaise lounge in Uncle Eddie's office. With her dark hair, deeply kohled eyes, and porcelain complexion, she could have been mistaken for Egyptian royalty awaiting the embalmers. Her arms were crisscrossed over her chest, but there were no scepters or papyrus beneath her long, chrome-tipped fingers. Instead they held the envelope containing the photos Officer Casey had said he'd be by to pick up.

"Chaiya," I repeated, giving her a heartier shake. "Wake up."

She sat up, her eyes large and a little glassy. "Is he here?"

"Yep," Delano said from the doorway. "I'm back at last. What are your other two wishes, Kewpie?" He loped across the room and dropped a folder onto Uncle Eddie's desk.

Chaiya frowned at him. "Not you. Thom Casey."

"He's not here," I told her. "And I don't think he's coming back tonight." I was pretty certain he would never come back. Surely he wouldn't help me now that I'd just finished demolishing his career . . . literally.

"You're waiting for Casey?" Delano asked, sitting on the edge of the desk. His forehead puckered. "Forget it, Coyote. He's not your type."

Chaiya sniffed. "That only shows what *you* know."

Delano's shaggy red eyebrows continued to move closer together, but he didn't respond. It was no secret to anybody but Chaiya that she was Delano's type. I smiled. There had been stranger couples in history, I supposed, although right off the top of my head I couldn't think of any. Oh, wait! I could—Lord Herbert and Wendela of the Welkin. In the last twenty-four hours the lord had sent her enough flowers to turn our tiny apartment into something resembling a prize-winning float in the Rose Bowl Parade.

"Anyway," I said, "Officer Casey's not coming for the pictures after all. You might as well go home."

"You're just trying to steal him from me," Chaiya said. "It won't work, Sammy. I'm positively snickered."

Delano grinned. "I think you mean snookered."

But *I* thought she meant *smitten,* and had a pang of something I couldn't name hit me. It certainly wasn't jealousy (was it?), so perhaps it was guilt for chasing Thom away before she could get to know him.

"Who's snookered?" a baritone voice asked from the outer office. "Besides you, Miss Shade."

This time I recognized the voice in a heartbeat. "Get out!" I said before the man had a chance to get in.

Heedless of my command, Barlow appeared in the doorway. "Is this the way she greets all your clients?" he asked Delano.

"You're not a client," I said as levelly as possible for the sake of professionalism.

"But I am," he continued. "I'm here to hire you to find a missing person for me. I believe you call her Wendela."

There wasn't enough money in this galaxy, or any other, for him to hire me to do that. I thanked my lucky stars my mother had kept Wendela after all—since she now believed the poor, sweet woman was safer climbing arbors than she was riding in a car with me.

"Get out!" I repeated.

"What do you want with Wendela?" the always-curious Delano asked.

Barlow smiled and extended his arms from his sides. "To make her a star!"

"You're a little late for that," Delano observed. "She already thinks she's a star." He pointed toward the firmament. "Although, personally, I think she's more lunar than stellar."

If I'd been closer to Delano I might have kicked him.

"At any rate," he continued, winking at me, "Nightshade reserves the right to refuse service to anybody—including nationally renowned crackpots. So beat it."

If I'd been closer to Delano I might have kissed him.

Barlow didn't move until he heard the door open to the outer hall. Then he glanced back over his shoulder before darting into Uncle Eddie's office. Although it looked to me as if Barlow was looking for a place to hide, Delano interpreted it as a full-out frontal assault and made a grab for him.

"Hello?" Thom Casey said from the reception area.

With a "see there" kind of look, Chaiya jumped to her feet and began to straighten her clothes and fluff up her hair. When I picked up the envelope of pictures she'd dropped, she slapped my hand and tried to wrest the envelope away from me. My fingers tightened on it reflexively.

At that moment Thom leaned around the doorjamb. "There's nobody in the outer office so—" His words ended abruptly.

It was impossible to say what he thought, or even where he looked. In the first split second he must have imagined he'd wandered onto the set of *Van Helsing II* or *III.* Before his eyes (very wide eyes, I might add) a vampire tussled with Cleopatra while a wolfman lifted a howling carnival barker from his feet preparatory to tossing him from the second-story window.

"Uh . . ." Thom said.

"Officer!" Barlow bellowed at the same time Chaiya called, "Sweetie!"

I will never understand why Thom Casey didn't act on his first instinct and flee for his life—or at least his sanity. Instead, he stepped into the room holding a sheaf of papers about as thick as a Phoenix metro phone book.

I let go of the envelope, and Delano released Wick Barlow with a growl to warn the guy not to make any more sudden moves.

"Thank goodness you're here, Officer!" the flustered radio host exclaimed as he edged away from Delano. "I—"

"What are *you* doing here?" Casey interrupted. "I distinctly remember telling you that if you weren't out of this neighborhood ten minutes after your show ended I'd run you in." He looked meaningfully at his watch.

"I was just on my way . . . elsewhere," Barlow said quickly. He backed away a little faster.

Thom stepped aside from the doorway to let Barlow pass, but not before adding, "I mean it, Barlow. If I catch you on my beat again I'll arrest you for being a public nuisance."

"You mean *creating* a public nuisance," I said helpfully.

The look Thom gave me made it clear that he meant what he'd said the first time—and that he didn't need my help with grammar, or anything else.

I could practically see Barlow's thought processes through his sweat-covered forehead. He was thinking that while spending a night in jail would be preferable to spending another three minutes with Delano, he'd best choose Plan C—beating it while he had the chance. He left posthaste.

When the nuisance was gone, Delano extended a hairy hand to the officer. "Good to see you again, Casey. Welcome to Nightshade."

Thom shook it. "Thanks." He looked around. "It's . . . uh . . ." Once again, words failed him.

"I knew you'd come!" Chaiya exclaimed, batting her eyelashes at Thom, and then turning to give me the evil eye over her shoulder. "I have what you want!"

While I wouldn't begin to guess what Chaiya meant, I was relieved to see that all she offered was the envelope of digital photos.

"Thanks," he said, accepting it, then taking a step back. (Chaiya has a tendency to invade people's personal space, especially people who look like Thom Casey.)

"She *is* snookered," Delano muttered.

"He means I'm snickered," Chaiya sighed, looking up into Thom's eyes.

If those gorgeous gray eyes of his got any wider, I thought they might just pop out of their sockets.

"Shall we go now?" Chaiya asked him sweetly.

"Uh . . ."

"You need to increase your word power," Chaiya admonished Thom, but fondly.

"Go where?" Delano asked in behalf of the rest of us.

"Thom is driving me home," she announced, although it was clearly news to the officer. To me she added, "I've put in fourteen hours of overtime this week, so it's time I left. Uncle Eddie isn't going to like paying time-and-a-half. Shall we go, Thomas?"

"Uh . . ." Thom said for the third or fourth time—I'd lost count. "I'm . . . on duty."

"I'm so glad!" I said, but not for the reason Chaiya thought. "I mean, I'm glad you still *have* a job after . . . after the run-in with the garbage cans."

He gave me a wry look. "It's the middle of the night on a weekend. There won't be anybody in Internal Affairs to fire me before Monday morning." He stepped around Chaiya. Carefully. "That's why I thought we'd better try to get to the bottom of this now, Miss Shade. If you have the time."

"I do!" I said, even before I knew what "this" he was talking about.

Chaiya scowled. "But I don't have my car!"

"That's because you left it parked around the corner," Delano supplied. "I saw you move it there hours ago, but I couldn't figure out why." He glanced at Thom and his eyes narrowed. "Until now." Turning back to Chaiya he said, "I'll take you to get it, Kit Kat."

"Blue Nissan?" Casey asked. When Chaiya nodded he said, "It's not there. It was illegally parked in front of a fire station. I had it towed."

Maybe if he'd at least looked sheepish she might not have scowled quite so ferociously. I was beginning to think this might be one of her shorter infatuations after all.

"Speaking of snookered . . ." Delano snickered. "Come on, Cuckoo. I'll take you home. We'll worry about getting your car back tomorrow."

"You're going to pay for this," Chaiya told me on her way out the door.

I wondered if she meant I'd have to pay the towing bill and the overtime—or pay in other ways for staying with Thom while she left with Delano. Deciding I probably didn't want to know which it was, I said good-bye, then led Officer Casey toward Uncle Eddie's desk and offered him a seat.

He looked at the black lacquer chair with the Chinese brocade, glanced around the room at the other options—chaise lounge, faux electric chair, and carousel unicorn—and remained standing.

I dragged Delano's favored Windsor out from behind the door with a smile. "Uncle Eddie's tastes are rather eclectic."

Thom didn't comment. He sat on the Windsor and put the sheaf of papers on Eddie's desk. I sat down and thanked him profusely for coming, especially under the circumstances.

"I'm only doing my job," he said, pushing the stack of papers in front of me. "These are mug shots of women picked up downtown within the last six to nine months."

I could scarcely believe there were that many women in the city, let alone in that line of . . . um . . . work.

He continued. "Do you have time to look for mug shots of the two women? If you do, maybe I can find one or the other of them tomorrow and get some help to clear this thing up."

"I thought you weren't working that area anymore."

"I'm not."

I waited for Thom to say more, but he didn't. He didn't have to. I'm a good enough detective to deduce that he hadn't learned his lesson when it came to moonlighting. At least he hadn't learned it well enough to abandon a cause he considered worthwhile. But I was willing to bet it would be a blue moon—or longer—before he worked for Nightshade Investigation again.

I looked at the first picture. It was of a brunette, so I flipped to the next thinking this might not be as daunting a task as it seemed at first. Since both the women in the pictures were blond, I could flip past all the brunettes and redheads. The next picture was of a blond, but not the right one. I turned the page. The next one was a blond, but still not the right one. The third was a blond and the fourth and the fifth and—no wonder Monroe mistook me for a "professional." I considered picking up a box of Miss Clairol on my way home just on general principle.

Ten minutes passed and I wasn't a quarter of the way through the pictures. Worse, they all looked so much alike I was afraid I wouldn't be able to positively identify either woman, even with the help of the pictures from my camera.

Aware that I was getting nowhere fast, Thom pushed out his chair and stood. "I have to get back out on the street." He glanced up at the grandfather clock on the far wall. There was a large, well-preserved crow perched on top of it. Judging by the look on Thom's face, it wasn't something he expected to see.

"That's Quoth," I told him. "The raven, I mean. He was the bane of Uncle Eddie's existence. My uncle loves his summer garden up in Payson almost as much as he loves Nightshade. He's especially fond of his sweet corn."

"And he shot the bird for getting into it?"

"Of course not! Uncle Eddie doesn't even spray for bugs. Besides, he's our stake patriarch. He couldn't even curse at Quoth."

Thom's eyebrows rose. "You're LDS?" he asked.

"Yes," I said, smiling. "Born and raised. Surprised?"

"Yes," he said. Then, realizing the truth was probably also rude, he backpedaled. "No. I mean . . ."

I watched him trying not to look at my all-black ensemble. Clearly he was endeavoring to think of me as someone other than a shorter, plumper, blonder Elvira—but failing. "I know what you mean," I said, the smile becoming a giggle. "You mean you wonder who'd baptize the Addams Family and call Morticia to teach Sunday School."

"No," he said. "I was thinking—"

"That my family is probably more like the Munsters?"

"No."

But he smiled when he said it, and that smile had the magnetic power to pull me from my chair. As I walked Thom to the door I told him the rest of Quoth's story. "The bird finally died of old age—or maybe it ate too much sweet corn and died of indigestion. At any rate, Uncle Eddie realized he'd miss his old nemesis so much that he had him stuffed."

"And 'quoth the raven, Nevermore.'" Thom quoted.

"Yes, but it's more like 'Quoth, the raven evermore,'" I pointed out.

"Now I've heard everything."

"No, you haven't." Sorry that we had already reached the door and he was about to exit, I could think of lots more to say. "Want to hear the story about the shrunken head there in the hutch? Uncle Eddie's mission was to—"

"Uh, maybe another time," Thom said, stepping into the reception area. "Finish looking over those pictures. Do it as fast as you can. I need to get that book back to the station."

He didn't say "before somebody realizes I took it," but I wondered. Testing my theory I said, "Do you want me to call the station when—"

"No," he interrupted. "I'll be back in another hour or so to pick it up."

In just twenty-four hours I'd come to know Dudley Do-Right well enough to believe he'd never steal the book from the precinct. On the other hand, I knew the circumstances well enough to know he'd just as soon not have anybody know why he'd borrowed it or where he took it. Somebody at the station had tampered with my camera, and Officer Casey was launching a one-man internal investigation to find out who it was.

"I can't tell you how much I appreciate your help," I said as he crossed the small room and pulled open the outer door. "But I don't want to cost you your job." I flinched. "If I haven't already, I mean."

He turned with his hand still on the knob. "This thing might be bigger than either of our jobs."

A real superhero wouldn't have let that man walk away without getting an explanation of his meaning. Of course, a real superhero would have probably already known for herself.

Me? I was left in the dark. In more ways than one.

ACROSS
    55 Any plant of the genus solanum, including
        belladonna; The best detective agency in the world!
DOWN
    33 Hebrew name meaning "life force"; Girl who needs a
        dictionary more than she needs another boyfriend

Chapter 16

Standing on the corner watching all the guys watching all the girls go by . . .

Although I couldn't get the lyrics out of my head, it certainly wasn't what I wanted to do with my Saturday night. I'd have rather been home watching a chick flick and painting my toenails purple like Chaiya. (I never paint my toenails, but even if I did, it wouldn't be purple.) I would have rather been at my parents' home playing Risk with Arjay. (I hate Risk. There is something about world domination by *any* color that just doesn't appeal to me.) I'd have rather been emptying bedpans in the acute-care ward of Shady Acres. I'd have rather been . . . Never mind. You probably have the general idea by now.

To make matters worse, I'd feared Knute was right that my car had been spotted by one of the councilman's minions on my first stakeout, so instead of driving to this awful neighborhood and thus providing myself with a relatively safe haven and a more or less reliable means of escape, I'd taken the bus. Let me tell you, if Wick Barlow wants to find alien life here on earth, he ought to spend his nights checking out Phoenix's buses instead of its skies. I was the *only* thing onboard that vehicle besides the driver who was undeniably human. And I'm not sure about the driver. I think I've seen him in a Raid commercial—and he isn't the one holding the can, if you know what I mean.

So there I was just before midnight, pressing myself as deeply as possible into the shadows, with no transportation, Diet Coke, or crossword puzzle. This wasn't staking out—this was staking my life on a lost cause. I had come to find two women I didn't know, and hopefully before someone awful I didn't *want* to know found me. Talk about stupid. If all that was left of me by morning was a blurry chalk outline on a skanky sidewalk, I'd have nobody to blame but myself.

As if my rising fear was a self-fulfilling prophecy, a big man across the street turned to look my direction. I flattened my back against the decaying brick wall and tried to make myself smaller and darker. The movement only made him more curious. He tossed his cigarette into the gutter and stepped from the curb onto the street.

I edged cautiously along the building toward a side street. If I could just make it the whole ten or twenty feet along the wall before he attacked me, maybe I could make a run for it. I tried not to think about where I'd run *to* since every street in a three-mile radius was equally sinister.

My heart hammered in my ears, but I scarcely heard it. I was listening instead to the eerie sound the man made walking toward me. The ghost of Marley in *A Christmas Carol* didn't wear as many chains as that man had hanging from his filthy clothing. Nor would a ghost have been half as terrifying.

As I groped my way along the side of the building, afraid to take my eyes off the approaching assassin, I fumbled in my jacket pockets for the small can of pepper spray I always carry. I found a comb, a package of powdered-sugar donuts, and enough change to get me home if another bus happened to drop out of orbit while I was still living. I also found out I don't *always* carry the pepper spray—I only *almost* always carry it.

I hadn't yet reached the corner when I realized the guy was now close enough for me to see, hear, *and* smell. Before I swooned, I grasped my cell phone and tried to remember the three numbers you press for an emergency and what order they go in. (If you think that's unbelievable, you try it some night under the same circumstances. On second thought, that's bad advice. Do not try this in your own city.)

Just as I'd given up on my brain, my feet got me to the corner. But before I could turn and run, the man stopped and stared at me—or past me—for several seconds before shrugging and walking away. For a really stupid half second I was offended. I mean, how bad do you have to be to be rejected by a modern-day Jack the Ripper?

I'd overcome my irrationality and almost managed to draw a ragged breath when a male voice from the side street at my back said, "What are you doing here?"

I am absolutely certain there was nothing slow about the way I turned, but he still caught my fist before it impacted with his solar plexus. I looked up at Thom Casey, unsure whether I should hit him with a left jab or wrap my free arm around his neck and never let him go.

When I didn't answer his first question, he glanced down the block and asked another. "Where's Knute?"

That question was enough to replace my fear with indignation. "How should I know?" I pulled my hand free from his grasp. "I don't need a babysitter!"

"You need something," he said. "Common sense comes to mind."

"*You're* here," I pointed out. "What's the difference?"

"If nothing else, I'm armed with more than a package of donuts and a pocket comb."

I mashed the donuts back into my pocket. "I have a cell phone for backup."

"Uh, huh. Do you know what the 911 response time is to this neighborhood?"

I didn't, but I didn't need him to tell me. If the police were smarter than me, they wouldn't respond at all.

"Where's your car?" he asked.

"At home. I came on the bus in case the councilman's lackeys recognized my VW."

I'm not sure what the look was on Thom's face. It might have been begrudging admiration, but more likely it was astonishment at meeting a creature with even more of a bird's brain than Quoth. What he said was, "I'll take you home."

I shook my head. "I haven't found them yet." I pulled the picture of the blond girl from my back pocket. My digital photo was all I had to go on since I hadn't been able to identify either woman from Thom's book of mug shots. I could only hope I might recognize the stand-in if I saw her again in person. "I have to talk to this girl," I said, extending the picture. "I have to find out who hired her. She's the only one who—"

"She's dead."

The shock of those words pushed me back against the building.

"A drug overdose," he said. "Earlier today."

"But—"

"That's what I think too."

I didn't know what *I* thought yet, let alone what Thom did, but I was too stunned—and too proud—to admit it.

"My car's this way," he said, turning back down the street I'd been edging toward to escape the odiferous guy in chains.

I glanced back over my shoulder as I followed Thom. My would-be assailant had gone back to smoking and watching for an easier target. Feeling his eyes on me, I hurried my steps to be at Thom's side. Close to his side, in fact. Casey wasn't nearly as big as Knute, or as reckless and caution-inspiring as Delano, but there was something about the way he carried himself that would make even tough men think twice about taking him on.

"You're a natural-born cop," I observed.

He missed half a step. "What makes you say that?" Then he recovered. "Right. You've been talking to Knute."

"I haven't!" I said. "I mean, I've talked to him, but not about you. I mean, not about you being a policeman. Well, I've talked to him about you being a policeman, but not . . . I mean . . ." My words trailed off. I had no idea what I meant. I had no idea what *he* meant.

(If you see a pattern developing here, you get a gold star for paying attention.)

We took a few more steps in silence before I decided a true professional would stick to the business at hand. Thinking about the drug overdose I said, "It wasn't an accident, was it?"

"No. As Knute told you, some people think I was born to it."

"Huh?"

Casey slowed his pace and looked down at me. "What are you talking about, Miss Shade?"

Instead of telling him, I blurted out, "Can't you call me Sam? Or at least Samantha?"

He blinked. "Just how many subjects are we discussing at once?"

"At least three, I think."

He shook his head and walked a little faster. When we arrived at his car, he unlocked the door on the passenger side and pulled it open.

I stepped back. "I don't want you to take me home."

"You want to stay out here on the street by yourself?"

"No. I want you to take me wherever you're going." I knew I sounded like Chaiya, but that wasn't the way I meant it. "I mean—"

"Get in," he said suddenly, his eyes on something happening down the street.

I glanced over my shoulder but didn't see whatever it was he looked at. In case this offer to get in his car was the only one I got, I tried to take him up on it.

"Get in," he repeated, circling the car to the driver's side. Thom had only spared me enough of a glance to see I was still on the sidewalk. He was focused on something—or someone—at least a block away.

"I'm trying to," I said. "But—"

He opened his door, saw my problem, and began shoveling books from the front passenger seat onto the back. When he'd cleared a spot almost big enough for a Weimaraner, I squeezed into it. After pulling Dante, Steinbeck, and Frost from between the seat and the door, I managed to close it.

"Do you drive a bookmobile, or what?" I asked, tossing Dante and Frost over my shoulder and allowing Steinbeck to fall on the floor next to Twain.

"No, they're mine." He pulled out onto the street before I realized he'd started the car.

I pulled Alfred, Lord Tennyson from the crack between the seat and the door and fumbled past Dickens and Wordsworth for the clip to my seat belt. In order to fasten it, D. H. Lawrence, W. D. Auden, e. e. cummings, and several other notable men of letters had to go too.

"Nobody reads this stuff anymore," I pointed out, moving my feet politely off Tolstoy and planting them instead on Hemingway, since I found him too dull in high school to care for whom his bell tolled.

"I read it."

"Then have you considered installing a bookshelf at home?"

"I have more than a dozen bookshelves. They're all full."

I pulled an author from behind me whose corner was putting uncomfortable pressure on my kidney. "George Eliot," I said, glancing at the cover. I tossed it over my shoulder and frowned at the sexist bibliophile sitting next to me. "Don't you read women authors?"

"Yes," he said. "That one, for instance. Eliot was born Mary Ann Evans."

Oops. I vowed silently to catch up on my literature reading just as soon as I polished off all the back issues of the *Ensign* and LDS romance novels that are stacked up beside my bed.

Thom whipped the car into a U-turn with one hand. With the other he pulled a blue knit stocking cap over his head and down past his ears.

"Would you mind ducking down a little?" he asked.

I lowered my chin onto my chest.

"A little more."

I scrunched.

"More. Do it now."

I bent double.

"Good."

"What's going on?" I asked my kneecaps.

"I don't know," he said, pulling to a stop about half a block down and across the street from a dimly lit bar.

(You've probably noticed that Thom Casey gives me that "I don't know" line a lot. Have you figured out yet if he's telling me the truth when he says it? Me, neither.)

I wondered if he'd chosen to park under one of the several broken streetlights for a reason and decided he probably had. "What do you *think* is going on?" I pressed.

"I don't know," he repeated, reaching for his door handle. "But I think that with just a little more luck we're going to find out."

Thom opened his door, but no overhead light came on to show me his face. Unscrewing the bulbs in one's car is an old trick practiced by PIs, movie directors, and, apparently, undercover police officers.

It was too dark to see a face on the floorboards too, even though I was scrunched over so far my nose was probably only a foot or so away from Anna Karenina's. I turned my head to look out the windshield and up at the streetlight. The bulb looked like it had been shot out, but not necessarily this week or this year. Unfortunately, the sound wasn't nearly as muted as the light. With Thom's door open, I heard people yelling at each other, even over the hip-hop music that blared from within a derelict flophouse.

"I need to take a quick look down the street," he said. "I'll be right back."

"What am I supposed to do?"

"Read Tolstoy." He locked and then closed the door. Then he tapped on the window. "Stay down. You stand out like a sore thumb in this neighborhood."

Despite the fact he'd probably paid me a compliment, I wasn't pleased. And I wasn't going to keep my chin on my knees and hold Tolstoy between my toes. I counted slowly to thirty, giving Thom time to be far enough away not to hear my door open, then I opened it. Poe fell into the gutter, but I figured he'd been there before, so I left him. I didn't want to risk losing sight of Thom.

He walked down the dingy sidewalk like he belonged there. Unlike certain private detectives, who shall remain nameless, he'd dressed to fit the neighborhood. He didn't wear chains, but he did wear clothes that were nondescript and a little threadbare. Nobody except women would look at him twice—and they'd look at him no matter what he wore. I frowned down at my black jeans, black silk T, soft leather jacket, and steel-toed boots and wondered if it was time to update my wardrobe. After all, I wear the same thing on stakeouts that I do to Enrichment Nights, and I probably look equally ridiculous both places.

I followed Thom at a discreet distance until he reached the door to the bar. When he pushed it open and went inside, I stopped in my tracks.

What now?

I'd been taught all my life to avoid the very appearance of evil and to never go anywhere the Spirit wouldn't go with me. I'd discussed this with Uncle Eddie, of course. If there were extenuating circumstances—say a life-or-death situation on the other side of the barroom door—then I wouldn't hesitate. But I had no idea why Thom had gone in there, so I couldn't be sure if I should follow him. He had told me to wait in the car after all.

What if he needed backup?

What of the Spirit?

I feared that because of the raucous noise and stench of smoke and booze that assaulted my senses, the Holy Ghost must already be waiting for me six or eight steps back. I took a step back myself. Then, worried about Thom, I took two steps forward. This left me in front of an all-night ethnic market where I paused to reconsider yet again.

Although we'd explored this ethic in Nightshade Training 101, ever since the discussion, Uncle Eddie and Knute had conspired to make sure I didn't find myself in a situation in which to test what I'd learned. But they weren't here now, and I was.

What to do?

Then I realized I must have caught up with the Spirit after all, because an unmistakable still small voice in my head told me that where I stood was a dangerous, evil place.

But it would be another few minutes before I knew just how dangerous and evil.

ACROSS

    51 Foot digit; "____ the line" (what Thom didn't do any of the times he went to Van Buren Street off duty)

DOWN

    42 Mythic bird that bursts into flame and then rises again from its own ashes; Capital of Arizona (so called because it's hot enough here to make one believe the bird story?)

Chapter 17

A sharp sound of breaking glass from somewhere down the street from whence I'd come made me cringe. It suddenly occurred to me that maybe there was a life-or-death situation here—and maybe it was on *this* side of the barroom door, so I should be in there with Thom instead of out here by myself. I ran toward the bar, but I didn't have to run into it because Thom was already on his way back out. I ran into him instead.

I waited for him to point out that he'd told me to stay in the car because I wanted to point out that he wasn't the boss of me, but all he said was, "I hope you didn't lock your car door."

"Of course I did," I said, turning to follow him back down the street. "I watched you lock your door."

"I locked it because I'd asked you to stay in the car," he said. "That's the same reason I left the keys in the ignition."

"How was I supposed to know that?"

"Keen powers of observation?"

If I could have walked fast enough to stay at his side, Thom might have seen me glare. Instead he was looking down the street toward a trio of hoodlums darting from one empty vehicle to the next. They'd just approached his Chevy and were trying to open the doors.

"Hey!" Thom hollered. In the next second, one of the thugs raised a tire iron. The driver's side window exploded into a gazillion pieces and Thom started to jog. As he ran, I saw him reach briefly beneath his jacket with his right hand to unsnap the shoulder harness that held his pistol. I brought up the rear. Even if I could have outrun him, I didn't want to. When you're armed with only a comb, a package of donuts, and a cell phone, discretion really is the better part of valor.

Casey stopped about eight feet from the front of his car and said, "Take all the books you'll read, guys, but I'll have to ask you to leave the vehicle." The biggest one turned and hefted the tire iron with an unmistakable "you're not the boss of me" look about him.

Thom reached into his jacket again, but he didn't pull a gun on the kid as I'd expected. Instead he withdrew a black leather wallet and flipped it open to show a badge. "Phoenix PD," he said.

Since the badge implied a service revolver and a whole lot of backup, and since the scratched and dented bookmobile he drove wasn't much of a prize to start with, the three boys must have suddenly remembered they'd forgotten to practice the piano and/or clean their rooms before going out to terrorize the city streets. They were gone before Thom could put his badge back in his pocket.

"They didn't take any of your books," I observed when we'd walked back to the car.

He reached through the broken window (I didn't comment on how convenient that was) and unlatched the door. Then he opened it, considered his traveling library for a moment, and finally chose a thin volume of Theodore Roethke to use as a scoop for the broken glass. When he'd swept most of it out onto the street, he climbed in, closed the door, and moved the keys from the ignition to the pocket of his jeans.

I walked over to the passenger side where I couldn't help but notice the door was still locked. I waited patiently for him to open it. When he didn't, I tapped on the window.

Thom drummed the three middle fingers of his right hand on the steering wheel while he gave his inherent decency time to reassert itself. At last he leaned over and unlocked my door.

I picked Poe up from the gutter and slid in next to Thom. "Your 'Tell-Tale Heart,'" I said, laying the book on top of the pile that was still between us. I didn't expect gratitude—or even a response—and that was a good thing because I didn't get either. Instead of speaking to me, he reached over to open the glove compartment and pulled out a small pair of binoculars.

There were so many things I wanted to ask Thom. I wanted to know why he had so many books—and why he had such *boring* ones. I wanted to know everything there was to know about that "born to be a cop" thing he'd alluded to. I wanted to know what he was doing here if the girl from the new pictures was already dead and he didn't know what the first one had looked like. I wanted to know what he thought about the overdose. Mostly, I wanted to know what he was looking for through those binoculars. That's what I asked. That and why he'd gone into the bar he was now staring at.

"I thought I saw a guy go in there," he replied.

"If that was all you wanted to know, you should have asked me," I said sarcastically. "I saw a whole lot of guys go in there."

He ignored the barb. "I wanted to make sure this guy was who I thought he was."

"Was he?"

"Yes. Harrison Mead. He's been hanging around down here tonight acting like he's waiting for somebody. I was keeping an eye on him when I spotted you on the corner. You must have just come off the bus."

"Harrison Mead?" I leaned forward, but it didn't make the bar significantly closer, nor could I see through the walls without super-vision—and if I'd had any kind of supervision I'd have never gone alone and unarmed to Van Buren in the first place. (Sorry. Bad puns are as hard for me to resist as good crossword puzzles and powdered-sugar donuts.)

"I'm watching now to see if I recognize the face of a fence—or a dealer—or anybody else he might be waiting for."

"You think Harrison is meeting somebody to sell the mummy?"

"Not necessarily," Thom said. "But I'm not discounting it, either. There isn't much in the world that can't be sold to somebody or other in this neighborhood if the price is right." He lowered the binoculars to look at me, probably because I'd shifted in the seat to try to get more comfortable. "Is there someplace you'd rather be?"

"No!" I said, dismayed at how quickly I'd said it and how much I meant it.

"Then let's watch for a while and see who else turns up." He reached over and removed a volume of *Walden* from between the seat and the small of my back. "'I'd rather sit on a pumpkin and have it all to myself than to be crowded onto a velvet cushion.' Thoreau." He tossed the book into the backseat with the rest. (If he stopped by any more book-sellers, the stack would be so high he wouldn't be able to see out his rearview mirror.) "Are you alone in the seat now?"

"Yes," I said gratefully. "Except for Jane Austen, and I don't mind sharing with her."

"You like Austen?"

I nodded. Gwyneth Paltrow's role in *Emma* made the film one of my all-time favorites, but I didn't tell Thom that in case he was unfortunate enough to be familiar with only the printed version.

I sat in silence for almost a full minute, fingering *Sense and Sensibility* and wishing I had some. Then I said, "Surely you didn't come down here tonight expecting to see Harrison Mead."

"No," Thom said. "He's about the last person I expected to show up in this neighborhood."

I pulled the donuts out of my jacket pocket. "Besides me?"

He looked over, but quickly away when he saw that I was looking back at him. "You, I wasn't surprised to see, but I thought Knute would be with you. Or at least trailing you."

"He doesn't know I'm here," I said, frowning. "I don't need a keeper."

"So you say."

"I'd planned to share my donuts." I raised the package to my mouth to open it. "But after that crack, you can forget it."

He made a face as I bit into the cellophane. "Didn't your mother ever tell you that's bad for your teeth?"

"Yes," I mumbled through the plastic wrap. "She's a very traditional, very good mother. You can't blame her for how I turned out."

Thom Casey was even better looking when he smiled. I regretted not giving him more reason to do it. "What does she think about you being a PI?" he asked.

"Well," I said, lowering the package and sighing over the little cloud of powdered sugar that hovered over it, "she and my father aren't absolutely sold on Nightshade as the career for me, if that's what you mean." I pulled out a donut and watched the white powder filter down onto my black pants like fairy dust.

Why did I open the stupid things? I asked myself. If there was a delicate way to eat them I'd never seen it. But it was too late to turn back now. I'd have to eat at least one of them as best I could or look even sillier than I did already. Besides, I wanted a donut.

"Of course, they didn't like my last job much better," I said.

"What were you?" Thom asked. "Foreman of a wrecking crew?"

I politely ignored his ungallant implication. "I was a psychology intern at the state mental hospital."

This time when Thom met my gaze, I was the one who looked away. I bit my lip instead of the donut. There was no reason for me to think he knew who Wendela was or to suspect me of kidnapping her—not that that's what I'd done exactly—but still I wished I'd never mentioned being within fifty miles of the hospital where she'd so recently been a patient. "I changed my mind. You can have a donut," I said to distract him from my goof-up.

He held up a hand to refuse, but then turned it over and extended it, probably at the desperate look on my face. I plunked the smashed donut onto his palm and stuffed part of a second one into my mouth. If I chewed slowly enough, I wouldn't have to speak again for a while. (And if I choked on the impossibly dry thing—which seemed likely—I might never have to speak again.)

"Thanks," he said, eating his donut in one bite and without the explosion of sugar and crumbs I was experiencing. (He didn't even have white powder left on his fingers when he was finished. If ever I could have hated Thom Casey, it would have been in that moment.) "But you want to be a detective?" he continued, sounding genuinely interested.

I nodded. When I'd finally managed to swallow, I said, "I want it more than anything. I've wanted to work with Uncle Eddie my whole life."

Thom leaned back in his seat, but his eyes were still on the street. If there was something going down, he wasn't going to miss it. "Why?" he asked.

Thrilled that the subject had become what I do now instead of what I did before, I told him all about growing up and adoring my Uncle Eddie and his offbeat office, and how working with him had been my fondest wish ever since I was old enough to lisp, "Star light, star fright."

"Did you say, 'Star light, star *fright*'?" Thom asked.

I nodded. "That's how I thought the rhyme went until I was six or seven. By then, I'd decided to become a superhero when I grew up, so I modified the whole thing to 'Star light, star fright, first star I see tonight, I wish I may, I wish I might, be given power, wrongs to right.'"

I expected him to laugh. I mean, I'd only recited it to two other human beings in my whole life, and they'd both laughed at me. But Thom Casey is one of those rare, natural-born listeners. And he's more besides. Anyway, I found myself telling him all about my childhood aspiration—or do I mean childish aspiration?—to become a superhero. He smiled as I spoke, but it was in a nice way.

"Not that I have any better chance of becoming Batgirl than I do CEO of Nightshade," I concluded, offering him the last donut and feeling ever so relieved when he took it.

"Why do you say that?" Kindly, Thom didn't mention that while I lack Batgirl's cool motorcycle, physical prowess, and mental acuity, I do happen to posses her wardrobe.

"Maybe you're not as astute as I thought you were," I replied, leaning against the door with a sigh. "Or you'd have noticed that I've recently bungled two of the biggest cases Nightshade ever had."

"I wouldn't write off the mummy just yet," Thom said. Apparently he had more optimism than I that this thing with Harrison would pan out. "And you can't blame yourself for losing the pictures of Mermann. Somebody set you up." The dimple winked into his cheek when he frowned. "And they probably used me to do it."

I sat up straighter. "What do you mean?"

"I mean that while I believe in coincidence, I don't believe in them falling quite as thick and fast as they seem to be doing right now." That didn't answer the question, but he continued. "Somebody went to a lot of effort, and more than a little risk, to smuggle your camera in and out of the police station, not to mention setting up the dummy poses."

"Knute says it's to discredit me," I said. "He says that nobody will believe the pictures were erased and replaced."

"They might believe it if you tell them you think I did it," Thom said.

"I'd never accuse—" He shot me a glance that ended the sentence abruptly. "I mean, I'd never accuse you now that I know you," I amended. "But somebody—"

"Yeah," he agreed. "Somebody. The same somebody who figured out real quick we could track down the girl in your pictures." His face grew grim. "I can't believe it's another coincidence she OD'd less than six hours after I took those galleys back into the precinct. That has to be the thing that tipped them off we were on to them."

"You think somebody murdered her before we could talk to her?"

"Yes."

Suddenly this was an entirely different case than the one I'd signed up for. "Who knew you had the galleys?"

"I don't know," Casey said. "I didn't check it out. Since it's a busy station and we have several copies of the same book, I didn't think anybody would miss one for just a couple of hours. Nobody *should* have missed it. Which means somebody must have seen me take it. Which means—"

"Somebody's watching us?" I supplied. I had goose bumps now—and they weren't the kind you get during general conference.

"Apparently."

As inane as it was, I looked around apprehensively. "Who? Why?"

"I don't know, Sam, but I figure it must have something to do with the Mermann deal. It's the only thing that makes sense."

He'd called me by my first name for the first time, and I was too spooked to savor it. "And you're down here tonight because . . . ?"

"Because I'd hoped one of my contacts could tell me what went down this morning. I've read the police reports on the overdose, but I don't believe them."

I shook my head, unable to believe what he was saying or fathom what he wasn't saying. A sleazy councilman buying drugs or being unfaithful to his wife was one thing, a cop tampering with evidence was another, but a police officer or councilman committing *murder?* There must be more to the story. My voice came out as a squeak. "Did you find out anything tonight?"

"No," he said, frustrated. "Now that the word's out I'm a cop, there's been a sudden epidemic of mass amnesia here on Van Buren."

"Did I blow your cover?" I gasped.

"No," he said. "The captain went out of his way Tuesday night to make sure of that."

I pictured Thom being dragged off in handcuffs and cringed. "Then how did it happen?"

"That's yet another thing I'd like to know."

The next few minutes passed in silence. At first I considered what he'd said, then I worried about how to broach the subject I'd been avoiding—the one that, despite everything, weighed heaviest on my conscience. At last I said, "I really *am* sorry, Thom. I feel terrible about what happened."

He glanced to his left. "It's no big deal about the window."

"I didn't mean that," I said. "I meant the other night when—"

"The squad car?" He shrugged. "At least nobody was hurt."

"I didn't mean that, either," I continued desperately. "I meant the night before that when—"

He pulled off the stocking cap and winced when his fingers made contact with the still-painful lump he'd received while guarding my mummy. "No permanent damage."

"I'm sorry about that, too!" I said, scarcely able to believe this man had taken donuts from me. After everything I'd done to him, you'd think he'd have expected them to be poisoned. "I'm sorry about *everything*, Thom, but I meant the night before *all* of that when I . . . when you . . . when I thought . . ."

Now that he knew I was talking about scaring off the runaway, he wasn't as quick to tell me it was no big deal. Probably because it *was* a big deal and we both knew it.

I watched him watch the street for as long as I could stand. There was something about the dimple that appeared in his right cheek when he frowned that made my heartache even worse. I looked out the side window at the litter-strewn sidewalk. At last I whispered, "You haven't found her yet, have you?"

"No."

"Maybe she went home to her family."

"She doesn't have a family," Thom said. "Especially not anymore." He lifted the binoculars when a pair of men approached the bar.

Even from here, the guys looked nervous. *Probably underage,* I thought.

When Thom had studied their faces and decided he didn't know either of them, he lowered the glasses and resumed our conversation. "And she doesn't have a home."

"But Knute said she was a runaway."

"Taryn ran away from a foster home. She's a ward of the state."

Not wanting to see the pained look on his face, I stared out the windshield. Only one of the two men stopped in front of the bar. The other continued walking toward us, then turned into the all-night market.

"Why would Taryn come *here?*" I asked.

"Looking for her sister," he said. "When her mother died, Taryn's sister was eighteen—too young to care for Taryn, but too old for the government to keep them together. There are no other living relatives. I checked."

It was too sad to think about. I closed my eyes as if that would block the girls' story from my mind, but it only made the picture more vivid. "How have they survived in this place?" I asked, even though I didn't want to know the answer.

"Petty theft," Thom said. "Panhandling. Odd jobs when they could get them."

I breathed a little easier since the answer was so much better than what I'd expected. But then I looked at Thom's face and couldn't breathe at all. There was more to the story.

"Unless I'm wrong—and I hope I am," he said, "Taryn's sister took on a 'modeling role' for a little spare cash. I think she's the one who posed for the fake pictures in your camera."

Dizzy, I leaned back in the seat. If that was the case, Taryn's sister was dead. I felt responsible. "What about Taryn? Is she dead too?"

The dimple in Thom's cheek deepened, and I looked away. "I hope not," he said. "I hope she ran scared. I hope she's only hiding from me now because she thinks I betrayed her by not telling her I'm a cop. I hope . . ." He didn't finish the sentence because he was focused on something going on down the street.

I heard yelling through the broken window. By the time I had pinpointed the source of it—an older man standing outside the market swinging a wine bottle at a kid who had run from the store carrying a paper sack—Thom had already reached for his phone with one hand and opened his car door with the other.

"Stay here," he told me. "Stay down." Unlike me, he had no trouble pushing 911. In the next second he said to a dispatcher, "Officer 683. We have a 211 in progress at—"

There were more numbers and words after that, but I didn't catch them. Thom was out of the car and running down the street.

"Stop!" he hollered. "Police!"

Miraculously, the lanky kid who had just robbed the store obeyed. He froze beneath one of the few operational street-lights in the neighborhood. Turning slowly as Thom approached, he dropped the sack. The shopkeeper rushed forward. In the next second I saw what Thom didn't because his eyes were on the suspect and the old man. Just beyond the kid, still in the shadows outside the bar, was the guy the robber had come with. In his hand was a gun. When he raised it toward Thom's chest I did the first thing that came to mind.

I screamed.

ACROSS
   12 *Rodent; Contemptible person (like Harrison Mead);*
        "I smell a _____"
DOWN
   56 *Yore; What you don't dwell on much if you're me*

Chapter 18

I have remarkable lung power. The single word which I screamed—*No!*—seemed to shake the dilapidated brick buildings up and down the block. For sure it affected the windows. At once, curious or guilty faces either appeared at the glass or disappeared from it, depending on the proclivities of the owners.

But my crying out had an opposite effect on Thom than I'd intended. While I'd meant it as a warning—if I'd had time to think it through enough to mean it as anything—he interpreted it as a call for help, and with the only suspect he'd seen immobile, he glanced instinctively in my direction.

I screamed again when the guy in the shadows wrapped both shaky hands around the gun as if it would take all ten of his fingers to pull the trigger. In the next second Thom would be dead, and it would be my fault because I'd distracted him from the real danger.

What neither I nor the gunman counted on was the involvement of the shopkeeper. The stooped, gray-haired man who had run from the store yelling for help and waving a bottle of cheap wine had just sent that bottle hurtling past Officer Casey's head and into the shadows where the gunman stood. It shattered against the wall, narrowly missing the would-be shooter and making a sound almost as sharp as the report of a rifle. When Thom spun back around, both the gunman and the robber ran.

"He has a gun!" I yelled after Thom as I struggled to open the car door. At last it gave way, and a half a dozen authors and I tumbled out onto the filthy sidewalk. I stumbled to my feet and ran after Thom. It didn't matter that I had no idea what help I could offer with only my pocket comb, because it looked like the chances of me catching up to him were nil.

As the three men rounded the corner, Thom was only a few yards behind and gaining. I saw he had drawn his pistol this time, but he was still outnumbered by men who were armed, probably whacked out on meth, and desperate enough to do anything to get away from the police. I wondered how long it had been since he'd called the dispatcher. Seconds? Minutes? Hours?

It was approximately forever before I reached the corner—about the same time as the store owner—and skidded to a stop to stare down the vacant street.

"Where'd they go?" the storekeeper asked between gasps for breath. The paper bag, along with the money that he had retrieved from the sidewalk, was now securely under one arm. In his free hand he held the neck of the broken wine bottle. The jagged glass glinted in the dim light. Although we were probably on the same side in this thing, I edged away from him.

"I don't know where they went," I panted from a safer distance.

As if in answer, Thom hollered, "Hold it!" His voice was muffled by the buildings between where we stood and the narrow alley behind the bar where he'd apparently cornered the criminals. Next we heard him call out, "Drop your weapon or I'll shoot!"

Less than two seconds later a single shot rang out.

This time I didn't scream. (Even though I wanted to.) Instead, I pulled the cell phone from my pocket and started pushing numbers. I didn't know the code for "officer down," but this time I could recall the 911 it took to get somebody's attention.

I tried to talk and run at the same time—which is actually quite a bit more difficult than walking and chewing gum, especially when you're terrified. When the dispatcher on the line told me to calm down and take a deep breath, I wanted to throttle her.

She was still counseling me to remain calm and act cautiously when I reached the mouth of the alley. Grasping the corner of the building for support, I finally followed her advice and took a deep gulp of air before sticking my head around the corner.

Thom stood about ten yards away, his gun trained on both suspects. The gunman was sitting on the pavement, his back against a garbage dumpster. His left hand was clasped to his right shoulder, and blood seeped between his fingers. His eyes were wide and glassy, but I didn't think he was in shock. More likely he was stoned out of his mind and feeling no pain. His friend crouched nearby, shaking like a bobblehead doll caught in an earthquake.

Speaking into my ear, the dispatcher had to ask me the same question six times before I was able to respond to it.

"It's . . . it's okay," I told her. "Officer Casey has them both in custody."

This time Thom accepted my presence as a given. "Tell them we need an ambulance."

"It's on the way," I said, but the reassurance was unnecessary since he could now hear the sirens for himself.

I slumped against the wall in relief. At the same time the bobbleheaded guy raised himself up on his hands and feet as if to scuttle away like a crab.

"Don't move," Thom warned him.

I watched the guy slump back onto the garbage-strewn asphalt. He was just a kid. Both of them were.

"It wasn't supposed to be this way, man!" Bobblehead told his companion. He seemed shocked at the turn of events. "I thought you were gonna—"

"Shut up!" his partner said. "Shut your stupid . . ."

A string of profanities followed, none of which seemed to register with Bobble. He whined, "But I was supposed to grab the dough and you were supposed to off the—"

The words ended abruptly when the gunman swung his bloody fist into the side of his companion's jaw.

"Freeze!" Thom commanded, but this time the men didn't obey. Bobble screamed and cursed and tried to cover his face while the other man ignored his wounded shoulder and used both arms to throw more punches.

Thom took a step forward, but before he could gain the upper hand in this new crisis, the old man from the grocery store ran past me brandishing his wicked, handmade butcher knife.

"Thom!" I cried, "Look out!"

I could never decide if the next few minutes passed in a blur or in slow motion. The only thing I knew for sure is that I'm probably smart to carry donuts instead of a gun. If I'd been the one holding a weapon, I would have used it—possibly on all three of those wildmen. It seemed like the only way to stop the writhing mass of bodies that had formed before I could blink.

"Get help!" Thom said, securing his pistol before wading fearlessly into the fray. "Go back to the corner and flag down those patrol cars."

I whirled and ran the short way back to the main street in what must surely have been Olympic-record time. The first of the vehicles with flashing lights had just turned onto the street. I waved my arms madly. The driver must have seen me because the car's speed increased as it came toward where I stood. I motioned frantically toward the alley, then turned and ran back to Thom.

By some miracle he had disarmed the adrenaline-pumped store owner and extricated him from the pile of rubbish— human and otherwise. He gripped the older man's upper arm securely with one strong hand to keep him from again trying to exact his own justice. In his other hand was the pistol, once again trained on the two youth. All four men were spattered in blood, but it was impossible for me to tell just whose blood was whose.

Within another minute, headlights illuminated the street and two uniformed police officers charged forward with guns drawn. It wasn't long before two others joined them. More came after that.

If you've ever seen an episode of *COPS* and used it to define police work in your mind, I'm here to tell you those guys' work seems fast paced and exciting only because they have a good video editor back at the studio. In real life, an armed robbery followed by a police chase and shooting, followed by an assault on the perps by one another and their irate victim takes a long time to sort out. A very long time. Too long to portray in a half-hour TV show, for sure. Too long for a docudrama, even. I was beginning to think we were approaching miniseries proportions. But then, I didn't really know what time it was, because I didn't pay a lot of attention to the police. My mind was on other things.

After giving a very detailed statement to two different officers, I'd been pretty much ignored. (It was little wonder. I was the only clearly innocent bystander within six blocks. The rest of the onlookers could probably have been run in on general principle and the police wouldn't have made a false arrest in the bunch.) Being ignored gave me the welcome chance to scan the crowd. I was looking for someone.

In the front row behind the police lines were the street people and drunks from the bars. They were the boldest because they were, by comparison, the "upstanding" citizens of the 'hood. They shouted obscenities at the officers and kibitzed while the dark shadows of dealers appeared at the periphery just long enough to see if anybody they knew had been busted or killed. After all, this would mean they could move in on new territory or perhaps help themselves to their associates' stashes while they were otherwise engaged.

No matter how long and hard I scanned the train wreck of humanity, I didn't again see the figure I sought. When I'd first come back down the alley from signaling the police, I'd thought I'd caught a glimpse of something small and slight slip behind one of the large dumpsters that lined the street—something with long, red hair and impossibly large eyes. But before I could refocus my vision from the corner of my eye, whatever had been there was gone. Then all my attention had focused on Thom, covered with blood and struggling to maintain control of the situation for the few remaining moments until his fellow officers arrived. In the hours I'd sat there since, I hadn't seen Taryn again—if indeed it had been the runaway in the first place—despite staring into the dimness until my eyes ached.

At last it occurred to me that it had been a very long time since the suspects and the store owner were taken away, but there weren't significantly fewer police on the street. Whereas up until now they'd been moving methodically back and forth across the crime scene, swinging the beams from their flashlights into every dark corner and picking up every piece of trash with gloved hands, now they were huddled together into two groups. One band had formed around Thom, who was picking unconsciously at a bandage that had been applied to his left forearm by paramedics, and the rest had gathered several yards away. They looked like opposing teams waiting for the whistle to blow so they could square off for a division basketball title.

In the next minute, the metaphorical whistle blew. A police captain arrived on the scene with another man in plainclothes. The captain was Dix, the same officer who had "arrested" Thom on Tuesday night. When he stepped over the police tape, I followed—far enough back to remain unobtrusive, but close enough to hear what he said.

What he said was, "Well, Casey?"

Thom straightened. Apparently everybody but me already knew what was going on because there were no preambles.

"He had a gun in his hand when I fired on him, Captain," Thom said.

"He says he didn't," the captain countered. "He says he dropped it as he ran. He says he was raising his arms to surrender when you shot him."

Thom shook his head.

"He's sixteen years old for gosh sakes!"

Now Thom's head dropped toward his chest. "I couldn't know that, sir. All I knew was that he was armed and preparing to fire."

"Where's the weapon?"

Thom didn't reply.

"As we reported, there is no weapon, sir," an officer from the "opposing team" said. "We've been over every square inch of this alley."

I couldn't stand it another second. I pushed my way into the circle around Thom. "That guy had a gun!" I told the captain.

Dix didn't spare me a glance at first, but when at last he did, he did a double take. "Aren't you—?"

"Yes," I said. "I'm Samantha Shade of Nightshade Investigation. We . . . spoke . . . on Tuesday night, and again at the precinct on Wednesday . . . and Thursday. (And I hadn't liked him on any of those occasions, either.) "I—"

"You saw the gun in the suspect's hand here in the alley, Miss Shade?" the captain interrupted impatiently.

"No," I admitted. "But I—"

"You saw the gun lying in the street when you arrived on the scene?"

I bit my lip. "No, but I—"

"As you said in your statement, the *only* place you saw the gun was in the suspect's hand outside the bar. Is that correct?"

"Yes," I said. "But—"

"But what?"

"But I know Thom wouldn't have fired if that kid hadn't been aiming a gun at him!" Too late I realized I should have said, "Officer Casey" because the captain's eyebrows rose at my use of Thom's first name. I talked faster, hoping to distract him from my gaffe. "Officer Casey didn't shoot him in front of the bar, and he didn't draw his gun on the kids who broke the window in his car earlier. There were three of them—and they had a tire iron!" Thinking the "earlier part" needed more explanation, I added, "We were parked around the corner . . ." My words trailed off at the urgent "Don't help me anymore, please" look on Thom's face.

"I can see your relationship has progressed from last Tuesday," the captain said sarcastically.

"It wasn't *parking,* parking!" I protested, feeling the color rise to my cheeks. This guy might be Thom's boss and all, but I didn't like him. I didn't like him at all. "Give me a break. Who'd date in this neighborhood? We were down here—"

"Captain," Thom interrupted quickly, "Miss Shade has given her statement. She didn't see the gun. When the suspect dropped it I kicked it under the dumpster. Neither she nor the store owner could have seen it there, and nobody knows where it went after that."

"Or if it was ever there," the captain observed.

The old adage "With friends like that, who needs enemies?" came to mind. I considered giving a piece of it— my mind, not the adage—to the captain, but forbore at the warning look on Thom's face.

Captain Dix turned to the man who had accompanied him to the scene and said, "He's all yours." To Thom he said, "This is Lt. Cassell from Internal Affairs. I trust you'll cooperate fully."

Thom nodded. The dimple in his cheek was as deep as I'd ever seen it.

One of his fellow officers clasped him on the shoulder. "Hang in there," the man said. "I'll nose around here a little longer, talk to some people, and see if I can turn anything up."

"You'll get back to your beat," the captain growled. "That goes for the rest of you yahoos."

Thom reached into his pocket, removed his set of car keys, and tossed them to me. "Take my car to your place, would you? I'll arrange to pick it up tomorrow or the next day." Then he shook hands with the officer who'd offered to help him and said, "Make sure she gets back to my car all right."

"But I want to help you," I told Thom. "I—"

"If you really want to help me," he said, "you'll take my car home. I don't want to lose my books."

The chance of anybody around here wanting those tomes of his was negligible, and we both knew it. "But—"

"Go home, Sam," he said as his friend took my elbow. "Harrison isn't within twenty miles of this place by now. There isn't anything to accomplish here."

Except find the gun, I thought as Thom followed the older men to the patrol car and got in the backseat. But even as I thought it, I recognized its futility. A dozen professionals had already searched every inch of this alley and come up empty-handed.

The gun was gone—and with it the last hope Thomas Casey had for a career in law enforcement.

ACROSS

42 *Deviate from truth; Something practiced by more than one person in this story under extenuating circumstances—and otherwise*

63 *With 58 ACROSS, what facts often fail to do (first word); What one must be able to do before moving on to algebra*

DOWN

51 *Opposite of "we"*

Chapter 19

"That's libel!" I said, tossing Monday's newspaper toward the wastebasket next to Uncle Eddie's desk. Since my mother dutifully saves the crossword puzzles for me, I don't subscribe to the paper at home. Thus, I hadn't seen the awful headlines and worse articles until I went into work that evening. Mercifully, I'd also missed the stories about Thom on the news—although Knute informed me they had headed every broadcast.

"Don't throw it away!" Chaiya protested, making a diving catch for the front page. "It's a great picture of Thom!"

It is a good picture, I thought as Chaiya laid the paper on the desk and smoothed out the wrinkles. Unfortunately, while Thom's photo was flattering, the headline accompanying it was beyond bad. *ROGUE COP SHOOTS UNARMED CHILD; MOTHER SUES CITY.*

"Isn't that libel?" I asked. "That 'child' was a monster, Knute. He was clearly on drugs. His eyes were glassy and weird—and you should have seen the way he beat up his own friend." I glared down at the headline. "And he *had* a gun."

"Not one anybody can find."

"If Thom says he kicked it under a dumpster, then he did," I insisted.

"Hey," Knute said, holding up a hand, "you don't have to convince me, Sam. It's the rest of metropolitan Phoenix you have to argue with."

I dropped into Uncle Eddie's chair while Chaiya disappeared into her office in search of scissors.

"It's unbelievable," I railed. "'Rogue cop'! And the way they skewed that article made it sound like Thom was drunk when he hit the garbage cans Friday night."

"Their version sells more papers," Knute observed.

"And they wrote about the assault charges I filed against him on Wednesday," I continued. "But they don't mention anywhere that I said I was wrong and dropped them thirty-six hours later!" Somehow, this last was the worst of all. I couldn't stand to be named as an accessory to Thom's newest problems—even though I was. "I'm surprised they don't know he was working for us at Graeme Manor the night an extraterrestrial mummy disappeared," I muttered.

"Give them time," Knute said. "They'll dig it up."

I was so angry over it all I couldn't think straight.

"I just hope this doesn't kill his father prematurely," Knute said quietly.

I looked up in horror. Unlike me, Knute never exaggerates or embellishes. He deals only in cold, hard facts. He wouldn't even *think* a thing like that unless there was a very real possibility.

"What do you mean?"

"Thom's father has pancreatic cancer," Knute said. "In his case it's a death sentence. Thom was finishing up in graduate school when they found out. He left right away and tested with the first group to leave the academy. His father pulled some strings that landed him on the force here in Phoenix."

None of that made sense and I said so.

"It sounds like a bad cliché," Knute said, "but all the Casey men have been cops—ever since the first of them emigrated from Ireland."

"All of them?" I repeated. No wonder Thom had said he was born to be a cop.

Knute nodded. "Six generations later, Thom's father was chief of LAPD when he was shot."

"Shot?" I was beginning to sound like a parrot.

"In the gut. It's how they found out about the cancer since the man was too stubborn to see a doctor outside of an emergency room. As I said, Thom was finishing graduate school when it went down." He leaned back in the electric chair. "Did you know that guy was a Rhodes scholar? He spent two years at Oxford in England. He has a master's degree and most of a doctorate. If it weren't for trying to please his dad, Thom would be Dr. Casey now—teaching English lit and writing obscure treatises on the collected works of Tennyson."

No wonder Thom had so darn many books. And he probably hadn't lied about reading them.

"But he's an only child and the last of the line," Knute concluded. "Under the circumstances, he couldn't bear to break his father's heart by choosing academia over law enforcement."

The dismal meaning to Thom's words came clear. He'd tried to make his dad proud, but his family's heritage had to stop somewhere. Unfortunately, the brick wall now erected before his career was mostly of my construction. "How do you know all this?" I asked, intrigue battling my guilty conscience.

Knute shrugged. "I like the guy. We got together for dinner one night."

Wait until Chaiya hears that, I thought. *She'll be more jealous than I am.* (Not that I was jealous, exactly. I was more like . . . surprised. Surprised and curious . . . and maybe jealous. It was hard to tell what all I felt when Thom's name was mentioned.)

"Have you talked to him recently?" I asked. Despite the fact I still had possession of Almost–Dr. Casey's bookmobile, I hadn't heard a word from him.

"No," Knute said. "I called a couple of times yesterday, but he'd taken his phone off the hook. Today I heard he was downtown meeting with Internal Affairs and the PD's legal eagles."

Chaiya returned before I could respond, trailed by Wendela who had been working on her needlepoint in the outer office.

"Do we have any more floss, Samantha?" Wendela asked. "I seem to be running a tad shy of what I need to finish my petit point."

"It would be in your basket," I told her.

Wendela went happily after it, trailing the gossamer strands of silver and gold that she used to highlight the spheres in her celestial designs.

While Chaiya cut out Thom's picture, I continued to frown at the headline above it and the bold type below. "It's awful, Knute!" I said again. "It's so bad that—" My words ended at the sight of Thom Casey filling the open doorway.

He raised his bandaged arm in greeting, then looked from my face to Knute's and back. Finally he said, "Am I interrupting a wake?" Then he saw what Chaiya was doing and smiled ruefully. "Oh, right. Mine."

"It's a great picture!" Chaiya assured him happily.

"Yeah," he said. "If you're looking for something to put up on a dartboard."

Chaiya ignored the comment and pointed to the Great Wall of Books Knute had helped me construct from Thom's classics. (Not wanting to leave them in the open car—and finding there was no room for them in his already book-filled trunk—I'd borrowed a dolly from the funeral home next door and loaded them onto it. Knute had wheeled it inside and onto the elevator for me and then helped me stack them in Uncle Eddie's office for safekeeping.) "Those aren't all yours, are they?" she asked.

Thom glanced at the books, then at me. "Thank you, Sam," he said. To Chaiya he said, "Yes, they're all mine."

"You haven't actually *read* them?"

"Uh, yeah. I have."

"*Why?*"

"Thoreau said to read the best books first or you might never read them at all," Thom answered. Probably due to Chaiya's quizzical stare, it almost sounded like the literate cop tacked on a question mark at the last moment.

When I had recovered from hearing Thom call me by my first name again, I said, "I'm so glad you're here."

"I'm sorry I left the car and the books with you so long," he began. "I—"

"No!" I interrupted. "I mean, I'm glad you're here because . . ." Looking up into his eyes, I couldn't continue. I couldn't even think what it was I might have been going to say. He, Chaiya, Knute, and even Wendela were looking at me and waiting for the end of the sentence. I felt the blood creep into my cheeks. "Because I . . . I mean . . . because *we . . .*" Inspiration hit at last. "Because we have your paycheck ready for the job you did for Nightshade last week."

His eyebrows rose. "Good timing. Turns out I'm unemployed at the moment."

I looked down at my hands. It wasn't inspiration that had hit me after all. (I didn't know what it was, but it felt like a truck.) How could I have said that when I knew he'd just been suspended without pay for the duration of the investigation or until the case against him and the city was settled? That would be weeks, at least. What would he do in the meantime—work at Barnes and Noble? The only other thing I knew he was qualified to do was teach, and I doubted many schools would look twice at a résumé from a man who had allegedly shot an unarmed kid.

"I'm sorry," I murmured. "I didn't mean—"

"I know what you mean," he said.

I hoped it was true.

"How bad is it?" Knute asked, motioning for Thom to take a seat.

He remained standing. "It's plenty bad. Believe it or not, the kid I shot was going to play in the NBA someday." His voice was rueful and his dimple was deep. "His mother wants $10 million compensation for the damage to his 'potential career' on top of $2 million for the 'physical pain and mental anguish' I've caused them both."

"That kid couldn't play basketball if his life depended on it!" I said. "He couldn't even walk straight." I turned to Knute. "And he probably won't live to see his seventeenth birthday. The only mistake Thom made was in just nicking his shoulder. He shouldn't have missed."

"He didn't miss," Knute said. "Thom did exactly the damage he intended to."

Casey cast him a grateful look, but said, "That's beside the point. He's just a kid and I did shoot him."

"Only because he was going to shoot you for stopping him from robbing a store," I insisted.

"I wonder," Knute mused.

Now Thom looked stricken. "He had a gun, Knute. I swear he did."

"I believe it," Knute said hastily. "And I think he was going to use it. At least I think he was *supposed* to use it."

All of a sudden the words of the bobbleheaded punk flashed into my mind. "Thom!" I said. "That other kid—the shaky one—remember?" I scooted forward in the chair. "What was it he kept saying about something his pal was supposed to do?"

"I don't know," Thom said slowly. "But I've been trying to remember."

"Whatever it was," I said, struggling to recall the exact words myself and failing, "it made the gunman beat him senseless rather than let him keep talking."

"Where is that shaky kid now?" Knute asked.

Thom shrugged. "If the department knows, I'm the last person they'll tell."

"Maybe I ought to see if I can find out."

I could practically see the cogs turning in the perceptive giant's head.

"What are you thinking?" I asked.

"I'm thinking maybe the robbery wasn't the point," he replied. "I'm thinking maybe it was staged. Maybe somebody's real intent was to get Thom killed in the line of duty. And maybe the only flaw in their plan was that the druggie they hired to do the job was either too scared or too stoned to pull the trigger."

It made sense. "That's what I saw!" I realized aloud. "When the one kid ran out of the store it was almost like he waited for Thom to give chase while his friend stood in the shadows with the gun." I turned to Thom. "He *would* have shot you, Thom, except the old guy threw that bottle at him and scared him half to death, so he ran instead."

Thom changed his mind about sitting down. He pulled up the Windsor and dropped onto it

"You've thought of this angle," Knute observed.

"It's about all I've thought about," Thom said. "But I hoped I was being paranoid."

"Why would somebody want to kill Thom?" Chaiya asked.

Clearly Thom wondered the same thing.

"Because they think he knows something," Knute said.

Thom shook his head. "They're wrong."

"Maybe," Knute conceded, "but they know a lot about you. They knew you were in the neighborhood that night. They knew you wouldn't stand by if a robbery went down. I'm thinking they saw a quick, permanent resolution to their problem—real or imagined. They just hired the wrong two guys to pull it off."

"The only thing your theory doesn't explain is the missing gun, Knute," I pointed out. "It's too complicated for a frame, isn't it?"

Knute scratched at his wooly head. "Yeah, it is. That gun just disappearing doesn't make any sense at all."

"None of this is going to make any sense to Internal Affairs," Thom decided aloud. "There's no way they're going to buy a conspiracy theory from me *or* Nightshade." He looked from one to the other of us sheepishly. "Sorry. No offense."

Knute rose. "'Course not." To me he said, "If you don't mind, boss, I'm going to do a little nosing around on this thing. Delano's all over the Hanley case, and Chaiya can check out the sites we're still watching for mummy auctions."

"About that," Thom said. "It's why I'm here, actually. Well, part of the reason at least." He stood. "I've managed to wrangle an invitation to Graeme Manor tonight, but there's a caveat."

"A fish egg?" Chaiya asked, turning up her nose. "Ick!"

Thom looked puzzled for a moment, then said, "There's a condition." He glanced across the room toward Wendela. "Lord Herbert specifically asked that I bring along Miss . . ."

"Wendela," I supplied.

"Yes."

Wendela's hand fluttered to her heart. I smiled. "We'd love to go."

Possibly I said it too quickly and too enthusiastically because the look Chaiya shot me could curdle milk. "Yes, *we* would," she said.

"But *you* have to work here, Chaiya," Knute interjected in a gallant attempt to save me from my roommate's wrath. "Besides the mummy research, you're still working on those transcripts for Delano, remember? He'll be very disappointed if you're not here with them when he comes in."

That was true on more than one level, and Knute and I both knew it. Chaiya didn't. Her lower lip curled outward and downward, just as it had when she was a little girl. But she raised her chin like a pro. "I'm sorry, Thomas," she said. "You'll have to go without me this time. I'm *indescribable* around here."

I knew she meant indispensable, but I didn't dare correct her. Besides, for once she was right.

Knute rose and clasped Thom's uninjured arm in a fatherly gesture. "You be careful," he said. "If we're right, you not being dead right now might be a real concern to somebody." He paused, probably considering if he should go along with us as a bodyguard. At last he asked, "You armed?"

"No," Thom replied. "They took my service weapon with my badge."

"They pull your license to carry?"

"No. At least not yet."

Knute nodded at me. I pulled open the top drawer in Uncle Eddie's desk and stuck my fingernail into a tiny crevice in the wooden pencil holder. A panel slid back to reveal a secret compartment below. I gingerly removed the gun and extended it to Thom.

He gave a low whistle.

"Yeah," Knute said. "She's a classic, but she still fires better than anything you'll find today. But only six shots." He grinned. "You need more than that?"

"Only if there are seven of them."

I tried to smile at the thin joke, but it wasn't funny. Nothing about this was funny. You'd think a mature, well-educated, reasonably intelligent young woman of discriminating taste would have wanted to distance herself from a man who was not only unemployed and newly notorious, but who might also be marked for murder. But since that man was Thom Casey, I *didn't* want to distance myself from him. I wanted to stand by his side no matter what.

And maybe . . . just maybe . . . I wanted to stand a little closer than that.

ACROSS

15 *Lacking intensity; What Shady Acres never is when Wendela is around*

21 *The thing that fits neatly around the picture they want you to see; Setup*

DOWN

6 *Sixth planet from the sun; Wendela's birthplace?*

10 *Gear; Wheel; Something I often think I can see turning in Knute's head*

Chapter 20

"Is that line from *Romeo and Juliet?*" I asked Thom as Lord Herbert waxed poetic over Wendela being "an angel! Or, if not, an earthly paragon!"

"No," he said. "It's from *Cymbeline.*"

The two of us were seated on a divan in Lord Herbert's lounge while a woman who resembled Mrs. White of Clue fame served us canapés.

Being a good detective—and a little paranoid besides—I deduced at once that not only did the maid not have a revolver, rope, knife, or even candlestick on her tray, there wasn't a single lead pipe or wrench in the room. Despite Knute's worries, Thom was probably safe here.

Across the room, Lord Herbert kissed Wendela's palm. She was speaking as earnestly as I'd ever seen her. Once again she reminded me of Lady Macbeth as she rolled the sash from her dress between her long, delicate fingers. I couldn't hear what she said, but I did manage to pick up a snatch of Lord Herbert's reply.

"'There's nothing ill can dwell in such a temple,'" he said. "'If the ill spirit have so fair a house, good things will strive to dwell with 't.'"

"*The Tempest,*" Thom said before I could guess wrong again.

Like most American high school graduates, I can quote the first line of Hamlet's "to be or not to be" soliloquy and name maybe four or five more Shakespearean plays besides.

(I've even seen the ones with Mel Gibson, Leonardo DiCaprio, and Kevin Kline.) The only one I've actually read, however, is *Macbeth,* and I've slogged through it twice—once in high school and again in college. (There is a scene in it I love—the witches on the moor. Now that's great literature.)

"What in the world is he doing?" I asked Thom as Lord Herbert struck a pose and said something florid about Wendela's eyes.

"'That man that hath a tongue, I say, is no man, if with his tongue he cannot win a woman.'"

That might not have been an answer (though it might have been), but it was a darn good Lord Herbert impersonation. I faked a frown when I'd have rather laughed out loud. "Don't tell me you can do that Shakespearean thing too."

"Yes," Thom said with a smile to which I could easily become addicted. "I can. When done for sport it's called barding, and the object of it is to see who can carry on conversation the longest using only Shakespearean quotes. It's 'a kind of excellent dumb discourse.' I was very good at it in school."

"Uh, huh." I pretended to pull away as if he had classical cooties, but I didn't actually move so much as an inch. "So, did Lord Herbert pick it up at Oxford like you did?"

Thom hesitated. "*Now* you've been talking to Knute."

I nodded. "Now I have."

Thom shrugged off my confession and answered my question. "I don't think so. In fact, I doubt he's ever lived in England." At my startled expression he added, "But, being a lord and all, he might tell you otherwise."

I could scarcely believe the implications of what I'd just heard. I'd asked the question in jest—or perhaps to draw Thom out about himself—but I'd discovered by accident he thought Lord Herbert was a liar. Why?

"Did you investigate him?" I whispered.

"Not thoroughly," Thom responded. "At least not yet."

"But *why?*" I pressed, forgetting for the moment to be grateful that he had probably done it to help me solve the mummy case.

"Curiosity, mostly."

All of a sudden, cat clichés began to pop into my head. The first was *curiosity killed the cat.* Somebody wanted to kill Thom. Could it be Lord Herbert? What if he had some deep, dark secret he was afraid Thom would uncover? I shook my head at the absurdity of the notion. The Easter Bunny has deeper, darker secrets than Lord Herbert.

The second feline cliché to come to mind was *don't let the cat out of the bag.* This one was likely more apt—especially as it pertained to me. Lord Herbert probably didn't have skeletons in his closet, but Wendela might. For sure Wendela and I together did.

Just how many people has Thom checked out already? I wondered as the canapé in my mouth began to taste like dirt, only drier and less tasty. *And how thoroughly has he checked them?*

I laid the remains of the stuffed mushroom back on the china plate and lowered it toward my lap. It hopped across the dish like a Mexican jumping bean. Either there was a very small, very localized earthquake just beneath my side of the divan, or my hands were shaking like crazy.

Despite the fact that curiosity could incarcerate this cat, I just had to ask. "Are you still checking out everyone who was here the night the mummy disappeared?"

Thom looked at Wendela for several long, terrifying seconds before he turned back to me. "Not everybody," he said. "Not anybody now that I've been suspended and lost access to the database."

I let out a breath, glad that he'd apparently been investigating his suspects in alphabetical order and hadn't yet reached the W's. If he had, I knew from what he'd told me about swearing to uphold the law, he wouldn't be sitting there with a common criminal (me) now. Thom's great misfortune, his suspension, could prove to be my greatest fortune. The thought was strange and not at all comforting.

I felt guilty without being charged. Then I looked across the room at Wendela and wondered, if I had it to do over, what I would have done differently. *Could* I have done anything differently?

To understand how Wendela came to live with me, you must first know that the months I worked at the state mental hospital were some of the worst in their history. (But not because of me!) Weeks after I left, there was a surprise inspection that resulted in the temporary loss of the hospital's accreditation. Although I hear it is much better now, during my internship it was like a prison—but with less hope for the inmates. Everything about the facility, inside and out, was old, gray, and dingy. The semester I worked there became the longest few months of my life.

In the first place, I had no actual duties to occupy my time. My assignments included working jigsaw puzzles, playing games, and visiting with the patients—at least those who were awake and coherent on my midnight-to-six shift. Then I wrote reports of my observations for the nurses to round-file before the doctors ever saw them. It was a waste of everybody's time except that it earned me a degree in the college of diversified studies as a psych major and increased my gratitude and compassion a thousand-fold.

Every night before entering the high, forbidding walls, I would search for the brightest star—or focus on a jet leaving Sky Harbor Airport if it was too cloudy to see a star—and recite, "Star light, star fright, first star I see tonight, I wish I may, I wish I might be given power, wrongs to right."

The greatest wrong I'd ever seen in my life was the one the system inflicted upon Wendela.

Wendela Doe—so called because nobody, including her, seemed to know her last name—was a patient in the long-term ward. In other words she was a "lifer"—an inmate without hope of release. An indigent, she'd been committed by the state because she was "mentally retarded, incurably delusional, and a danger to herself." But she was incurable only because there was nothing clinically wrong with her aside from an uncomplicated mind and a strong, if fanciful, belief she came from the stars. Possibly she was a danger to herself. Even then she had a tendency to climb billboards and power poles—but only to search for a way back to the happiness she had known in whatever place she'd called home.

Since the doctors hadn't determined that her condition could be improved by medication, she was mostly spared it. This was a mixed blessing. Although it would have been a crime to sedate her, it might also have been kindness. Confinement in an ugly, eight-by-ten room made Wendela despondent and restless, especially at night. Add to her emotional distress a gift for escaping and a perpetual wanderlust, and she was more than inconvenient to the understaffed, overtaxed workers who had no time to watch her. Thus, she was restrained.

To be perfectly graphic, she was handcuffed to her metal bed frame.

It broke my heart. I had never met a person who radiated a gentler, more Christlike spirit, and yet she was treated worse than a rabid dog.

Night after night I talked to Wendela. I read to her. I listened to her tell me nonsensical stories and sing haunting melodies in a language only she understood. When I couldn't stand it a moment longer, I hand-carried my most scathing report to the hospital director—and threatened to take it to the *Arizona Republic* as well. I was thus granted permission to unchain Wendela while I was with her and to walk with her up and down the halls. Eventually I even received permission to take her outdoors. (And, yes, I almost lost her a couple of times before I learned where all the fire-escape ladders were located.) I loved every moment we spent together.

You've already figured out the end of the story, haven't you? On the last night of my internship I took Wendela out walking, but I never took her back. It wasn't something I planned—it was just something that seemed like the only thing I *could* do. I'd plagued the doctors and director to reopen her case but was told over and over again that without relatives to intervene in her behalf, their hands were tied. Her case could not be appealed and she could not be released, no matter what I said or did.

I'd gone to Uncle Eddie for help in uncovering Wendela's past, of course, but after weeks of searching, not even he and Knute working together could turn up a clue about her origins. They wouldn't even hazard a guess. For all anybody could prove, she really *had* dropped from the Milky Way.

It was hopeless. *I* was without hope because I knew that when I left the state hospital, Wendela would remain chained to that bed until the day she died.

What would you have done?

Maybe I didn't think of that, so I did the first impulsive thing that came to mind. I kidnapped an inmate.

At least one doctor, a nurse, two nurse's aides, and three security guards saw us leave the hospital, but nobody tried to stop us. It wouldn't surprise me to learn the staff cheered as we left. Like me, they often felt powerless and trapped in an untenable situation—good people bound by ethics on one hand and miles of red tape on the other. How could they *not* be pleased to see one small pinprick of light break through that black universe of misery and despair?

I drove Wendela back to my apartment with my heart pounding, listening for police sirens, but hearing only the raucous sounds of city traffic and Wendela's soft singing.

Like a common kidnapper, I hid out for a few days, listening to news broadcasts and scouring the papers for any mention of missing women. Days passed and nothing appeared anywhere. Whether the hospital administration didn't notice, didn't care, or didn't want to call attention to its facility for fear of the censure that eventually happened anyway, not one word was ever said nor any investigation launched. I told myself there was no harm, no foul, and started to breathe again. The hospital was glad to be rid of Wendela and I was glad to have her.

I told my compassionate, Christian parents that Wendela had been freed from the hospital and had nowhere else to go, so I took her in. (And I used precisely those words because they were true.)

Uncle Eddie and Knute—who I'm sure made note of the coincidence of me asking them to investigate an inmate one month and then showing up with her as a roommate the next— never asked me the circumstances of Wendela's miraculous release, and I never offered to tell them. Since then I'd never told *anyone* my secret, but now I thought I would tell Thom Casey.

As I turned toward him, the maid reappeared, carrying the same silver platter. This time it held glasses of punch.

"The platter isn't real silver," she said to Thom with a great deal more volume than was necessary. "The *sterling* platter wasn't in its place this evening."

If her intention was to be overheard by Lord Herbert, she was successful. He and Wendela left off their romantic murmurings and strolled over to sit on a love seat across from us.

"It's no matter," Lord Herbert said to his servant. "This tray is fine."

"Fine is it?" she grumbled. "Is it 'fine' when a family heirloom disappears?" She set the tray on the low cherry table with a thump. "And, I might add, it's run off with the salt cellars and good candlesticks." Before Lord Herbert could respond, she'd planted herself in front of Thom again. "It isn't my place to say," she said, "but the lord here is being robbed blind. I thought that with you being a policeman and all, you might—"

"Mrs. Blanco," Lord Herbert said good-naturedly, "Officer Casey is paying me a social call. As much as I appre-

ciate your good intentions, it is *not* your place. Thank you for
the refreshments. That will be all."

Despite his jovial tone, this must be what passed for a
stinging rebuke in Graeme Manor, because the faithful maid's
lips formed a thin, unhappy line. As she left the room I heard
her murmur, "I'm just saying . . ."

"I think she's right," Thom told our host.

"Of course she's right, Thomas," Lord Herbert agreed. I
almost spit my punch into my lap, but Lord Herbert
continued to smile serenely. "My nephew has been clandes-
tinely cashing in his inheritance since before he could grow a
decent beard. He'll be lucky if there's anything left to steal by
the time he turns thirty-five."

"And you don't have a problem with that?" I asked.

"'The most peaceable way for you if you do take a thief,
is to let him show himself what he is and steal out of your
company,'" Lord Herbert replied.

"This isn't *Much Ado About Nothing*," Thom said. "This
is grand theft." He leaned forward. "And outside of the
theater, men like Harrison are seldom 'condemned into
everlasting redemption' no matter how good your intentions."

"Ahh," Lord Herbert sighed as if the punch was much
tastier than it was.

(I think he reveled in barding, and really, how many
people could he possibly have met in the course of his life
who could do it as well as Thom?)

"But don't you agree, Thomas," he continued, "that 'our
wills and fates do so contrary run that our devices still are
overthrown'?"

"What I believe," Thom countered, "is that 'some rise by
sin and some by virtue fall.'"

I watched the contentment fade from Lord Herbert's face
a millimeter at a time. He forced a smile and said hopefully,
"And by that you mean Harrison?"

Even as Lord Herbert said it, he looked as guilty as I felt. Despite myself, I began to wonder if I'd misjudged him and the Easter Bunny. Maybe he *did* have a deep, dark secret or two.

"'Men's judgments are a parcel of their fortunes,'" Thom said.

Lord Herbert looked steadfastly down at his punch as if deliberately trying to misunderstand.

I didn't have to pretend to misunderstand.

"It's a harmless diversion, Thomas," Lord Herbert said at last. "'To have what we would have, we speak not what we mean.'" He leaned forward. "Trust me, sir."

"'He's mad that trusts in the tameness of a wolf,'" Thom said, but he said it with a smile.

Lord Herbert returned the smile with a wink. "'Though this be madness, yet there is method in 't.'"

"Then may I suggest 'more matter, with less art'?"

"Harrison is stealing from you, Lord Herbert!" I interjected at last, hoping to steer the conversation back to the point at hand—if indeed it had ever left it. Honestly, I wished they would modernize their English by about five centuries. The three witches in *Macbeth* had made more sense to me than those two barders.

"Mere baubles," Lord Herbert told me. "The items with which Harrison amuses himself are scarcely worth the trouble to take. I have carefully tucked away everything of real value."

"But the mummy!" I said, catching the sardonic look on Thom's face but not knowing what to make of it. "Isn't your nephew the most likely suspect? I mean, the doors were open in the conservatory. Who would have had access to a key besides Harrison? He probably gave it to an accomplice who—" I stopped myself midsentence as Lord Herbert's head continued to move back and forth. "How do you *know* he didn't steal it?" I concluded in frustration.

When Lord Herbert didn't reply, Thom said, "Could we take one more look at your study, Lord Herbert?"

"I would delight in showing it to you!" the lord exclaimed, rising with his punch glass still in hand. "I think you will be as pleased with the results as am I."

"Results?" Thom asked.

"Why, yes," Lord Herbert said. "Didn't I tell you? It's been completely refurbished."

And it had. Minutes later I stood in the doorway in front of Thom and admired the transformation of the former mummy room. There was a massive lacquer-and-glass display case where the dais had once stood. Within the case were two finely crafted geisha figurines. The Oriental theme was repeated on the walls in subtle red and black watercolors done on cream silk and centered in ebony frames. The effect was exquisite.

"Can you see the 'pride peep through each part of me'?" Lord Herbert asked in satisfaction.

I could. And I could see incredulity peeping through each part of Thom. The barding had been startled right out of him. "Who did this?" he asked in plain, understandable, modern English.

"Why, Hedda," Lord Herbert replied. "She has a fine eye for interior design, don't you agree? She's done many of my rooms. Most of them, in fact."

"When did she do it?" Thom asked. His eyes were on the carpet. It was new—cream colored and nondescript, the last thing most people without a vacuum cleaner would look at in a room filled with such beautiful things. But it was the only thing Thom looked at.

"Friday, I believe," Lord Herbert said. As if anticipating Thom's next question he added, "My dear sister is somewhat obsessive/compulsive, I'm afraid. She abhors the sight of blood—the thought of it, even. She didn't sleep a wink because of the stains on the carpet. The least I could do for her was to have it replaced as soon as I returned home." He looked about the room. "And as long as we no longer have

Hermes, it seemed that a change was in order. I do think it's quite satisfactory, don't you?"

It was more than satisfactory, anybody could see that. Anybody but Thom. "Who replaced your carpeting, Lord Herbert?" he pressed.

"I couldn't tell you." The lord smiled sheepishly. "I was led to them, Thomas. My hand was guided upon the leaves of our own modern-day Delphic Oracle."

"He found them in the yellow pages in the phone book," I explained. "That's the same way he found Nightshade."

"Uh, huh," Thom replied, as if it wasn't much of a revelation. "And you paid in cash, no doubt."

"Why certainly."

"He paid *us* in cash," I said as if to defend Lord Herbert's peculiarities.

Thom shook his head. "'If this were played upon a stage now, I could condemn it as an improbable fiction.'"

Lord Herbert turned away, but I turned back toward Thom as if looking up into his face would tell me what was in his head. Did he believe Hedda had insisted on new carpet and redecorated the room to cover her tracks after the theft of the mummy? That would support my theory as to why she was so quick to help Wendela set the room aright after the mummy's disappearance on Thursday night. On the other hand, a tendency toward being obsessive/compulsive and revolted by blood explained it just as well. Who, I wondered, was Thom going to accuse here?

He didn't accuse anyone. Instead, he changed the subject.

"I asked if I could come by tonight because I need to talk to Harrison," Thom said. "But not about stealing the mummy," he added hastily. "Or even about 'cashing in his inheritance,' as you call it. I want to see him because he might be able to help me with a personal matter."

"I have great faith in your better nature, Thomas," Lord Herbert said genially, squeezing Wendela's fingers before releasing them to move toward the intercom. "I trust it is not unfounded."

He pushed a button and spoke to his nephew in another part of the house, asking him to join us in the study. The reply was crude, but affirmative. Before long we heard Harrison snap at a servant whom he must have encountered at the end of the hall.

"'By the pricking of my thumbs, something wicked this way comes,'" I murmured. Then I clasped a hand over my mouth, both in dismay that now *I* was doing that stupid barding thing, and mortification that the only quote I remembered from *Macbeth* was an inexcusably rude one. I glanced at Lord Herbert who looked surprised and a little shaken. "I'm so sorry," I began. "I didn't mean . . ." My words trailed off. After all, I probably *did* mean what I'd said about Harrison, and lying on top of being rude would only compound my sin.

"Lord Herbert doesn't quote *Macbeth*," Thom observed in the ensuing silence. "Do you, Lord Herbert?"

The lord's bright blue eyes met Thom's for only a moment before lowering. I thought by the look on his face he might send us packing, but instead he said, "No, Thomas, I don't. As you must know."

Now Thom was the one who wouldn't look at Lord Herbert. Once again the new carpet held his full attention.

"Then 'the play's the thing,'" the elderly man said softly, "'wherein you'll catch the conscience of the king.'" He took a step closer to the young police officer. "*Do* you know my conscience, Thomas? *Am* I a suspect in your mind?"

Thom raised his chin. "There is no crime to suspect you of," he said. "Is there, Lord Herbert?"

I heard the words. I saw the looks that passed between the two men. I even felt the tension in the air, but I didn't understand what was going on. What did Thom know about Lord Herbert Graeme that I didn't? Was whatever it was damaging enough for the lord to want Thom never to speak of it? Is that why he agreed to let him come back to the manor tonight? After all, Thom's blood had already been spilt here by *somebody.* What if his attacker's only regret was that they hadn't done a more thorough job of spilling it?

ACROSS

   46 *Put out of sight; What I suspected the Meads had done with the mummy*

   47 *Abbr. for "darned convenient"—what too many "accidental" deaths were believed to be*

DOWN

   37 *_____ of Avon; The art (sport?) of quoting Shakespeare (_____ing)*

Chapter 21

Harrison Meade leaned languidly against the study's door-jamb and glowered at Thom, me, and even Wendela. "You called, Uncle Herbie?" he asked in a tone that dripped scorn.

"Only because I asked him to," Thom said.

"Well, well—the rogue cop," Harrison sneered. "Judging by the public outcry, I'd have expected them to have locked you up by now, Casey." His eyes narrowed as an insincere smile spread across his face. "Or lynched you."

Thom didn't react, but Lord Herbert did. "Thomas?" he exclaimed.

"He's referring to an incident on Saturday night," Thom said. "I shot an armed robber."

"An unarmed teenager," Harrison countered.

"My question for you," Thom said, again ignoring the barb with patience that would have done credit to Job, "is who called and asked you to meet them on Van Buren Saturday night?"

Perhaps it was because he was so tall and lean, but Harrison looked like a snake when he recoiled. I expected a forked tongue to dart out from between his white teeth as he said, "You've lost it, Casey."

"No," Thom said. "According to the records at the phone company, somebody called here from a pay phone on Van Buren just after ten. About an hour later, you showed up. You hung around the phone booth for a while, and then you entered a bar. You were still there when the robbery went down."

Harrison was livid. "Did you come here to accuse me of something?"

"No," Thom said again. "I came here to ask you a question. I'll repeat it. Who called you on Saturday night?"

"Nobody called me," Harrison hissed. "But even if somebody had, what's it to you?"

Thom glanced at Lord Herbert. "Let's say I'm naturally curious."

My mind raced. Was Thom's question to Harrison a way to gauge his reaction to us knowing he was on Van Buren Saturday night, or an honest request for information? In other words, did Thom suspect Harrison of conspiring to have him killed, or did he think somebody had used Harrison as bait?

Either way, I reasoned, if Harrison was involved in setting Thom up, the caller was somebody who had known Thom was here at Graeme Manor last week. Nothing else made sense. I glanced at Lord Herbert and couldn't help but note the beads of perspiration that glistened on his balding forehead. I hoped he had nitro handy. My own heart skipped a beat as I realized just how short my list of possible assassins had become—and how nervous a couple of the men on it were right now.

I was still telling myself to suspect the Tooth Fairy before Lord Herbert when Harrison said to Thom, "You've got it all wrong, Casey. I've never been to Van Buren. Don't know where it is, even."

The boldfaced lie delivered so coolly left Thom with few options. He could pretend to believe the lie, expose the guy as the liar and thief he was, or he could rearrange Harrison's face until the creep suddenly remembered who he'd gone to meet Saturday night.

I was hoping to see Thom wipe the sardonic, self-satisfied grin off Harrison's face when my cell phone rang. It was Delano.

"Bertram called in," Delano told me without preamble. "He's on the gate at Graeme Manor tonight. Says he thinks he saw a guy sneak onto Lord Herbert's estate while he was checking out one of the servant's cars. Bert claims to have called out to him, but says the guy disappeared into the shadows."

My heart rose into my throat. Had Thom's enemy followed us here or been summoned after we arrived?

"How long ago?" I asked.

"I dunno," he said. "Just a few minutes, I think. I know we've told the guards to only worry about the cars leaving the manor, Sammy, but I think maybe we oughta check this out. It feels wrong. I just called in to tell you I'm not far away and I'm on my way over there."

"I'm *at* Graeme Manor!" I told my associate, casting anxious eyes toward Thom. "And—"

"I'll call the police," Delano said.

"What's up?" Thom asked.

I filled him in and felt the blood leave my face when he instinctively reached under his jacket to assure himself that Uncle Eddie's gun was still tucked into the waistband of his jeans.

"Description?" he asked.

I relayed the question to Delano, but thought as I did so that it was probably futile. Bertram had grown up in my ward, so I knew that while he was the salt of the earth, he was also about as bright as a rock.

I was right to doubt his abilities. When Delano finished interrogating Bertram we knew only that the intruder was a man (Bertram guessed) dressed in black (or dark blue or brown or green or plaid) who was average build (or a little heavy) and short (unless he was average or tall and just scrunched down to better disappear into the bushes).

"Armed?" Thom asked.

I didn't have to relay the question to know Bertram wouldn't know.

Delano must have heard Thom's voice when the latter had stepped closer to my phone. "Casey's there with you?" he said into my ear. "Good."

Not good, I thought. *Not good at all.*

"Thom!" I cried as he turned and headed for the door. "Wait for the police. Or at least wait for Delano. We don't know who's out there."

"Yeah," Harrison smirked. "It might not be a kid this time, Casey. What if it's a real bad guy?"

Thom shouldered past Lord Herbert's nephew and entered the hallway almost before I could blink. Closing my cell phone and thrusting it in my jacket pocket, I followed.

"Move!" I commanded Harrison who continued to stand insolently in the doorway, blocking my path.

"What's the magic word?"

More words came to my Sunday School–teaching mind than really should have, but I didn't utter a single one of them. Instead I executed a perfect tae kwon do move and was most of the way to the conservatory before Harrison knew what hit him. As fast as I was this time, I wasn't fast enough. The double doors were open and Thom was nowhere to be seen.

***

"Thom!" I yelled into the darkness.

Admittedly, that wasn't how I'd been taught to conduct a stealth operation, but I'd been searching for Thom for more than half an hour now and "antsy" didn't begin to describe the pinpricks of fear that jogged up and down my spine. Things didn't feel right. They didn't even *smell* right. I wrinkled my nose at a musky, foul odor on the cool, night breeze.

"Thom!" I repeated, louder. Maybe if I made enough noise, he would give up his self-appointed, possibly suicidal mission and come back to the manor—if only to tell me to be quiet.

"Thom!" I said a third time, but not as loud. Calling him wasn't going to work. He wasn't a Weimaraner, and he wasn't coming back. I shuddered and quickly amended the thought to he wasn't coming back *until* he knew who was prowling the estate. In the meantime, he could be anywhere.

And he wasn't the only one. The prowler could be anywhere as well. I glanced over my shoulder, blessing the moonlight. I was alone. Too alone. I wanted company. Preferably armed and able company. But the police could be anywhere too. Clearly they were anywhere but here.

I stared across the pool and into the open desert. Shadows danced and darted among the cacti and mesquite and palo alto trees, but even staring couldn't make those shadows separate themselves into clear, recognizable forms.

Unless you grew up around here, you probably think "desert/deserted," right? Wrong. Dozens of species of plants are native to Mummy Mountain—many of them large enough to conceal a man. And it's home to scores of critters that, like Arjay, live nocturnally to escape the bright, searing rays of the Phoenix sun. Thus, from where I stood, it was impossible to know if the rustlings in the bushes were caused by coyotes, javelina, or armed assassins.

I pushed away the thought of assassins and replaced it with a prayer for the arrival of the cavalry. Soon would be good. Now would be better. I hadn't heard a gunshot, but that didn't mean Thom wasn't hurt, and there was just too much property to search by myself.

Not that that stopped me from searching.

Another ten minutes later I leaned cautiously around a corner before moving forward. Everything was as still on this side of the building as it had been on the other two. The gravel in the path crunched beneath my feet and further irritated my raw nerves, so I sidestepped into the soft loam of newly planted flowerbeds.

Up ahead, a light glowed through an open window. I'd long ago lost my bearings—and I didn't know the manor well in the first place—so I had no idea what room it was. Nor did it look as if I could find out by peeking in the window. It was high up and well protected by rosebushes below.

Just before I stepped back onto the path to avoid the thorns, I heard a woman's voice carried through the stillness. Even if I'd been unable to recognize Lord Herbert's sister by her voice, I could never have mistaken her vocabulary. When the tirade ended, Hedda spoke softly again—too softly to be heard from where I stood.

I had to know what that woman was saying. I pressed myself into Lord Herbert's prize-winning roses (they smelled better than they felt), and eavesdropped on Hedda's side of a phone conversation. It was soon apparent she wanted something done that somebody else didn't want to do.

"I don't care about the risks!" she said, her voice rising loud enough to make the self-piercing I was experiencing unnecessary. "I want it sold *now*. Do you understand me?"

I drew a breath.

Okay, it was more like a gasp.

I didn't bother to search my pocket for a tape recorder because I knew I'd only come up with a small can of pepper spray and a partially completed crossword puzzle.

And a cell phone. I pulled it from my pocket and called my home phone. With me and Wendela here and Chaiya at Nightshade, the answering machine would pick up. It was several agonizing seconds before it did, but they were seconds in which Hedda was silent, listening.

At about the same time I heard the soft beep to indicate my machine was ready to record, Hedda said, "If you can't do the job, I'll find somebody who can!" She paused, listening to the brief response. "That's what I thought. Do it!" There was another pause, then, "I'll take care of Herbert, thank you. I've always taken care of Herbert."

The sound of Hedda slamming down the receiver rang in my ears. I could only imagine how it must have sounded to the person on the other end of the line. I made a mental note to start looking for a browbeaten, deaf pawnbroker, because when I found him, I'd have Hedda's lackey.

I shifted from one foot to the other, but I didn't move away and I didn't lower the phone. I hoped Hedda would make another, more incriminating call so I could record something that would impress a district attorney. I had no such luck. There was only the sound of a chair being pushed back. Seconds later the light went out in the room and she was gone.

I couldn't wait to tell Thom what I'd heard.

Thom!

I couldn't decide whether to scream for him again or to call the police and scream at them for not responding to our emergency call. Or maybe I'd just scream.

I flipped my cell phone closed. Before I could complete another action—desperate or otherwise—it rang.

"Thom?" It was more of a wish than a rational guess.

"Delano," came the answer. "Where are you?"

"Where are *you?*" I countered. "I thought you were coming. I thought—"

"I'm here," he said. "Down at the guardhouse."

Thank goodness for that. "Is everything—"

"Everything was over when I got here."

"You mean Thom had already caught the prowler?" I asked in relief.

"Unfortunately."

Unfortunately? "Is Thom there?" I asked, the anxiety returning threefold.

"He's here," Delano said. I could have sworn he chuckled, but perhaps he choked on emotion. "Unfortunately."

That awful word again. I began to jog toward the driveway leading down to the front gate. "I'll be right there."

"I wouldn't recommend it."

"Is Thom hurt?" I gasped. Visions of it came at once to my overactive imagination. Why else would it be "unfortunate" that Thom had caught the prowler if the man hadn't injured or—

"Delano!" I cried. "Is Thom—?"

"He's putrid," Delano interrupted with what was definitely a laugh. "That's Casey's word, by the way, not mine."

"Putrid?" I asked as I ran. Even if he was dead, Thom hadn't had time to rot. And as for a dead man calling himself putrid . . . this made no sense at all.

"It pays to increase your word power, Sammy," Delano said into my ear. "Casey is malodorous, rank, stinky . . . get it?" Not yet I didn't, but Delano painted me a word picture. "He caught the skunk he was after, but that wasn't necessarily a good thing, considering the skunk had already run afoul of one of its own kind—a four-footed, white-striped variety, that is."

I remembered the foul odor I'd whiffed earlier, and skidded to a stop on the wide drive. It is one thing to be willing to stand by a man who is unemployed, newly notorious, and possibly marked for assassination, but it is another to stand by—or even near—a man who's had a close encounter with the wrong end of a skunk.

Some things, after all, are beyond loyalty, compassion, and even infatuation.

"What happened?" I asked, catching my breath and imagining I smelled skunk even though they were far enough away that I probably didn't.

"Barlow got sprayed. Thom got Barlow." Delano paused. "I'd say they're both worse off for the experience."

"Wick Barlow!" I couldn't believe it. I would have preferred to hear there really *had* been an armed assassin on the property instead of that slimy radio-show host.

My mind worked overtime. Had Barlow trailed us to Graeme Manor tonight because he was stalking Wendela? Because he was stalking Thom? Or had he shown up without knowing we were here, hoping to get one more crack at convincing Hedda to let him examine the mummy before she sold it on the black market?

"What's he doing here?" I demanded as if I believed Barlow would have already given a full, honest confession.

"He says he's paying a social call on Lord Herbert."

"Sneaking through the desert?"

"Says he wasn't sneaking," Delano replied. "Barlow claims he just didn't want to take the time to have that big van of his inspected on the way out, so he left it down on the road to walk up to the house."

"It's more than a mile."

"I asked him about that," Delano said. "He says he walks all the time because he never knows what he might see when he's out under the stars. Things are always looking up in his line of work, you know."

"Then his is the only one," I muttered. In my mind I could hear Barlow deliver the explanations with the sincerity of a newly scrubbed deacon out collecting fast offerings. "What about the guard? Why didn't he walk right past him?"

"Says he did," Delano reported. "Says the guard was busy. Says he waved at the kid, even." His voice lowered. "It was Bertram, Sam. Might have happened."

I stamped my foot in frustration. Wick Barlow was the kind of man who could steal the moon from the sky in front of the whole world and still come up with a plausible alibi. He wasn't worth the effort it had taken the skunk to spray him.

"Casey wants you to find out what Lord Herbert has to say about all this," Delano continued. "Try to get him to press charges for trespassing at least."

"He won't," I guessed aloud.

"You're probably right, but ask anyway." He paused for a moment and I heard Thom's voice. "Good point," Delano said. To me he added, "Tell Lord Herbert you think Barlow is stalking Wendela."

I nodded, but Delano couldn't hear what was left of my marbles rattle around inside my head.

"The police are here," he continued, "but they're not sold on the idea of putting Barlow in the squad car." I could tell from his voice Delano was enjoying this a little too much. "Not that I blame them. Anyway, after you've talked to Lord Herbert I'll come up and drive you and Wendela back to Nightshade. In the meantime, I told Casey I'd run into town for some tomato juice and that de-skunk gunk."

"Get lots," I suggested, remembering how many times we'd had to douse Clueless after a camping trip on which the Weimaraner had advanced when she should have retreated. "Get gallons."

So Thom had had to take out a guy recently sprayed by a skunk, I thought on my way back inside to see Lord Herbert. *Unfortunate, indeed.*

My mind reviewed Thom's life since he'd met me: faux arrest, cracked skull, job demotion, totaled squad car, broken window, murder attempt, suspension, and now being rendered putrid. Talk about a series of unfortunate events. Thom probably thought he'd be better off hanging out with Lemony Snicket's Count Olaf than he was with me.

And if he did think that, I'd think he was probably right.

ACROSS
　　18 Negative correlative used to connect two alternatives:
　　　　"Wick Barlow has neither sense _____ sensitivity"
DOWN
　　24 Eccentric; With "ball," it would describe most of the
　　　　characters in this story

Chapter 22

I sat at Uncle Eddie's desk the next night frowning down at the pencil in my hand. Like many of its boxmates, the writing utensil had been new when I took it from the drawer, and now it was ruined. At the rate I was going, Uncle Eddie would think his desk had been ransacked by a roving pack of ravenous beavers. At least that would be better than him finding out the truth—that I'd chewed his pencils to bits in fits of angst.

I reached for the legal pad and added "buy new pencils" to the bottom of my To Do list. If I added one more thing to that list I'd have to turn the paper over and use the back—or else continue it on something longer, possibly a roll of paper towels. So far, besides the many tasks associated with trying to keep Nightshade from folding before Uncle Eddie's next daily phone call from Paris, there were these items:

23) *Convince Delano that Chaiya is not in love with Thom Casey.*

24) *Convince Chaiya that I am not in love with Thom Casey.*

25) *Convince* myself *that I am not in love with Thom Casey.*

26) *Convince Wendela that despite her being in love with Lord Herbert, she can't marry him because the state of Arizona does not issue marriage certificates for the uniting of minor lords and missing persons.*

27) Tell Thom Casey and Lord Herbert who Wendela is and where I found her before request for said marriage certificate arises and they find out for themselves.

28) Buy dental floss to remove pieces of wood from between teeth.

29) Buy new pencils.

Number twenty-seven was circled and had an arrow indicating it should be moved up my list of priorities. The last thing I'd heard Lord Herbert say as we left the manor the night before was, "Ah, Samantha! 'That I should love a bright particular star, and think to wed it.'" I didn't need Thom to tell me Lord Herbert was barding again. Nor did I need him to tell me what the quote meant. It meant trouble.

It was trouble I didn't know how to handle. Who could have predicted that after only three dates (if you counted the Mummy Mystery Dinner, the visit to the hospital, and the canapés and punch as dates), twelve dozen roses, and innumerable sighs of bliss, Lord Herbert Graeme and Miss (Ms.? *Mrs.?*) Wendela Doe would resurrect a geriatric version of *Romeo and Juliet* and want to take it on the road? Talk about a tragedy with comic overtones. Or maybe it was a comedy with a tragic outcome. Whatever it was, it was impossible to produce.

I crossed out number twenty-seven and put a star by number twenty-six instead. Then I circled the star. Then I underlined the task. Then I thought about it for another minute before wadding up the To Do list and chucking it across the room. I may not be good at guarding mummies, but I am terrible at breaking hearts. I'd go back to number twenty-seven after all. I'd confess to Thom the very first chance I got. That way, I could be tucked safely away in a jail cell while somebody else explained to Lord Herbert and Wendela why they could never wed.

I stuck the pencil back in my mouth and pulled out the second list I'd been working on. It was labeled "People Who

Might Want to Kill Thom Casey," but it was essentially a roster of people who had attended Lord Herbert's mummy unveiling—the host, the guests, the servants, and even the people employed by Nightshade. I'd already crossed most of the names off the list; only about a half dozen remained.

I stared down at the list for a full minute. Then I took the pencil from between my teeth and crossed out the violinist. I'd now eliminated all the people I thought had only *one* possible reason to use Harrison as bait to kill Thom. In other words, if the *only* motive I could establish for a person wanting to get rid of Casey was fear he'd finger them for stealing the mummy, I crossed him or her off my list.

I wanted to discuss my theories with Thom. If only he would call me. How long was he going to hold a grudge about that stupid skunk—and the window and the squad car and the knot on his head and the false arrest and the still-missing runaway—anyway? Or if, as Knute said, he wasn't holding a grudge, what *was* he doing?

I looked at the telephone for the tenth or twelfth time that night, but staring at it still didn't make it ring. I looked back down at my list and frowned. Some of the remaining names weren't plausible suspects—Lord Herbert, for instance. On the other hand, if whatever it was Thom seemed to know about him was bad, then he, Hedda, and Harrison all had motive for wanting Thom dead. I left the odd trio at the top.

Then I looked at the next name: Wick Barlow. I hadn't crossed it out yet because . . . well, mostly because I disliked and distrusted the man. At least I'd had a measure of satisfaction (read: *revenge*) for him tailing me and Wendela. His scheduled live broadcast the night before had been replaced with a "Best of Barlow"—what with the host being busy avoiding arrest and having to deodorize himself and all. Believe me when I say Barlow was so putrid even his listeners on the East Coast could have smelled him through their radios. (Okay, don't believe me. But it *was* bad.)

The next name on my list was Delano's. Despite the fact he didn't seem quite passionate enough about Chaiya to actually commit a crime of passion, the motive was there.

I had my own name too. After all, who had a stronger motive to wish Thom Casey off the police force—if not the planet— than me? But I crossed myself off the list in the next second because not only did I know I hadn't set Casey up, I knew absolutely that I didn't want him dead. I wanted Thom . . .

Maybe that last sentence should have ended with a period instead of ellipses.

Or maybe it shouldn't. Maybe what I wanted was for him to go safely back to a university somewhere and stay out of my life.

Or maybe I wanted . . .

Frustrated and not knowing *what* I wanted, I wadded up the stupid list and tossed it across the room after the first. As I did, the door opened, hitting the ball of paper and bunting it into the electric chair.

"Am I out?" Knute asked from the doorway. As always, he was right on time for our nightly staff meeting. He ambled over to the chair and picked up the "foul ball" rather than sitting on it.

I bit my lower lip as he unfolded it. "That's nothing important," I said, hoping he'd throw it away without looking at it.

"'People Who Might Want to Kill Thom Casey,'" Knute read aloud. "I see you've crossed off your own name. Change your mind, did you, Sam?"

"Yes," I said. "I mean, no. I mean . . ."

"I know what you mean," Knute said.

I hoped it was more a platitude than a statement of fact.

He scanned the rest of the names, then looked up, bemused. "Delano?"

I should have known better than to jot my random thoughts down on paper. At least when I keep them in my head nobody but me knows how stupid they are.

"Well, Chaiya thinks she's in love with Thom, and we all think Delano's in love with Chaiya, so—"

"So who's in love with Kodiak?" Delano asked from the doorway. "Casey?"

"No!" I said too quickly and too loud besides. "Nobody's in love with Chaiya!"

"What's *that* supposed to mean?" Chaiya asked. She'd slipped past Delano to stand just inside the door with her fists on her hips.

Her eyes narrowed like those of a cat about to pounce, and I knew I was in trouble. Like any intelligent mouse, I instinctively shrank down in Uncle Eddie's chair. "It doesn't mean anything," I squeaked. "Nothing I say means anything."

"Amen!" Knute and Delano cried out.

Okay, they didn't really say it, but I know they thought it.

One side of Chaiya's burgundy lips rose. "Then you *do* think Thom Casey is enameled with me."

"Yes," I said, inching up a little and thanking my lucky stars Chaiya's tenuous grasp on word power—mistaking *enameled* for *enamored*—had offered me an easy out. "If ever I've seen someone enameled with you, it's Thom Casey." That was the gospel truth. Every time Chaiya approached Thom he had a definite glazed look about him. (When I approached him, he looked terrified. Or he should have.)

"Hmm," she said. "That could be a problem for him."

"It could?"

Chaiya unclenched her fists and used her fingers to tangle her hair. As she did so, she sighed melodramatically. "See, I've been thinking . . ."

(This was a dangerous thing since my cousin is about as good at it as I am.)

" . . . when I marry Thom . . ." She reconsidered and started the sentence again. "*If* I marry Thom, I'll be Chaiya Coco Casey. Does that sound poetic to you?"

"It sounds like you've got whooping cough," Delano said.

I expected Chaiya to turn on Delano. I didn't expect her to turn toward him and giggle. "You're right." Then she sighed again, but deeper. "Poor Thom. I'll have to tell him it's over between us. Do you think he'll ever reconnoiter from being enameled with me?"

"Yes," I said. "I mean, no. I mean . . ." It was long past time to change the subject. "Is Wendela all right out there?"

Chaiya leaned out the door to peek into the reception area. "Are you all right out there, Wendela?"

I'd meant it as a hint to go tend the woman, not a request for information. I tried again. "Would you keep a close watch on Wendela while I meet with Knute and Delano? Don't take your eyes off her, okay?"

It wasn't something I could explain, but after months of getting to know Wendela I'd come to recognize the peculiar "time to climb a billboard" glint in her eye. The glint was growing brighter every night, as was my concern.

"Keep her occupied doing her petit point," I suggested, although I knew using some of the soft floss to tie Wendela's ankle to the desk would probably have been an even better idea.

Chaiya nodded and took a step backward. "Are you through with the computer, Sammy, or do you want me to leave that Shakespeare page open?"

"I'm through," I said, embarrassed I'd forgotten to exit the website. In the next second I wondered *why* I felt guilty for "getting caught" cramming a little culture into my brain. How would any of them know I was trying to take up the arcane sport of barding, hoping to impress a guy I hardly knew?

I looked into three separate sets of eyes and knew they *all* knew. Heck, Quoth the raven probably knew I had a major crush on a certain literate police officer.

But I was not going to confirm it. "I was, um, looking for a quote to open with tonight," I said.

Knute played along. "'Course you were. Find anything appropriate for Nightshade?"

"Well," I said, returning the smile he was hiding behind his fist, "I did happen upon, 'True is it that we have seen better days' from *As You Like It.*"

Delano grinned. "'The worst is not so long as we can say, this is the worst.' *King Lear.*"

I ask you, can *everybody* in the world quote Shakespeare except for me? (And then tell me what Delano meant by that crack.)

"But the quote I wrote down," I continued, "is from *Much Ado About Nothing.*" I looked at Knute, remembering what he'd told me the night we first met Thom. "'O, what men dare do! What men may do! What men daily do, not knowing what they do.'"

It was profound. Probably.

"I know what we're doing," Delano said, rolling his eyes. "We're wasting time. Doesn't anybody but me work around here?"

"Yes," I said, reaching for the notepad and picking up my masticated pencil. "You should see *my* To Do list." My eyes narrowed as I waited for him to make another crack—about much ado about my nothing—but he forbore. Mollified, I said, "You go first, Delano."

Twenty minutes later, Delano and Knute had reported the status of their current cases and were ready to go to work on their next. As the younger man loped out into the reception area, Knute approached Uncle Eddie's desk with my crumpled suspect list still in hand.

"I wouldn't throw this away quite yet," he said, smoothing it out in front of me.

I looked down at it sheepishly. "I don't really think Delano wants to kill Thom."

"No," Knute said, "but a good detective would list him just the same."

It might not have been a full-blown compliment, but I chose to take it as one and smiled up at my colleague. "Thanks, Knute."

When he sat on the edge of Uncle Eddie's desk, I half expected it to tilt like a seesaw, but it didn't.

"I may have found that kid who robbed the store," he said, his face now grim. "But I don't know for sure since all his records have been sealed."

"Well, he *is* a juvenile," I pointed out. "How did you find him? Did you talk to the gunman?"

I knew that set of records couldn't have been sealed, not when the loser had already spoken to reporters and had a lawsuit filed in his behalf. It was crazy, but nobody seemed to remember that *he'd* been the one caught committing an armed robbery—or worse. The way the press told it, he came off as a hero while Thom was made to look like a villain.

"Yeah, I talked to the punk," Knute said.

I wondered where the customary eighteen-page report was and said so.

Knute shook his head. "What I got from him wasn't worth a report. It wasn't worth the ten minutes I invested." His thick lips turned down in disgust. "He didn't say anything you haven't read in the papers, Sam. He's rehearsed every syllable some lawyer's fed him, and he repeats them over and over like a trained parrot. I don't know where they dug him up, but he's a cocky little—"

Knute stopped himself midword, but I already knew the appellation wouldn't have been positive. Frankly, I was surprised. Knute Belanoff was the least judgmental person I'd ever met. As far as I knew, despite working in a business where lowlifes populate much of the territory, he'd never met a person he didn't like—or at least try to understand and pity. This kid, apparently, was a first.

"At least he told you who his friend was," I said.

"Not a chance," Knute said. "That's the last thing he'd tell me. That's the last thing he'd tell anybody, most likely."

The way he said it—and the look on his face—gave me the creeps. As usual, he was telling me something without telling me.

"But you said you thought you found the other kid," I reminded him. "How could you have done that with nothing to go on?"

"I had plenty to go on," the big man said. "I had about two dozen eyewitnesses at the scene before the punks were hauled off."

"That's true," I admitted, knowing I should have realized it sooner. "Then somebody else ID'd him for you."

"Nope," Knute said. "Nobody on the streets would talk. Not to me and not to Andrew Jackson."

Now that was strange. With the right denomination bill in his pocket, there was nothing Knute couldn't find out.

"That was strange," Knute said, echoing my thoughts. "At least it was until I factored in that girl you and Thom were looking for. All she did was pose for a picture, and the next thing you know she's dead of an overdose. With just one needle mark on her arm, I might add. You can't blame the people, Sam. They're afraid."

"Of what?"

"Of this." He pulled an envelope from the pocket of his jacket. "I played a hunch. Fortunately, I have friends in low places."

The envelope in his hand was county stationery—from the office of the coroner, in fact. I felt the blood drain from my face and pool in my throat.

"Think you'd recognize the kid?" Knute asked.

I couldn't swallow, but I managed to nod.

Knute removed two photos from the envelope. "This first one is the most likely. He's a John Doe. Druggie. Runaway. Lived on the streets."

He held the picture in front of me, but it was a couple of seconds before I opened my eyes and looked at it. The photo was black-and-white and grainy, but there was no doubt in my mind. That corpse was Bobblehead. I nodded and closed my eyes until Knute took the picture away.

He frowned. "That's what I thought. Poor kid." He was his old, sympathetic self again when it came to this half of the robbery duo. "He was desperate for money and had the added convenience of not being missed if he turned up dead."

And he *had* turned up dead. Almost immediately—just like Taryn's sister. If Chaiya were here to call it convenience instead of coincidence, I knew she'd be right. What I didn't know is what kind of monster was loose on the streets.

"What did Thom say?" I asked at last.

"I haven't talked to him."

I looked up in surprise. "You have to tell him what you found."

Knute shook his head. "Thom knows. According to my contact in the morgue, he'd already been there and seen the body."

"Working a hunch?" I asked.

"Probably a tip," Knute said. "Casey still has a whole lot of friends in the Phoenix PD."

"And maybe an enemy?" I whispered, knowing that no other answer made sense.

"Yeah," Knute said, his dark face sober. "And maybe an enemy."

ACROSS

33 With *"word,"* it's the type of puzzle I love; With
   "double," it's what was about to happen to Thom—
   again

49 Kind of list which, for obsessive people like me, tends
   to become very long (two words)

DOWN

7 Unless you're like Chaiya, crossword puzzles and Reader's
   Digest help increase this (two words)

20 Edgar Allen Poe: "__ the raven, 'Nevermore!'"; Beloved
   stuffed bird in Uncle Eddie's office

Chapter 23

It was a dark and stormy night.

Not really. I just couldn't resist slipping that in somewhere.

But Friday night *was* dark, if dry and mostly cloudless. And my mood as I sat at Uncle Eddie's desk was decidedly stormy.

It had been four days since we'd visited Graeme Manor. I hadn't seen or heard from Thom since. Knute said it didn't have anything to do with our series of unfortunate events, but rather with the danger Thom faced since the death of Bobblehead. He said they had agreed I should "concentrate on other cases" besides the councilman and the mummy, since Mermann and Harrison were both implicated in this thing, one way or another.

Despite myself, I had to admire Knute's nerve in telling me this to my face. (Knute Belanoff is a very brave man.) I did not, however, appreciate the decision they had reached, no matter Knute's insistence that they both wanted only to "protect" me.

After Knute left the office on Wednesday night (and after I stopped throwing things at the door he'd exited), I tried to feel "protected" in a good way. But not even my crush on Thom could help me pull it off. Unlike Chaiya, I know what protected means. It means secluded, sheltered, *confined.* While I felt all those things, mostly I felt furious. Then I felt

offended. Then I felt rejected. Then I felt humiliated.
Then—

Never mind. It would take a thesaurus full of negative
adjectives to describe me on that night and the days that
followed. Over and over I mentally recited the Prayer of St.
Francis of Assisi:

> . . . *where there is injury, (let me sow) pardon; where*
> *there is doubt, faith; where there is despair, hope; where*
> *there is darkness, light; and where there is sadness, joy. O*
> *Divine Master, grant that I may not so much seek to be*
> *consoled, as to console; to be understood as to under-*
> *stand; to be loved as to love; for it is in giving that we*
> *receive; it is in pardoning that we are pardoned . . .*

I've loved the words of that creed ever since a friend gave
it to me in high school. (And I'm not alone in admiring it.
It's been quoted in general conference several times.) I've
written it in every one of my journals and, hopefully, onto
the tablets of my heart. If superheroes are required to take an
oath of office, I think this must be what they say.

As always, St. Francis's prayer—and prayers of my own—
helped. By Friday night I was no longer angry at Knute and
Thom. I still didn't feel protected, but I didn't feel resentful,
either. I'd settled on two different things to feel—resigned
and dejected.

As negative as they were, I just couldn't get over those
last two no matter what I did. How could I believe in
myself when two men I respected and admired and even
loved had made it clear they didn't believe in me? Neither of
them thought I was a decent detective, let alone a superhero.

I stared out the window, wondering if I'd been wishing
on the wrong star all these years.

Or if I'd had the right star but the wrong wish.

I leaned back and let the soft leather of Uncle Eddie's chair swallow me whole. Maybe this career didn't fit me any better than the chair. Maybe I'd had the right star and the right wish, but I'd gone about it the wrong way. Maybe my father was right. Maybe I should quit Nightshade and go back to school. I could get a master's degree and work at Camp Sundown with kids like Arjay. Or I could get a doctorate and maybe help right the wrongs at a mental hospital somewhere.

Or maybe I should just give up star-wishing, take off the mask, fold up the cape, and get a life. Who was I to think I could fight crime, right wrong, and vanquish evil anyway?

Not that I hadn't tried. I'd tried, all right. Tried and failed.

Instead of crying (which was my first choice), I started a letter of resignation. I got as far as "Dear Uncle Eddie" when the intercom buzzed.

"I'm leaving early," Chaiya said. "I have a date with that buff extenuator."

"Extenuator?" I asked, because I just had to know.

"You know, Sammy. A guy who extenuates bugs."

"Right," I said. I'd seen the guy around our apartment complex and knew Chaiya had accurately noted his physique even if she was a little hazy on his job description. I sighed. "Does he have a brother?"

"I don't know. Want me to ask?"

"Yes, please." If necessity is the mother of invention, desperation is the sister of stupidity. (And don't bother reading that last sentence again. It won't make any more sense the second time around.) In other words, I needed to assure my heart that my mind was serious about writing off Thom Casey, and a date might help. Since Chaiya manages to come across more men in a day than the average Marine Corps recruiter, she was my best bet to set one up.

"Anyway," Chaiya said, "which car do you want?"

"Mine," I replied. "But thanks for asking."

Forty-eight hours earlier—back when I still had delusions of grandeur and dreams of showing Knute and Thom I could hold my own as a private investigator—I'd borrowed Chaiya's Nissan, dropped Wendela off at Graeme Manor, and gone downtown to stake out the red-light district where once before I'd scared off a runaway kid and caught Councilman Mermann red-handed.

This time I had no luck—bad or good. Taryn was nowhere to be seen. The councilman had learned his lesson, and by the end of a long, depressing night, so had the detective. I was through with stakeouts. I was through keeping vampire hours. I was through with Nightshade. And there was *one* perk. If I started going to school days and sleeping nights, I'd never have to hear another of Wick Barlow's broadcasts.

The radio-show host had been even more pompous than usual the last few nights, but his vow to give his listeners "a real scoop" had taken on a desperate edge to my ear. The desperation didn't surprise me. It was a pretty safe bet he didn't have Hermes—and couldn't interview a mummy if he did have him—and I *knew* he'd never get Wendela because I would remove his vocal chords with my bare hands before I'd let him chat her up coast-to-coast. So, like the rest of the insomniacs in America, I waited for Wick Barlow to reveal his hand.

Unlike the rest of America, I also watched for him. Just in case.

But I never saw him. Either he'd stopped tailing me or he'd gotten better at it.

The intercom buzzed again. "Don't forget that Arjay's playing video games in the research room," Chaiya reminded me. "I took him to pick up some more of those magazine prescriptions of his, but you're supposed to take him home."

"Like I would forget Arjay," I told Chaiya, feigning offense to cover my guilt. I already had forgotten him.

"And Wendela's leaning out the window staring at billboards again."

Uh, oh. I pushed back Uncle Eddie's chair.

"I'm leaving now, Sammy," Chaiya said, clicking off the machine to prove she meant it.

"I'm leaving too," I told Quoth, as I picked up the beginnings of my letter of resignation and stuck it in my jacket pocket next to the donuts and crossword puzzle. "And I'm not coming back."

***

"I have to stop at the police station," Arjay announced as we neared the brick building on our way home to Shady Acres. "Officer Casey took my brochure last Friday for the other guys to look at. I reeeeeeeeally need it back," he added when I didn't slow the car. "The subscriptions are due Monday."

"There won't be any subscriptions, Arjay," I said reasonably. "Officer Casey meant well, but he hasn't been to the station except to defend himself. He certainly couldn't have sold magazines for you."

"Those magazines sell themselves," Arjay insisted, reciting the company spiel I'd heard so many times before. "All you have to do is leave a brochure and let people know it's for a good cause."

I couldn't argue with the "good cause" part, and he knew it. The money raised went to a summer camp for children with XP where the campers sleep days and get up at sundown to ride horseback, swim, race go-carts, and do all the other fun activities most kids can do while the sun shines. Camp was one of the highlights of Arjay's life. Although our parents paid his way, Arjay was a perpetual fund-raiser-in-progress who donated every penny he earned to "camperships" for needy kids. Who was I to discourage such irrepressible charity—and free enterprise?

I slowed and pulled into a loading zone, hoping he wouldn't be too discouraged when there were no takers on his brochure. "Hurry up," I said. "I'll wait here with Wendela."

I leaned back in my seat with a smile as I watched my little brother run up the wide stairs. The smile was short-lived.

"Hello, pretty lady," a semifamiliar voice said, tapping on my window.

You know why most superheroes wear masks? It's so their facial expressions won't give them away.

"Hey," Bob Monroe said, making a motion for me to roll down the window. "I'm a good guy, remember?"

Probably he was a good guy—or at least a good-enough guy. On the other hand, I'd seen *The Wolf Man.* Remember that rhyme the old gypsy recites? *E'en the man who is pure in heart and says his prayers by night may become a wolf when the wolfbane blooms and the autumn moon shines bright.* The autumn moon was plenty bright, and no wolfbane would be required to turn Thom's ex-partner into a wolf. I'd figured that out at Graeme Manor the night the mummy disappeared.

But since I'm no Red Riding Hood, I'm not particularly afraid of wolves. I rolled down the window. "Hello, Officer Monroe," I said. It was then I realized I was illegally parked. "Shall I move the car before or after you give me the ticket?"

"You have me confused with Dudley Do-Right," he said, leaning against the door. "I came over because I'm glad to see you."

If this was a continuation of last week's come-on, I was not interested. "Because?"

He grinned. "Because you saved me a call to Nightshade to ask you to meet me later."

"Business or pleasure?"

"It's always a pleasure to see you."

"Uh, huh." Monroe was flirting with me again, but there was an edge to his voice and something about his face that told me flirtation wasn't the only thing on his mind.

"It's business," he said.

Now I was interested. Maybe he knew something that could help Thom. For Thom's sake I would have flirted back, but frankly, I'm not very good at it. "What kind of business?"

He leaned into the car and lowered his voice. "I may be able to help you find something you've lost."

"What?" I asked, thinking the only thing I'd lost recently was my mind for letting him get this close to me.

"Meet me tonight and find out."

I drew in a breath. Bob Monroe smelled of cologne, tobacco, and self-confidence. It wasn't an aroma I trusted.

"No," I said. "Tell me here and now or don't tell me at all."

His eyes flicked toward the police station then back to me. "We can't talk here. There are eyes everywhere."

My own eyes widened. It sounded like a line from a movie, but it was delivered with the sincerity of a Jimmy Stewart one.

"Nightshade?" I suggested.

"They're watching Nightshade."

Who? I wanted to cry out. *Who's watching me?* But I knew Monroe couldn't—or wouldn't—tell me, so I said instead, "Where, then?"

"I'm working undercover tonight, but I can slip away for a few minutes. You know the old Estrella Planetarium downtown?"

I nodded. The erstwhile museum had stood empty on Van Buren for more than a decade after its holdings were moved to a new, state-of-the-art facility. The city argued to raze it, and the historical society argued to restore it for listing on the National Register. While they debated, the once-spectacular edifice bided its time, housing vermin and falling into ruin. It practically defined creepy.

"How about a Wendy's?" I suggested, thinking the more light and people around when I met Monroe the better.

"Too far out of my area." He acted genuinely sorry, but it might really have been an act. "I understand if you don't trust me," he said, reading my face like a comic book. "And you're right—it's not a good idea for you to go downtown. Forget it."

"No," I said, angry at myself for hesitating in the first place. Until I turned in that letter of resignation to Uncle Eddie, I was still an investigator. If Monroe knew about something I'd lost, it had to be either the mummy or the pictures of the councilman. Either way, I ought to hear what he had to say, no matter where he wanted to say it. "The museum is fine. What time?"

"One? One-thirty?"

"I'll be there."

I waited for him to say, "Come alone," like in the old detective movies, but he didn't say it. He winked at me and walked away.

I would go alone, of course—no matter what Monroe said or didn't say. I mean, who would I take? Wendela? Arjay? Not likely. And I couldn't call Knute or Thom. They'd lock me in Uncle Eddie's office and go in my place. There was no way I'd let that happen.

Dark or light, stormy or clear, this was in all likelihood the last night I'd be a private investigator. I'd darn well better make the most of it.

ACROSS

   1   End of day; Camp in New York state for kids with XP

  60   Portent; Something sometimes associated with ravens or bluebirds

DOWN

   2   "The _____"—fanciful ghost story about kids with xeroderma pigmentosum (starring Nicole Kidman)

  23   Private Eye; The "I" in PI

Chapter 24

As it turned out, I didn't go alone to meet Bob Monroe at the planetarium.

That's because I took Arjay and Wendela to Shady Acres first and found the place in an uproar. One of the residents had suffered a heart attack, and although the paramedics had just left with the patient, my mother and Consuela had their hands full comforting the other residents who had been awakened by lights and sirens. I knew Arjay wouldn't be a problem. In fact, he pitched right in making hot chocolate and helping out the way I wished I could have.

But I couldn't stay long, and I couldn't leave Wendela behind. At least I couldn't leave her behind and expect to find her any closer to the ground than the satellite dish when I returned. So, as unlikely as our partnership was, I took her downtown to help me sleuth. Actually, I was glad she was there, since a line Thom had quoted to Lord Herbert kept going through my mind: *It's mad to trust the tameness of a wolf.*

Something like that.

So, just after 1:00 A.M. I parallel-parked my prized V-dub in a tiny open space between a pile of broken bottles and a wino sleeping it off in the gutter. (It was the best spot on the street.) Then I picked my way carefully to the curb and opened the door for Wendela.

"We're here?" she said, looking around happily. "How nice."

(I think I've already mentioned Wendela is very easy to please.)

I looked up at the imposing façade of the old Estrella Planetarium and regretted not asking Officer Monroe where, specifically, I was supposed to meet him. Choosing the most obvious rendezvous site, I led Wendela up a few wide stairs to the point where thick chains and a rusty padlock held the front doors closed. I waited there for less than a minute before I changed my mind. It was too open between the high columns and too near the main street besides. I felt vulnerable even *with* the pepper spray I *hadn't* forgotten to tuck into my pocket.

"Let's go around to the side," I told Wendela.

She followed obediently and silently. Her eyes didn't widen at the incredible sights there were to see in these surroundings. Instead she seemed to take it all in and look for more.

I reached for her hand when she lagged a half-step behind. "Stay with me, okay?"

"Yes, Samantha," she said, but her head turned back as we rounded the corner. I knew she was looking at the long, narrow fire ladders and judging the distance of the lowest rungs from the ground.

"Stay with me, Wendela," I repeated, and tightened my hold on her fingers. "This will only take a few minutes, then we'll drive up Camelback Mountain and look at the stars."

"Lovely!" she said, her head swiveling back into place.

I sighed in relief. "Let's wait here," I suggested, stepping into a narrow alcove. It was much quieter on this side of the building. We could wait in the deep shadows without being seen by passersby.

I positioned Wendela by a door and released my hold on her hand, but I still took the precaution of standing in front of her to block any attempt she might make to wander.

"May we go inside?" she asked.

"No," I said, staring down the alley to watch for the undercover officer. "The doors are all locked. This museum's been—" Before I could add, "locked up tight for almost twenty years," Wendela had opened the door. I hesitated, then pulled a flashlight from my pocket and shined the beam into the room.

Was Monroe already in there? Had he left the door open for me to follow?

Wendela's eyes followed the beam of light. "Why, Samantha," she exclaimed. "It's beautiful! How thoughtful of you to bring me here."

She slipped through the door while I was still deciding if we should go inside. I watched her glide across the room and stand in its center, bathed in moonlight from a circle of windows in the rotunda high above. It was so surreal I almost expected an unseen orchestra to strike up a new tune—"Wendela of the Welkin"—as she stood, enraptured, among the stars.

Someone, sometime had painted an incredible mural of the galaxy in the lobby of the planetarium portion of the museum. The colors had faded with time, and now, under the moonlight, the effect was ethereal and otherworldly. I could almost believe we'd stumbled through a portal into another galaxy.

Suddenly, a thought came to me that could explain at least part of the enigma that was Wendela.

"Did you work here?" I asked breathlessly.

She smiled but didn't stop twirling slowly in circles to take it all in. "Why, no, Samantha. Did you?"

I shook my head, but pressed on. "But you've *been* here?"

"Oh, never. But I do love it! Let's come back often." She stopped twirling and swayed a little on her feet. "Have you been here before?"

"Once," I admitted. To give her mind time to think this through and possibly catch up, I explained, "I was here on a field trip. I think it was in second grade. It was a long time ago—just before they closed the planetarium and museum for good. I barely remember it."

"Why would they close a place so grand?" Wendela asked. "Why . . . why . . . I could *live* here!"

"But you didn't live here?" I asked, trying one last time to jog her memory.

"No."

"I just thought . . . Well, you do say you came from the stars." I waved a hand up at the painted galaxy.

Wendela looked around and laughed. Even in this large, empty room the sound was clear and melodic. "I lived among the *stars*, Samantha," she said. "The *real* stars."

I nodded and forced a smile. At least I tried to force a smile. I'm afraid it looked more like a grimace.

"Herbert says he'll take me back there for our honeymoon," she confided. "But only to visit because he'd miss Graeme Manor so. And I'd rather live with Herbert than with the stars, even."

My head hurt. Or was it my heart?

"Oh, Samantha!" she cried. "Don't pucker your face so. You'll come to live at the manor too!" She clapped her hands in delight. "You will, won't you?"

I didn't respond because I couldn't. How could I ever explain to this sweet, guileless woman that not only would she and Herbert never honeymoon among the stars, they couldn't go as far as the local courthouse for a marriage license.

"We must bring Herbert here, Samantha!" Wendela exclaimed. "He'll love it as I do."

As Wendela held out her long, slender arms to embrace the faux cosmos, there was a loud thud and a small, startled cry from an adjacent room.

"This way," I said, training the light on the hall from which the sound had come and moving toward it. In the next moment I remembered *again* that discretion sometimes really is the better part of valor and stopped to call out, "Hello? Officer Monroe?"

There was no answer.

I pulled Wendela from her welkin and led her cautiously down a short hall into the next chamber.

It was a burial chamber.

A chill ran down my spine at the sight of the ochre-and-umber walls. Maybe I remembered this place better than I thought I did, because I knew at once I'd been here before. Unlike the rotunda, I'd never forgotten this room.

A priceless display devoted to the Egyptian Book of the Dead had been the last traveling exhibit to visit Estrella before its closure. The mummy and its spooky trappings for the next world had terrified me and given me nightmares for years. (Possibly this was because the sadist docent had gone out of his way to mention that child slaves were occasionally sealed alive into tombs to serve their mummified masters.) I had cried and hidden behind my mother when I was seven and, frankly, I didn't like the feel of this place much better at twenty-three.

I looked around. Since the museum had been slated to close as soon as the exhibit moved on, nobody had bothered to take away the high columns or fake funerary jars. Nor had they painted over the hieroglyphics. After sixteen years, I still remembered that those symbols were a portion of a prayer designed to bring the dead back to life. With the plaster sarcophagus set into one wall open and filled with snack-food wrappers, it looked as if the incantation had worked and the mummy had just stepped out for another Hershey bar—or to murder an unsuspecting archeologist—and would return momentarily for me. My mind went into imagination overload. It wouldn't have surprised me in the least if a panel had opened in the wall and Boris Karloff, as Imhotep, appeared. Or Imhotep himself, for that matter.

Just before I screamed for my mommy, a man's voice called out for me. "Here!" I croaked. "We're in here."

In another minute Bob Monroe strolled into the room. I've never been happier to see a man in my whole life. (Of

course, at that point I would have cheerfully welcomed the
Wolf Man himself, if only to get my mind off mummies.)

"I thought I was early," he said.

"We're earlier," I said with an emphasis on the "we" so
he'd see I'd brought a chaperone. "The side door was open."

"I saw that," he said. "The lock's been broken. I'll have to
see what I can do about securing it when we leave."

"Someone else is here," I told him. "We heard—"

"Rats."

"No," I insisted. "Something fell. Something big. Too big
to be knocked over by a rat."

"Did you see somebody?"

"No, but I heard—"

"Rats. The place must be full of them."

While I am normally capable of carrying on an "is so, is
not" conversation for hours if not days, I don't argue about
rats—or with them—so I dropped it. I wanted to hear what
he had to say, and I wanted to hear it fast so Wendela and I
could get out of there.

Maybe I wasn't the only one in a hurry, because Monroe
looked at his watch.

"I thought you said we were early," I said suspiciously.

"You're the only ones coming?"

"You were expecting someone else?"

"Your partner," he said, as if it should be obvious. "You're
in this together, right?"

I frowned. "Partner? You mean Knute?"

"Don't be coy."

"Forget coy," I said. "Think clueless."

Okay, I didn't say it. I didn't say anything because that
usually works better than spouting off—when I can
remember to try it.

"Casey didn't come with you?" he continued.

I figured I could now rule out Monroe as my "watcher."
Anybody who'd been spying on me would know by my

melancholy expression I hadn't spoken to Thom for days. But what did he mean by calling him *my* partner? The last partner Casey had was Monroe.

A light came on in my brain, but it was as dim as the moonlight filtering into the chamber from the hall—maybe dimmer. "You didn't want me to meet you here so you could tell me your theory about the missing mummy," I realized out loud. "I mean Lord Herbert's mummy," I amended, casting worried eyes toward the empty sarcophagus in the corner.

"Mummy?" Monroe said. "What would I know about that freaky mummy?"

"And you didn't . . ." I began again, but to myself. "And you said . . ." I paused, trying to sort out what he had said and done and what I had merely assumed. When Wendela moved away from me to examine the blue-glass scarabs on the far wall, I scarcely noticed. Instead I looked at Monroe. "Anyway, I'm here. What do you want to tell me?"

His momentary confusion faded, and his native self-confidence reasserted itself. "I might be able to get you what you need, Sam."

I wondered what that was if not Lord Herbert's mummy. A new job? Two aspirin and a good day's sleep?

"You know," he prompted. "What you 'lost' down at the police station last week."

The light in my head grew a little brighter. He *did* have the pictures. Or at least he knew who did.

Monroe smiled. "I bet you're having a tough go black-mailing the councilman without them."

At that moment, if I'd seen the mummy waltz in with the bride of Frankenstein's monster I would have believed my eyes more than I believed my ears. Blackmail? What was he talking about?

"I know what you and Casey are doing," Monroe said, his face leading me to believe he thought he was making sense. "All I want is a piece of the pie."

All of a sudden the light in my head was brighter than the flashlight in my hand. This was a sick game. Hoping to beat his partner out of the detective job, Monroe had stolen the pictures himself to frame Thom. Now that the shooting had put Thom out of the way for good, he no longer needed the pictures. His newest plan was to sell them back to me.

Or was it?

What if this wasn't a game? What if Monroe was the enemy Thom had on the force? What if, after coming to Graeme Manor, he'd had a better idea than the frame? What if he'd set up the robbery and called Harrison down to Van Buren as bait? If that was the case, Bob Monroe played for keeps.

Now that the metaphorical light was on, all the clues began to assemble themselves in my mind like in a crossword puzzle. Monroe *must* have been the one who set Thom up. Who else would know to drive the police captain by in a squad car on the very night Thom broke the rules to try to help a runaway girl? Who else could have seen the pictures on my camera? Who else but his partner knew Thom well enough to know he'd stick with the runaway girl, the Mermann deal, and the mummy case until they were solved? Certainly *nobody* else would know one phone call to Harrison Mead would keep Thom on the street long enough to be shot in cold blood.

Horrified, I backed away. Bob Monroe was no wolf. He was a monster.

As I retreated, he advanced. Since his legs were longer, we'd taken only three steps before he had hold of my elbow. "Don't you want the pictures, Samantha?"

"No!" I said, wresting my arm out of his fingers. "Get away from me! You're not going to use me the way you used those pictures. Thom didn't know who was in them, but you did! You must have conspired with the councilman to fake new ones."

"New ones?"

I ignored him. "Then you killed that poor girl who posed for you so nobody would find out what you'd done." It was like somebody had injected me with truth serum. I knew it was stupid to tell Monroe I was on to him, but I couldn't seem to close my mouth. "But that wasn't enough," I continued. "You were afraid Thom would find Taryn or figure it out himself when you followed him to Van Buren last Saturday, so you called Harrison and got him down there to keep Thom on the street until you could hire somebody to kill him. When the boys couldn't do it, you had to murder the nervous one—the one you thought would squeal."

Something flickered across Monroe's face. I couldn't positively identify it in the dim light, but it looked like the dawn of revelation. Why didn't I pay more attention to *The Incredibles*? I'd probably just written my own death sentence by monologuing. I fumbled in my pocket for the pepper spray, knowing as I did so it wouldn't be enough. "You might have used Harrison and that poor girl, but you're not going to use *me* to get another shot at Thom!" I told him, backing up against the empty sarcophagus. "You're not!" I pulled the canister from my pocket and leveled it at his wide, staring eyes.

But now I recognized the look on his face for sure. It was fear.

Not that that made any sense. Was he deathly allergic to cayenne pepper, or what?

The next thing Monroe did made even less sense. Just as I began to lower my thumb onto the button, he yelled, "She's got a gun!" and threw himself forward.

I thought he was diving for me so I fired. I missed by at least three feet, but the spray hit a column and spread out into the room. I sneezed just as Monroe lunged into one of the tall, fake funerary jars. It started a chain reaction. Before the last piece of heavy pottery crashed to the floor, Monroe had ripped open his shirt and grabbed wildly at a thin, black wire taped to his chest. Yanking the microphone free, he tossed it into the rubble and again grasped my elbow.

"Don't say anything," he hissed into my ear. "I've got to get you out of here. Now."

"Wendela!" I gasped through the burning sensation in my mouth and throat. In the few horrible minutes it had taken me to figure out Monroe, I'd forgotten her.

I cast the beam of my flashlight wildly around the chamber and tired to peer through the pepper-induced tears in my eyes.

Wendela was gone.

***

"There's no time to look for her," Monroe said. His voice was low and urgent. "Stop fighting me until I can explain."

He'd dragged me from the burial chamber in the opposite direction from where Wendela and I had come in. I had little choice but to follow since this time his grip on my arm was ironclad and I'd blinded myself with the pepper spray. I didn't know where we were. I only knew it was dark—after breaking the urns, he'd flung both our flashlights into a corner and clasped a hand over my mouth when I'd tried to protest. Moreover, somehow I'd lost my pepper spray along with my flashlight, not to mention my best friend and my bearings.

All I had left was my fear.

"Your friend will be okay," Monroe said into my ear. "It's you and Casey they want." He removed his hand from over my mouth, but kept it near my cheek in case I screamed.

I didn't scream. I could barely whisper. "Thom doesn't know I'm here."

"I hope you're right."

I had to get away from him. I had to warn Thom. I had to find Wendela. I had to call the police. The *right* police. I had to do *something* to help somebody.

As if reading my thoughts, Monroe pulled the cell phone from my pocket and laid it next to his own on the first thing we passed. "You can't help anybody if you're dead," he said, continuing to pull me along the wall where the shadows were the deepest.

He was right, but that didn't tell me if he'd meant the remark as a truism or a threat. "I won't—"

Once more Monroe's hand clamped over my mouth. I would have bit him, but my jaws don't open wide enough. My only consolation was that the watery discharge from my hopelessly running nose was sliming his smelly, rotten hand.

"Listen to me," he hissed, pulling me down behind a dais that—according to its plaque—once held the earthly remains of a wooly mammoth. He held me there and spoke in my ear, very fast and very low. "If you want to help Casey—if you want to live another ten minutes—you've got to calm down and shut up."

There was just enough light to show me his white teeth and the glint of desperation in his eyes. He looked like a wolf, but there was something about this wolf that almost inspired trust. Maybe it was his tears and swollen eyelids (he'd taken more of the pepper spray than I had). At any rate, I quit struggling to listen.

"I'm an idiot," he whispered. "They used me, Sam. I thought I was helping bust a bad cop, not setting up a good one."

He sounded sincere. Heck, he sounded anguished. I tried to nod my understanding from beneath his hand.

"This isn't a sting operation like I thought," he concluded. "It's a deathtrap. We can't call for help. Nobody will believe what we're up against."

This time I couldn't nod. I couldn't even breathe. And it wasn't because of Bob's hand or the pepper spray.

Me being stunned speechless worked well for both of us. He pulled me back to my feet and released his hold. Together we ran.

In the hall we had just exited someone brushed against a long-forgotten exhibit. Something long and hard and probably wooden crashed to the floor. It was no secret that we were being followed. Still, I'd have thought that even a maniacal, murderous stalker would at least have had the presence of mind to be subtle about it.

***

We moved through the museum in the dark, skirting an obelisk and ducking down behind an abandoned display case when Monroe heard a rustling in the corner. "Rats," he said under his breath. But he'd drawn a gun.

Normally I would be more afraid of rats than almost anything, but nothing about this night was normal. I didn't know *what* to fear—rabid vermin with inch-long fangs, Bob Monroe, or whoever he was trying to elude.

"You're going to shoot rats?" I whispered.

He didn't reply. He just pulled me back up and we kept moving.

What seemed like hours later, I realized we'd left what had been the public portion of the museum and stopped at the foot of a metal spiral staircase leading up into blackness.

"Take off your boots," Monroe instructed in a voice I hardly heard. He had removed his own shoes and slid them silently into a corner.

I tugged off my boots and pushed them after his.

"Good," he said, urging me ahead of him. "They'd make too much noise." He looked toward the top of the wrought-iron stairs. "If we make it up there, I think we can hold him off long enough."

Hold who off long enough for what?

To keep myself from screaming, I concentrated on climbing—running—up the narrow, twisty stairs. *If we make it,* he'd said. I expected at any moment to hear the blast of a revolver and feel the bullet rip into my heart.

Except for an incipient attack, my heart and I made it to the top just fine.

I practically fell onto the catwalk, and Monroe had to climb over the top of me to get off the stairs.

Whether by serendipity or design, our wanderings in the bowels of the museum below had brought us in a circle—back to the rotunda of the planetarium. But now we were high above the lobby, just beneath the small windows. Ahead, an open doorway revealed a control room for the planetarium's show. Behind us was the high, curving wall, and in front of us was another low, but blessedly solid wall. Our little catwalk circled the rotunda, but was so narrow, and had been painted to blend so perfectly with the main walls, as to be almost unnoticeable from below.

Monroe leaned back to catch his breath. "This is good," he said, swiping at his still-running nose with the back of his shirtsleeve. "There's no other way up here but those stairs."

Which goes to show what he knew.

I too had leaned back and gazed up through one of the skylights. What I saw stopped my rapidly thumping heart. There was at least *one* more way to get up this high without wings. Outside the window, Wendela clung with both hands to a weather vane that extended six or eight feet from the top of the copper dome. With her gray-streaked, golden hair and long, flowing dress billowing behind her in the breeze, she looked like a baroque angel about to take flight over the city.

"Wendela!" I cried out in horror.

Monroe clasped a hand over my mouth, but it was too late. Wendela and everybody else on the block had heard me. Wendela released one hand from the pole and used it to wave gaily at me through the window. At the same time, somewhere in the mostly empty—and surely deadly—halls below, Thomas Casey called my name.

ACROSS

    22 Symbolic carvings on sarcophagi; Chaiya's hand writing?

    44 Expire; What I sometimes said I was going to do, but
        didn't really want to

DOWN

    35 Weds; Links by commitment or custom

    36 Phoenix mountain range over which UFOs supposedly
        appeared in 1997; Fictional, erstwhile planetarium;
        Spanish for "star"

Chapter 25

If I'd still had doubts about Officer Monroe when we reached the catwalk, they evaporated the instant he saw Wendela above and heard his partner below. I stared into his shocked, frightened face and thought it was probably a mirror image of my own. (Except for the five o'clock shadow on his chin, of course.)

Before I could react—or even draw a breath—Monroe rose, leaned over the low wall, and hollered, "Casey! Get out of here! It's an ambush!" Ducking back behind the wall, he asked me if Thom was armed.

"I don't know," I said. "I gave him my uncle's gun a few nights ago."

"Good." Figuring he'd done all he could for his partner, Bob looked up at Wendela. She'd returned her free hand to the weather vane and stood with her head back, enraptured by a nightingale's view of the stars. "I'm no hero," he muttered. Another minute passed in which he alternated grinding his teeth with cursing under his breath. Then he said, "I might be able to reach her from the window. But if I startle her . . ."

He didn't have to finish the sentence. I already knew the top of that dome was at least three stories above the ground. If he couldn't reach her—or if Wendela struggled—they might both lose their balance and plunge to their deaths on the filthy streets below.

"She's done this before," I said, my heart racing with fear for her and for Thom and even for Bob. (He'd left out the part about how likely it was he could be shot from below in the rescue attempt.) "But she's never gone so *high.*"

Heedless of a bullet that could come at any moment now that we had alerted our hunter to our hiding place, Bob stood and reached for the window frame. This far above the floor, the skylight wasn't the type that could be opened. "Stay down," he told me. "But call to her and tell her I'm going to break the glass so I can pull her inside."

While I crept to the window and did as he instructed, Monroe removed his jacket and wrapped it around his fist and upper arm. "Get back," he said. As soon as I had scuttled backward to the top of the spiral stairs, he shattered the ancient pane.

Bits of glass fell gleaming toward the tile floor below like a meteor shower. I chose one bright, twinkling shard and wished the wish I always wish. Then I called out as calmly and reassuringly as I could, "A nice policeman is coming, Wendela! Do what he tells you, okay? As soon as you're inside, we'll go visit Lord Herbert and you can tell him about your adventure."

If that didn't get her to come down, nothing would.

As soon as Monroe put his head through the skylight, I started down the steps. Sure, Bob had warned Thom to get out of here, but Thom had also heard me cry out in fear for Wendela. I knew he would never leave us. What I didn't know was how I would find him—or how I could help him if I did find him.

Sometimes when the going gets tough, the tough can't go for ice cream—or even stop to consider all the whys and wherefores of their actions. They just have to believe that faith really does manage, then get going. This was one of those times. I practically flew down the stairs in my stocking feet.

Although it was hard for me to tell for sure because of the way sound echoed through the empty building, Thom's voice had seemed to come from somewhere beyond the Egyptian burial chamber, so that's where I went.

Fake tombs are plenty spooky when your imagination conjures up images of the walking dead. When you don't need an imagination to scare yourself because there really is somebody roaming the halls hoping to kill you, fake tombs are petrifying. I probably looked like a mummy myself as I approached the chamber, because I was so frozen with fear I could scarcely bend my joints.

I leaned around the corner of the doorway. The flashlights were still against the wall in one corner, so that part of the room was partially lit. But it wasn't a comforting kind of light. You know how eerie a face looks when there's a flashlight held under the chin? Well, this whole place looked like that. The hieroglyphics on the Book of the Dead seemed to twist and turn, while the plaster-and-glass scarabs set into the walls took on an unearthly, sinister glow.

I stood transfixed and stared. Unnatural light and broken funerary jars aside, there was something different about the room. I blinked and looked harder, but still couldn't place it. (The truth is that while I'm very good at crossword puzzles, I am very bad at those things in the newspaper where they show you two nearly identical pictures and challenge you to find the six differences between them. This was like that.) There *was* a difference, but I didn't know *what* it was.

At last I stepped cautiously into the room and picked my way through the debris. I'd neared the center when I thought I heard a soft scraping sound. With my heart pounding louder than any other sound, real or imagined, I squeezed myself between the column and the wall, vowing as I did so that if I lived through this I *would* give up donuts if that's what it took to pare those extra twenty pounds from my hips.

Unfortunately, I didn't realize the place I'd chosen to press my face against was the same place I'd earlier doused with pepper spray. With my nose already running, I did the only thing I could do under the circumstances. I sneezed.

Then I sneezed again.

This time I was certain I'd heard something, and it came from the hall on the other side of the chamber.

"Thom," I said. I didn't say it very loud because I was talking to God. And I didn't say it like a question because it was a prayer—and a fervent one at that.

Like all sincere prayers, this one was answered. Thom appeared in the doorway.

"Sam," he whispered.

When the right man says your name in the right way with the right look on his face, that one word is better than any love sonnet William Shakespeare ever wrote. For the first time since I'd started to fall for Thomas Casey, I had an inkling the feeling might possibly, maybe, someday—if I continued to say my prayers every night—be mutual.

Assuming we lived long enough to develop a meaningful relationship, that is.

Gun drawn but pointed carefully toward the floor, he took a step into the room and glanced toward the closed sarcophagus. That's when I knew what was different. That sarcophagus had been *open*. I remembered the empty wrappers inside it and how I'd wondered if the mummy had gone out for another snack. Now it was closed.

It must be a trap! I saw what would happen next as if on a movie screen. Thom would pass the sarcophagus on his way to sweeping me into his arms, and the lid would swing open behind him and . . .

And I would never be held in Thom's arms or hear him say my name the way I wanted him to say it forever.

That scenario wasn't going to happen as long as I was still alive and fantasizing.

Afraid to tip off the assassin I was on to him, I raised both my hands with the palms forward and used my facial expression to warn Thom to stop where he was.

He got the message and paused with Uncle Eddie's gun still in his hand.

I sprinted across the room and leaned all my weight against the ornate lid of the sarcophagus. This, I hoped, would keep the murderer inside from opening it before Thom was ready for him.

With my rear pressed against the case, I pantomimed pushing to urge Thom to find something with which to brace the lid closed.

Clearly Thom thought this was an odd time and place for charades, but he once again got the message and scanned the room.

"A column," I whispered. "Can you move it?"

Thom hesitated a couple of moments, then stuck the gun in the waistband of his jeans to tackle a column. He slid it a couple of feet, then stopped as if it had just occurred to him that he was taking directions from a lunatic.

But I knew I was right. As if to confirm my suspicions, the person inside the sarcophagus tested the lid.

"Thom!" I said urgently—and aloud this time. "Help me hold this closed! The man who wants to kill you is inside it."

"No," a deep voice said from the shadows of the opposite doorway. "He's right here." A tall man with a mustache entered the room with his gun drawn and leveled at Thom's chest. "Thank you, Miss Shade," he said. "I hadn't yet figured out how to unarm Casey. I appreciate you doing it for me."

The chuckle that followed was the worst sound I've ever heard. My stomach dropped to my toes, and I had to dig my fingers into the sarcophagus behind my back to remain upright.

Even in the dim light, the man with the evil laugh looked familiar to me—and he didn't. I thought I should know him—but I didn't know why I should. I looked then at Thom and watched the incredulity on his face change to horror. He knew this guy even if I didn't.

"Drop the weapon, Officer," the mustached man said. "Do it slow, but do it now."

My breath caught in my throat. Suddenly I *did* know who it was. The man with the gun was Captain Dix, Thom's superior on the Phoenix police force.

Clearly stunned, Thom obeyed without a word.

"Kick it toward me," the captain commanded.

Again Thom did as directed, but as he did it he stepped between me and the rogue cop.

"How chivalrous," the captain said in a tone that sent chills up my spine. "But I'm afraid you'll both have to die just the same. It turns out, Casey, that your integrity and tenacity have proven to be quite inconvenient for some very important people I know."

Dix bent to pick up the second gun, but did so without lowering his own weapon or taking his eyes off Thom. "I should have known you'd be trouble when I took you on the force. You're too much like your father."

"One of your oldest friends," Thom said. He'd found his voice by now, but still looked like he believed this was a bad dream from which he'd eventually awaken.

I knew better. This nightmare was about the realest thing I'd ever experienced.

"Yes," the captain replied. "My old friend. It's my only real regret. It will break Martin's heart when he learns that after extorting the good councilman, you and your pretty little partner here died in a sting that went south." He smiled at the expression on Thom's face.

"It won't work," Thom said, probably to convince himself. "Monroe's not the man you think he is."

I wished *I'd* shared Thom's confidence in his partner's character. It would have saved me a nasty reaction to pepper spray—not that I believed a little cayenne pepper in my face was the worst thing that was going to happen to me.

The captain's eyes narrowed. "Unfortunately, you're correct. If nothing else, he and Miss Shade turned out to be a little smarter than I'd bargained for. But it won't matter in the long run. A couple of key men down at the station think I've been working with Monroe to expose you. They won't have any trouble believing you killed him before I could get to you."

"And if they don't believe it?" Thom said. "How many people can you kill to cover your tracks, Captain?"

"As many as I have to."

No wonder I'd disliked this man since first arguing with him over Uncle Eddie's camera. (Do I have good instincts, or what?) Everything of which I'd suspected Monroe—and probably more—had been done by his boss. Now the veteran cop would kill us all to cover his tracks and keep whatever racket he and Mermann had going secure. I couldn't believe it. I'd had a lot of unlikely suspects on my "List of People Who Might Want to Kill Thom Casey," but I hadn't had *him*.

And it didn't look like there was anything anybody could do to stop him.

I don't know if what came to me then was a flash of deductive reasoning, divine inspiration, or sheer desperation under pressure. I only know that another crossword puzzle began to form in my mind. It looked like this:

```
S U R P R I S E     V             A
      A   W R A P P E R S     A C
W I L D C A R D     G     Y       T O
E     I     C   B R O K E N L O C K
N   V   D O O R     A           R
D   E     P   U   N       G R A B
E B R A S H   N   T H O M       Z
L   S     A       S   U   W   Y
A   D I X G           M   A
      O   U           M U S E U M
    O N L Y S H O T     M Y
```

Let me explain.

If you figure that, to start with, (ACROSS) you have evidence of pilfered candy *wrappers* and a *broken lock* on a *museum door,* then factor in that (DOWN) you have a street full of hungry *vagrants,* an open *sarcophagus,* and a missing *mummy,* it isn't hard to fill in more blanks (ACROSS) to determine that inside that formerly empty sarcophagus you might have a *wild card* you could use for your *only shot* at surviving the night and (DOWN) helping *Wendela* if you could *act crazy* enough to create a *diversion* and thus (ACROSS) give *Thom* one *brash* chance to *surprise* Captain *Dix* and *grab* his gun.

Got it? (That's okay. It was a little hazy in my mind too. But (DOWN) it *was* the only thing that came (ACROSS) *to* my mind's (DOWN) *eye* so I had to *run* with it, OK?)

Not that I would use an innocent bystander at their peril, of course. A self-respecting superhero would never do that. But I was desperate for a momentary diversion, and temporary insanity was the only one I could manufacture. If Thom caught on right away and acted as quickly as I knew he could, nobody had to get hurt—or murdered.

I used the heel of my foot to rap on the sarcophagus and said, "Excuse me, Mr. Mummy, sir. Sorry to bother you, but there's a guy out here with a gun who's going to kill us."

The captain took a step to the side for a better view of the crazy lady talking to a fake coffin. Even Thom made a half-turn to stare at me.

"The museum forgot to take their mummy when they moved," I said, pounding on the sarcophagus again. I sounded like a well-rehearsed "insane tour guide" at one of those haunted houses set up for Halloween. (Or maybe I sounded genuinely insane.) Either way, for a split second I had the captain's undivided attention. It was Thom's chance to make his move.

Unfortunately, I also had Thom's undivided attention, and he was too stunned to move.

"I'm getting help," I warned the captain, hoping Thom would take the hint very, very soon that this was the best—and probably only—distraction he would get. I knocked a third time. "Anybody in there?"

From inside the sarcophagus, somebody knocked back.

That was way creepy, even to me.

"I—Imhotep, I presume," I said, thinking what a nice, theatrical touch it was that my voice shook and my teeth chattered.

"Get away from that thing," the captain said, waving the gun at me and the sarcophagus.

"You can't kill a mummy," I told him. I didn't move for fear of exposing whoever was inside the crypt to the wrong side of a loaded revolver. "I mean, the thing about mummies is that they're already dead."

The captain advanced. As he neared me I felt the lid of the sarcophagus push against my hips. I leaned back to keep whoever it was inside, even though I'd probably already sealed his death by exposing his hideout.

And I'd done it for nothing. With the gun now pointed squarely at my face, Thom had lost his chance. The captain was going to kill everyone in sight and figure out how to explain all the bodies later.

Hamlet had ended better than this.

"Move!" Dix commanded me.

"Let me out!" an oratorical bass voice demanded from within the coffin.

Thom stood perfectly still. He looked like he might just be ready to die now that he'd seen and heard everything.

Right when I knew it couldn't possibly get any more bizarre, it did.

"Don't move!" a high, frantic voice called from the farthest doorway. "I have a gun! I'll shoot you! I will!"

Before anyone could take a breath, the wraithlike figure fired into the ceiling. Plaster rained down, and the sound of the shot reverberated through the empty museum like a clap of thunder.

The captain dropped a gun.

But the wraith dropped hers as well.

With a mighty shove, the occupant of the sarcophagus opened the lid from within, propelling me forward and into Dix.

We stumbled backward a couple of feet where Thom—finally proving he was as quick as I'd hoped—took away the captain's remaining gun. Then he threw Dix into the wall for good measure and whirled back toward the sarcophagus, ready to next take on whatever undead thing had exited its tomb.

It wasn't a mummy. It wasn't even the vagrant I'd expected. It was a rumpled, middle-aged UFOlogist with a microphone in one fist.

"Barlow!" Thom and I said together.

"Live and in person with a national exclusive!" the show host declared. "Every word anybody's said here has gone right from this mike onto the airwaves." He twirled the microphone like an Old West gunslinger and pointed it toward the floor. "Anything you'd like to add, Captain?"

From his place amid the rubble, the captain swore.

"The FCC's gonna slap you with one heck of a fine for saying that," Barlow observed dryly.

I turned, expecting to fall blissfully into Officer Thomas Casey's open arms. (Forget flying off like a superhero. I had new dreams now—dreams that centered on a certain well-read, gray-eyed cop.) But Thom's arms were already full of girl.

"My sister's dead!" the redheaded wraith sobbed onto his broad shoulder. "*He* killed her!"

Thom stroked the tangled mass of dirty red hair. "I know, Taryn. I'm so sorry."

"That's why I followed you," the girl moaned. "I was going to tell you what happened. I was going to ask you to help me. But when I first saw you that night, you had that woman with you and I was afraid. I kept watching, so I saw the two guys who robbed the store." Taryn's sobs increased. "I'm sorry I stole that gun you took from him, but I *had* to. Even more people were coming, and I was scared to be alone. I was scared of *him*. So—" The rest of her words dissolved into a torrent of tears.

Thom held her in his strong arms. "Everything's going to be okay now," he said.

"Do you hear sirens?" I asked suddenly. Judging by the volume coming through the thick museum walls, they were already close. Probably just outside. Had somebody called the police after all or—

Wendela!

***

It probably won't surprise you to learn that a lovely, elderly lady in a long, flowing dress can draw quite a lot of attention to herself in downtown Phoenix—even at three o'clock in the morning. At least she can if she's swinging from the top of a copper dome two hundred feet above the sidewalk, calling out to the street people to join her, and singing to the stars in a language known only to her.

But if you really want to attract a crowd, throw in a live radio remote from a widely popular, nationally syndicated talk-show host who claims to be broadcasting from within a sarcophagus and murmuring something about police corruption and mass murder.

In other words, without ever calling 911 or anybody else, we'd managed to attract almost every fire truck and patrol car in the Phoenix metro area—not to mention every insomniac and night worker. It was almost dawn before the excitement at the old Estrella Planetarium began to die down.

Exhausted, I plopped down next to Bob Monroe on a dais that—according to the plaque—had once held an ancient Roman sundial. In the middle of the room, Lord Herbert waltzed with Wendela beneath the starry, painted ceiling. Since he never missed one of Barlow's broadcasts, Herbert's limo had arrived not long after the first fleet of squad cars—well before Knute and Delano. Chaiya, who had probably been home from her date with the "extenuator" and asleep before Barlow's broadcast began, would have to read about it in the morning papers. (That's what she gets for being the odd one in the family who sleeps nights.)

"You hear any music?" Bob said, his eyes on the dancers.

"They hear the music of the spheres," I said, believing it was true. But as romantic and touching as the pair was, my eyes were on Thom. His arm was still around Taryn as he coaxed her to go with the kind, maternal social worker who had arrived more than an hour before.

"Jealous?" Monroe asked with a teasing grin.

"Of course not!" I said. Then, "Maybe a little." After all, since his last look of incredulity at me talking to a "mummy," Thom Casey hadn't glanced my way again.

"The poor girl's had it tough," Monroe said, looking around distastefully. "Can you imagine her and her sister living all alone in this big, spooky place? They were probably the only ones who knew about the broken lock." He shook his head. "I tell you, Sam, it would give me the willies."

I nodded and felt guilty. What did it say about my creed to "not so much seek to be consoled, as to console" and "not to seek to be loved as to love" when all I could do was sit there and feel overlooked and underappreciated? I should be pleased Taryn was safe at last. (And I was.) I should be pleased Thom and Bob were safe—and would probably be decorated as heroes on the force besides. (And I was.) As for Wendela . . . well, she was back on the ground and that was something. I'd still have to tell her she couldn't marry Lord Herbert, but I didn't have to tell her right now.

"It's been a long night," I said.

"Tell me about it." Monroe looked up at the high, broken skylight and gave a theatrical shudder. "Hey, that reminds me. I'm a hero! Doesn't that deserve a reward?" He pointed to his cheekbone.

Smiling, I kissed it. But when he turned his head and offered me his lips, I pulled back and scooted away for good measure.

"I said I was a hero," he said with a grin. "I never claimed to be a saint."

"You're a wolf."

"That, too." He chuckled and leaned back on his elbows. "Tell you what, pretty lady, when you're through mooning over my partner, get back to me."

Before I could reply, Wick Barlow approached. "That's a wrap," he said, stuffing the microphone into the pocket of his jacket. "I'm going back to the motel to get some sleep and figure out how I'll ever top *this* show." He turned and looked hopefully toward Wendela and Lord Herbert. "On the other hand, there is still the reason I followed you here tonight."

"I'll go on your show!" I volunteered. I would never let him interview Wendela, of course, but I did owe him something for saving all our lives. (If it hadn't been for him, we'd have all been unidentified dying objects.) As much as I hated to admit it, as stalkers go, Barlow turned out to be the kind to have. "Your listeners will be amazed by the story I'll tell about my UFO experience."

"You were abducted by aliens?" Bob asked as though it didn't surprise him much to hear it.

"No," I said. "But I've seen almost every episode of *X-Files*. I'll make it up as I go along. Barlow won't care. I mean, it's not like the woman he had on in August *really* bore Bigfoot's baby."

"I'll be in touch," Barlow chuckled. After tipping an imaginary hat to me, he sauntered off. "Stay tuned. Stay awake. Stay alert," he called back over his shoulder.

"Things are looking up!" I called after him.

And at that moment I almost believed it.

ACROSS

   39 Something upon which both waiters and policemen rely

   43 When Arjay gets up; With "Zone," it's one of the best
       TV series ever made!

DOWN

   46 Word to describe Phoenix, Thom Casey, and NONE
   of my dates

Chapter 26

About sixty-three hours later (9:00 P.M., Monday, for those of you who don't want to do the math), things were no longer looking up. I'd taken Wendela to Graeme Manor and asked Thom to meet us there. Before the night was over I expected to solve "The Mystery of the Missing Mummy" and break three hearts—my own included.

High atop Mummy Mountain, I stood on the balcony with Thom in front of the open French doors. In the ballroom at our back, a string quartet played while Herbert waltzed Wendela gracefully around the otherwise empty room. Below us in the valley, the lights of the city seemed to reflect the stars in the sky; it was like a vast mirror.

I might have been awed by the incredible beauty of it all if I hadn't already been struck by dread of what I had to say to Thom before he walked out of my life forever. (I'd heard from Knute that he had finally spoken candidly with his father and received a blessing to return to academia.) Moreover, Lord Herbert had asked him to be the best man at a wedding that could never take place. I had two tasks before me, then. I had to tell Thom about Wendela, and then I had to tell him good-bye—whether or not he turned me in for kidnapping.

"Thanks for coming tonight," I said, clutching the balcony's low wall for support.

"Thanks for asking me," he replied. "I wanted to talk to you, Sam. I—"

"No, I need to talk to you," I interrupted. "Before Lord Herbert and Wendela get their hopes up even more, there's . . . there's something you need to know." I cleared my throat, but it sounded like a whimper. "Their wedding can never happen. You—"

"'Let me not to the marriage of true minds admit impediments.'"

I looked away, unable to bear his incredible smile when I knew it would be the last time I saw it. "You don't know what I've done—"

"Yes, I do." Thom looked up into the sparkling sky. "You've wished on every star in the galaxy for the power to make the world a better place."

My heart turned over. I couldn't stand for him to say such things to me. I couldn't stand to be so close to him knowing how far apart we'd be in another moment. "But you don't know about Wendela," I murmured. "You don't know who she is because you never checked her out."

"I didn't have to check her out," Thom said. "I know who she is."

"You *couldn't* know! Uncle Eddie couldn't find out anything about Wendela's past or—"

"I had an advantage," he interrupted yet again. "I knew where she came from."

"You . . . *where?*"

The dimple I would miss so much winked into his cheek. "Wendela came from the stars." When I sank back against the wall he added, "Have you ever been to Hollywood and Vine? That's where the little brass plaques are set into the sidewalks, each bearing the name of a movie star." The dimple deepened. "Wendela lived on those streets, Sam. Literally on the street—not far from where I grew up in L.A. I met her when I was fourteen and handing out blankets for my Eagle Project. She doesn't remember me, of course, but I recognized her the first night I saw her at Graeme Manor."

"That's why you couldn't stop staring at her!"

"Yes, and I was naturally curious how she ended up with you," he said.

This was my cue to confess. I took a deep breath, but Thom pressed a finger to my lips. "Let me tell you Wendela's story," he said. "She arrived on the West Coast from Armenia in the '40s. She didn't speak English, but she was very young and beautiful, so more than one producer didn't care. Over the years she acted in a string of B movies—mostly science fiction things, though her last few films were more the Robin Hood genre, which I suppose explains the way she dresses. Those must have been the last, best days she remembers."

"You've seen her movies," I guessed.

"Every one," he admitted. "I have most of them on video. I'm undoubtedly her biggest fan."

If I hadn't already loved Thomas Casey to distraction, I would have fallen for him then and there.

"What happened to her, Thom?" I asked, amazed to be hearing the truth about Wendela at last.

"She learned to speak English, but nobody could teach her to act."

I wasn't surprised. Wendela could never pretend to be anybody but who she was.

"When she finally got too old to be a pretty extra, the jobs became fewer and farther between," Thom said. "She moved from an apartment to a boarding house to a flophouse and finally ended up on the street. She lived that way for years, Sam. But, you know, I think she was happy. She thought she was still in the movies—and she was still living amid the stars."

I smiled at how well everything fit. No wonder Wendela sang in a language I didn't understand. It wasn't gibberish, it was Armenian. And she really *had* lived among the stars. I leaned toward Thom. "Do you know how she ended up in Phoenix?"

"Yes. As she got a little older she got increasingly confused and lived more in past roles than in the present."

He frowned. "The police don't like run-of-the-mill street people, but ones who climb billboards attract even more negative attention. It isn't uncommon to buy the most colorful offenders one-way bus tickets to the next big city, hoping to make them somebody else's problem. That's what happened to Wendela just after I left on a mission in early 1997. I'm sure my father considered the warmth of Phoenix's climate a kindness over cold, wet San Francisco."

"And so she arrived the same night the strange lights were seen in the sky," I marveled. "And what with all the uproar about UFOs and her insisting she'd come from the stars, the police took her to the county hospital." I sighed. "I don't blame them, but I do blame the mental health care system. They—"

"They did what they could." His voice was tender when he added, "It takes a superhero to do more."

I looked up into his eyes and tingled all over. "But I—"

"That's the end of Wendela's story," he said. "Except for her marrying Lord Herbert and living happily every after."

I smiled. Now we *could* find an ID that would allow for a marriage surely made in heaven. Looking up at Thom, my smile widened. "Would you believe I once suspected Lord Herbert of wanting to kill you? I thought you'd discovered some deep, dark secret about him."

"You mean the deep, dark secret that he isn't who he says he is?"

My smile disappeared.

"Herbert's an actor too, Sam," Thom said, lowering his voice. "A classical stage actor, and a good one. His name is Herbert Stemple."

"How did you know?" I gasped.

"I didn't know," Thom admitted. "I only suspected until that night you quoted from *Macbeth.*"

"*Macbeth?*"

"Most Shakespearean actors are very superstitious. One of the oldest superstitions, dating back to the first performance, is that it's unlucky to quote from *Macbeth*. When I saw how he reacted, I asked my father to have any and all British Lord Graemes checked out. Sure enough, the last of the impoverished line died about a decade ago in Leeds—very comfortably—after 'selling' his title to an American actor."

"But where did Herbert get all his money?"

Thom smiled. "What Herbert lacks in sense, he makes up in luck. He invested most of his meager earnings in lottery tickets. One paid off royally—or lordly at least. The last Lord Graeme was more than happy to trade his pedigree and a manor full of assorted junk for half of the millions Herbert won." Thom turned to look into the ballroom at the dancers. "If you ask me, the Graemes got the best of the arrangement. With all his good works, our Lord Herbert has done more for their family name than any of them ever did."

"And he hasn't lost the rest of his money?" I asked in surprise.

"It's probably doubled or tripled," Thom said. "Thanks to his sister."

"Hedda?"

"What *she* lacks in personality she makes up in shrewdness. Because of her investments, Herbert and Wendela are assured a very comfortable 'lord and ladyship' for the rest of their lives."

I thought of the list in Hedda's hand at the dinner party and the phone call I'd overhead the night Thom was sprayed by the skunk. While I was suspecting her of selling off Lord Herbert's treasure, she was merely bullying his stock brokers into amassing more of it. It was all incredible . . . and reasonable . . . both at once.

"And the mummy?" I asked.

At last Thom looked perplexed. "I have no idea where that mummy came from. Maybe it was in the estate, but for all I know Herbert could have picked it up at a yard sale in Roswell."

He had missed my point. "Forget where it came from. Where do you think it went?"

Thom didn't reply, but his eyes were still on Lord Herbert.

"He has it, doesn't he?"

"Go on," Thom said.

I did, glad to be able to finally share my theory. "I think Lord Herbert planned to donate it," I said. "But he changed his mind at the party when he realized everybody wanted to *use* Hermes." I shook my head. "Or maybe he changed his mind when he met Wendela and saw how much she loves it. Most likely they did it together."

Thom grinned. "Tell me, Ms. Shade, how did they pull it off?"

"I think Lord Herbert used the music as a cue for one of the servants to cut the power," I said. "Remember, he asked the quartet to play a particular piece. And there's an intercom throughout the manor. I heard it when I was in the hall with Knute. Anyway, when the lights went out, Wendela hit you with the chair while Lord Herbert moved the dais and stowed the mummy in a secret compartment underneath. That's why when you looked at the carpet later, he faked a heart attack. After all, you said he's a good actor. Hedda probably knew he was faking but backed him up to give herself a chance to either talk him into selling the mummy, or to look for it herself while he was in the hospital. But he was still afraid you were on to him, so he had the dais removed and the carpet replaced."

Thom's grin was broader now. "And the open door to the conservatory? Harrison skulking around all night?"

"There was another theft that night," I said. "That was probably when the silver disappeared. Harrison took it, figuring if anybody noticed it was gone he could blame the caterers. He opened the door to the conservatory to stash the silver, but left the door open in his hurry to get back to the study when dinner ended so abruptly."

Thom leaned back against the wall, looking self-satisfied. "He's not going to be looting Graeme Manor much longer. The authorities have him nailed. I consider it my own little wedding gift to Lord and Lady Graeme."

"They won't nail him if Lord Herbert insists he's been giving him things," I pointed out. "Harrison will swear every penny he has is his inheritance."

"Oh, I hope so," Thom said. "That's exactly what I want him to insist. Between the money Herbert gives him outright and the things he cashes in himself, he must have passed the million-dollar mark in net receipts. Most of which has gone for cocaine." I gasped, but Thom was still smiling. "And yet he hasn't paid a cent in income or inheritance taxes."

This was all too good to be true. "And you think I'm right about the mummy?"

"I think you're right."

I'd solved "The Mystery of the Missing Mummy"! All that was left was to produce the sarcophagus and dazzle Uncle Eddie, Knute, and Delano with my skill and cunning.

"Do you think it's still hidden here in the manor?" I asked Thom.

He didn't answer. He'd turned his attention back to the sky above Mummy Mountain. I edged closer and stargazed with him until I knew what he was thinking. "It isn't *my* priceless, uninsured Egyptian mummy that's gone missing, is it?"

Thom shook his head.

"And the world doesn't need to know what's inside that sarcophagus," I continued. "At least not right now."

"Not right now," he agreed.

"But if I don't say anything I'll look like a failure, Thom. I'll—" My words ended when he looked down into my eyes.

"You've saved lives, Samantha Shade," he said, "including mine. And you've proved to yourself you have what it takes to be a top-notch private investigator. Maybe there are some mysteries better left unsolved, even by superheroes."

I knew in that moment Thom would never tell anybody else what he'd told me. He'd keep it to himself because all that mattered about Herbert and Wendela's lives was that they were together now in the twilight. Thomas Casey was an incredible man. And he was right.

He was also leaving. It was time, I knew, to say good-bye.

I clutched the top of the wall and looked down at the city lights. If anything, the blur of tears made them lovelier still. "I hear you're leaving Phoenix to finish up your doctorate."

"No."

I couldn't believe I'd heard the word correctly, but I couldn't ask him to repeat it for fear the magic "no" would dissolve in the cool night air. As long as I was silent I could pretend he was staying. Maybe I could pretend long enough for my heart to shrivel up and die instead of breaking into a million pieces as it had been threatening to do.

"I hear Phoenix PD might offer me a detective job," he said.

I blinked twice and swallowed three times, but I still couldn't speak. Finally I managed a tiny squeak of acknowledgement. "Why?"

He chuckled. "Probably because Monroe wants to leave for the bright lights of L.A. and I'm all they have left."

"I mean, why would you even consider accepting it?"

"Because I figure police work makes me closer to a super-hero."

There was more than one way to take that. I was still hoping and praying he meant it the way I wanted him to mean it when he suddenly moved closer and every coherent thought left my mind.

Thom pointed to a bright pinpoint of light in the north. "See that?" he asked. "When I got the tip you were in the planetarium, the first thing I did was look up into the sky for the brightest star. You know what I said?"

With him so near, I couldn't speak. I couldn't even think. I shook my head.

"I said, 'Star light, star fright.'" Thom smiled down at me and the moon was eclipsed. All that was left in the universe were two star-gray eyes I could wish upon forever. "That's when I knew that despite my better judgment, if I ever saw Samantha Shade again, I'd stick around awhile to see how things turn out for her and that nuthouse she works at."

"'Awhile'?" I repeated, leaning as close as I dared. "Tell me, Detective Casey. How long is 'awhile'?"

"Six months," he said. "Six years." He put his hands on my shoulders, and I thought I might melt beneath his touch. "Forever, maybe."

"C! And that's my final answer!"

Okay, I didn't say that. I didn't say anything because, in a classic example of the worst timing ever exhibited by a human being with a telephone, Chaiya called.

"Aren't you going to answer it?" Thom asked, moving his hands back where they had started.

I wouldn't have. Not in a million, billion, trillion years would I have answered that stupid cell phone except for the fact it plays *The Addams Family* theme song. (If you're ever looking for a quick, foolproof way to annihilate a romantic, moonlit moment, that's it.) Thom was already snapping his fingers in time with the digital tones.

"What?" I snapped into the phone. Then, wanting Thom's "awhile" to last longer than the time it would take him to realize I'd just sprouted fangs, I retracted my claws, softened my tone, and said, "I mean, what is it, Chaiya? I'm a little busy here."

"Good for you," she said. "But my father . . . no, my mistake . . . your father . . . no . . ." I heard her cover the phone to seek advice. "*The* father," she continued. "Father Rodriguez . . . anyway, he needs to talk to you . . . *tonight.* There's a ghost in his vestry."

More likely there was a bat in his belfry, but I hesitated to mention it. "There's a ghost in a priest's vestry?" I repeated. "And he's come to Nightshade about it?"

Thom rolled his eyes. "Who else?"

I frowned at him, but couldn't reply because Chaiya was still talking in my ear. "I told Father Rodriguez I don't think we do exercises at church," she said.

"No," I agreed. "And we don't do exorcisms, either. Besides, isn't that *his* line of work?"

While Chaiya shared my sarcasm with the holy potential customer, Thom took a step toward the doorway.

"Wait!" I protested. For the first time in my life, I didn't want to go work at Nightshade Investigation, Inc. I wanted to stay on the balcony where the moon and stars seemed close enough to touch—and where Thom was closer still. "Where are you going?"

"Ghostbusting, apparently." He motioned gallantly for me to precede him into the manor. "Mummies . . . haunted churches. Are all Nightshade's cases this strange?"

"Only the ones *I* get," I muttered. But as I joined that handsome, intelligent, soon-to-be-detective in the ballroom, it was all I could do not to throw my arms around him and dance for joy. I had solved the mummy mystery, found the runaway girl, and helped right the wrong in Metropolis after all. (Don't tell me that's not pretty darn good for a girl whose thighs are too pudgy for colored tights.) Moreover, Wendela had a bright future at last, and for the first time in months my conscience was clear. Life was about as good as it could get—without Thom's arms around me, of course.

I raised the phone back to my ear to hear Chaiya still chatting away. "She's saying something about poultry guests now," I reported.

"Poltergeists," Thom supplied.

Hey, he was getting pretty good at this.

After promising Chaiya and the priest we'd be there in thirty minutes, I hung up and looked up at Thom. "I guess I just accepted another case. Maybe I *will* own Nightshade someday."

He reached for my hand. "'Build on, and make thy castles high and fair, Rising and reaching upward to the skies; Listen to the voices in the upper air, Nor lose thy simple faith in mysteries.'"

"Shakespeare?"

"Longfellow."

I intertwined my fingers with Thom's, admiring the fit and imagining the eternal kingdom I could build with a man like this. "Me? Lose my faith in mysteries? Never!"

It was simply a mystery to me how I'd managed to find a man like Thomas Casey while looking for an extraterrestrial mummy. But if I could do that . . . well . . . the skies really were the limit!

I couldn't wait to don my cape and tackle the next case.

ACROSS

   64 With 53 DOWN, to deceive by false appearances (second word)

DOWN

   53 With 64 ACROSS, to deceive by false appearances (first word)

   59 A Lord Herbert word for when my next case would come along (soon); Abbr. for how this book should have been written?

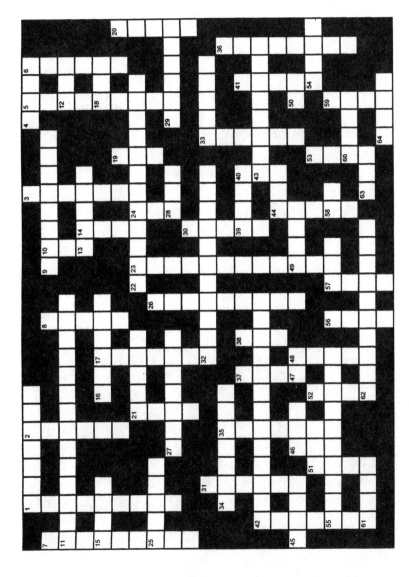

CROSSWORD PUZZLE CLUES

Note: Most (not all) of the answers are contained within the book, but not necessarily in the chapter they head.

ACROSS

1   End of day; Camp in New York state for kids with XP

4   Abbr. for mysterious lights in Phoenix sky in March 1997?

9   Made up of the best of varied sources; Uncle Eddie's office

11   Where Lord Herbert's mummy came from? (four words for "unearthly")

12   Rodent; Contemptible person (like Harrison Mead); "I smell a ____"

13   Small yard statuary; What Lord Herbert resembles

15   Lacking intensity; What Shady Acres never is when Wendela is around

16   In Greek mythology, the winged messenger of the gods; Lord Herbert's mummy

18   Negative correlative used to connect two alternatives: "Wick Barlow has neither sense ____ sensitivity"

21   The thing that fits neatly around the picture they want you to see; Setup

22   Symbolic carvings on sarcophagi; Chaiya's handwriting?

25   Lord Herbert's sister?; "Wicked ____ of the West"

27   Teutonic name meaning "wanderer"; Woman of the Welkin (welkin: arbor of heaven; stars)

28   The kind of light Arjay prefers; The bulb in my head sometimes?

29   Accept or agree; What I probably shouldn't do when asked to take on bizarre cases

32   Institution, museum, magazine; Professor Northcutt's domain

33 With "word," it's the type of puzzle I love; With "double," it's what was about to happen to Thom— again

34 Fictional (TV) detective who makes crime solving look a lot easier than it really is

39 Something upon which both waiters and policemen rely

42 Deviate from truth; Something practiced by more than one person in this story under extenuating circumstances—and otherwise

43 When Arjay gets up; With "Zone," it's one of the best TV series ever made!

44 Expire; What I sometimes said I was going to do, but didn't really want to

45 Word to describe mummy, runaway, and (once) Wendela; Obscured; Missing

46 Put out of sight; What I suspected the Meads had done with the mummy

47 Abbr. for "darned convenient"—what too many "accidental" deaths were believed to be

49 Kind of list which, for obsessive people like me, tends to become very long (two words)

50 Abbr. of rare genetic affliction; Why Arjay will never sunbathe

51 Foot digit; "_____ the line" (what Thom didn't do any of the times he went to Van Buren Street off duty)

54 What Knute and the Jolly Green Giant are

55 Any plant of the genus *solanum,* including belladonna; The best detective agency in the world!

57 Me and Chaiya: "We _____ family!"

58 Above the horizon; Where things are always looking in Wick Barlow's line of work

60 Portent; Something sometimes associated with ravens or bluebirds

61 One modern technique to determine contents of sealed sarcophagi

62 Where Arjay and thousands of other children learn algebra

63 With 58 ACROSS, what facts often fail to do (first word); What one must be able to do before moving on to algebra

64 With 53 DOWN, to deceive by false appearances (second word)

Down

1 Man-made object orbiting Earth; Wendela's favorite dish?

2 "The ____"—fanciful ghost story about kids with xeroderma pigmentosum (starring Nicole Kidman)

3 Cretin; Creep; Miscreant

5 Formal argumentation from Barlow; Evidence sought by Thom

6 Sixth planet from the sun; Wendela's birthplace?

7 Unless you're like Chaiya, crossword puzzles and *Reader's Digest* help increase this (two words)

8 Foreign; Strange; Extraterrestrial

10 Gear; Wheel; Something I often think I can see turning in Knute's head

14 Soon; Approaching; My career often seemed ____ its end

17 One of the mythical founders of Rome who was raised by wolves; What Lord Herbert calls Delano

19 Private Utah (Idaho, Hawaii) university; Thom Casey's alma mater

20 Edgar Allen Poe: "____ the raven, 'Nevermore!'"; Beloved stuffed bird in Uncle Eddie's office

21 Locate; What we couldn't do with regards to a certain priceless Egyptian antiquity

23 Private Eye; The "I" in PI

24 Eccentric; With "ball," it would describe most of the characters in this story

26 Of or relating to night; What Arjay, me, lemurs, owls, and vampires are

30 Giant, philosopher, saint, ace detective, and (sometimes) the most annoying man I know

31 Teacher/lecturer/museum devotee

33 Hebrew name meaning "life force"; Girl who needs a dictionary more than she needs another boyfriend

35 Weds; Links by commitment or custom

36 Phoenix mountain range over which UFOs supposedly appeared in 1997; Fictional, erstwhile planetarium; Spanish for "star"

37 ____ of Avon; The art (sport?) of quoting Shakespeare (____ing)

38 My odds at the end of Chapter 9 of someday becoming CEO of Nightshade Investigation, Inc.

40 Three probably unrelated letters that are proof positive that writing crossword puzzles is harder than it looks!

41 Ancient land of pharaohs, pyramids, and puzzles

42 Mythic bird that bursts into flame and then rises again from its own ashes; Capital of Arizona (so called because it's hot enough here to make one believe the bird story?)

44 Vital piece of "equipment" on stakeouts; Powdered sugar ____

46 Word to describe Phoenix, Thom Casey, and NONE of my dates

48 "When the going gets tough, the tough go for ice ____"

51 Opposite of "we"

52 Mathematician with a "beautiful mind" rather like Wendela's; Author of "I never saw a purple cow . . ." poem

53 With 64 ACROSS, to deceive by false appearances (first word)

56 Yore; What you don't dwell on much if you're me
57 Throb; With "head," it's what Thom must have had most of the time after he met me
59 A Lord Herbert word for when my next case would come along (soon); Abbr. for how this book should have been written?